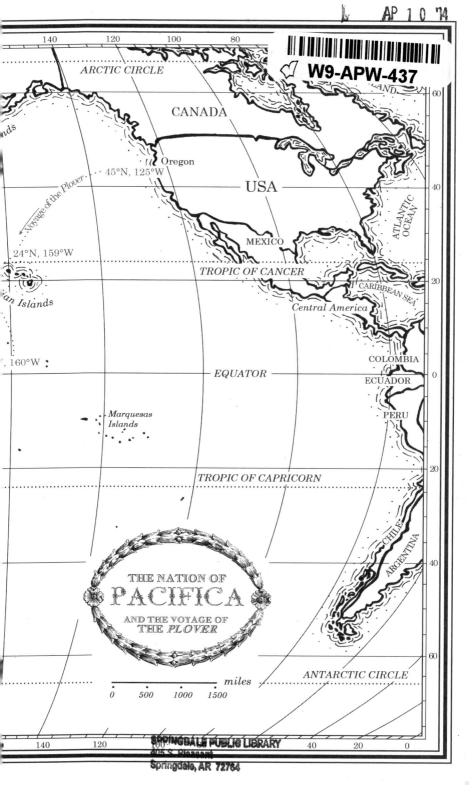

140   120   100   80

ARCTIC CIRCLE

CANADA

Oregon

Voyage of the Plover

45°N, 125°W

USA

24°N, 159°W

TROPIC OF CANCER

an Islands

MEXICO

CARIBBEAN SEA

Central America

160°W

COLOMBIA

EQUATOR

ECUADOR

PERU

Marquesas Islands

TROPIC OF CAPRICORN

ATLANTIC OCEAN

60

40

20

0

20

THE NATION OF
PACIFICA
AND THE VOYAGE OF
THE *PLOVER*

CHILE

ARGENTINA

40

miles

0   500   1000   1500

60

ANTARCTIC CIRCLE

140   120   100   40   20   0

THE PLOVER

BRIAN DOYLE

THOMAS DUNNE BOOKS

ST. MARTIN'S PRESS

NEW YORK

THOMAS DUNNE BOOKS.
An imprint of St. Martin's Press.

THE PLOVER. Copyright © 2014 by Brian Doyle. All rights reserved. Printed in the United States of America. For information, address St. Martin's Press, 175 Fifth Avenue, New York, N.Y. 10010.

www.thomasdunnebooks.com
www.stmartins.com

"Ke Hoʻolono Nei": music by Leokāne Pryor, original lyrics by Suzanne Case, Hawaiian poetic adaptation and translation by Kaliko Beamer-Trapp

Chapter illustrations by Katrina Van Dusen

Endpaper map by Cameron Macleod Jones

Designed by Jonathan Bennett

Library of Congress Cataloging-in-Publication Data

Doyle, Brian.
    The plover : a novel / Brian Doyle.—First Edition.
        p. cm.
    ISBN 978-1-250-03477-9 (hardcover)
    ISBN 978-1-250-03478-6 (e-book)
    1. Sea stories.   I. Title.
PS3604.O9547P56 2014
813'.6—dc23
                                                    2013032101

St. Martin's Press books may be purchased for educational, business, or promotional use. For information on bulk purchases, please contact Macmillan Corporate and Premium Sales Department at 1-800-221-7945, extension 5442, or write specialmarkets@macmillan.com.

First Edition: April 2014

10 9 8 7 6 5 4 3 2 1

For Mary

These last two years I have been much at sea, and I have never wearied; and never once did I lose my fidelity to blue water and a ship . . . my exile to the place of schooners and islands can be in no sense regarded as a calamity.

—*Robert Louis Stevenson to Henry James, 1890*

Every one of us has within us a drop of [the] ocean . . . just like a drop of the ocean has the same qualities as the whole ocean.

—*George Harrison*

The sea pronounces something, over and over, in a hoarse whisper; I cannot quite make it out.

—*Annie Dillard*

45° NORTH, 125° WEST

WEST AND THEN WEST for weeks and weeks or months and months sweet Jesus knows how long. A lifetime of life-times. On the continent of the sea. A pair of shaggy claws scuttling on the ceiling of the sea. The silent She.

West and then west! says Declan aloud, startling the gull sitting atop the *Plover*'s tiny cabin, her feathers ruffling in the steady wind. Onward twisted soldiers! The gull launches without the slightest effort, sliding into the welcoming air. Declan laughs. Go ahead, bird, assume the position, he says, and as if in obedience to the man's command the gull wheels behind and over the stern and hangs exactly nine feet above the boat without even a shiver of her wings. Sweet Jesus, says Declan, I would ask you how you *do* that, but you know and I know that there are more things than we know, as you know. Onward whiskered soldiers!

The *Plover,* out of Oregon, skippered by O Donnell, Declan, no fixed address or abode. Last registered midcoast, in Depoe Bay. Originally a small trawler, much amended and edited by its owner, who installed a mast and rigged the boat for coastal cruising. Wrecked once near Neawanaka, minor damage, repaired by owner. For some years a fishing boat bringing in regular catches, occasional permits filed for charter fishing, one permit filed for whale-watching cruise, a number of gratuitous permit applications filed in last three years apparently for the amusement of the owner: for flossing the teeth of unsuspecting whales, in search of Robert Dean Frisbie on account of incontrovertible evidence of his faked demise in the South Seas, in pursuit of the magnetic West Pole, in search of the names of god in the languages of the invertebrates west of the Mendocino Fracture Zone and east of the Emperor Seamounts, and etc. in that vein. Flurries and then blizzards of permit applications filed in the last six months, each more fanciful than the last. Last seen heading directly west from Oregon coast. Captain reportedly stated that he was going to "glom on to the 45th parallel and ride that sucker right onto the beach of some godforsaken island being bickered over by the Japanese and the Russians and claim it anew for Saint Mary Magdalene while none of the formerly murderous imperial powers were paying close attention." Also heard stating that he was going to "turn sharp left at 150 degrees longitude and snatch a Society island, naming it fresh for Saint Catherine of Siena, why should bold imperialism die ignominiously during my brief lifetime, and there were not enough celebrations of and monuments to Catherine of Siena, fine woman, twenty-fourth of twenty-five children, who are we not to sing her praises assiduously with gratuitous acts of theatrical foolery," and etc. in that vein. Conclusion: no destination known. Coast Guard reports no sightings. U.S. Navy Pacific Command alerted. General marine bulletin posted. To be considered lost at sea pending further information if any. Notice of same sent to next of kin. No estate. Three survivors, a sister of age and two minor brothers. No plans for funeral or memorial at this time.

★

What's on board: two hundred gallons of fuel, stashed in every conceivable nook and cranny. One hundred pounds of rice. Magellan survived on rice and so dammit will we. More onions and heads of garlic than a man can count in an hour, as I well know, having tried. A man is like an onion, is he not, a layered and reeking thing? Fifty boxes of cookies, fifty lemons, fifty limes. An enormous tin of marmalade. Fifty oranges. An enormous tin of olive oil. Fifty small bags of almonds scattered variously throughout the vessel so that a man will constantly be discovering a small bag of almonds no matter where he is on board, good idea, hey? Element of surprise, hey? Not that there is all that much board on board, or surprise neither. Twenty feet long by eight feet wide by seven feet deep. The size of a roomy coffin. But few coffins have fifty limes aboard, hey? Life raft, life jacket, foul-weather gear, medical kit, complete set of spare parts for engine, complete set of tools for fixing the fecking engine, complete set of fishing gear.

One, two, six, seven, why do I have seven fishing rods? Radio, charts, graphs, sextant, compass, flashlights, soap, baseball bat (Dick Groat model), set of Edmund Burke's speeches, sails, rigging, backup sails, backup rigging, a trumpet, excellent knives, bow and arrows? Who the hell put a bow and arrows on board? I don't remember putting a bow and arrows on board. Am I losing it already? A bow and arrows . . . what am I going to do with a bow and arrows, shoot flying fish? Sweet Jesus. Binoculars, backup binoculars, mirrors, sounding lead and string, flares, pencils, batteries for flashlights, sweet Jesus, arrows, I cannot believe I am shipping arrows, is that even legal? Am I considered armed? Can I get pulled over by the fecking Coast Guard and busted for harboring unregistered weapons? What is this, the fecking age of Magellan? Almanac. And, most important of all, boys and girls, your six-volume set of sight reduction tables! Never leave home without it! Because why? Because sight reduction tables are your handy solutions to problems of spherical trigonometry, which is to say problems in observed latitudes, celestial declinations, and computation of your azimuth! Exactly! The azimuth is *important*! Also do not leave home without Edmund Burke's speeches. Burke is *important*. Burke is an ocean whose depths are in general unplumbed. Everyone thinks they know what Burke said and wrote and meant and means and no one has the slightest idea what he actually wrote because no one fecking reads old Edmund Burke anymore but *I* will address and redress this problem. *I* am going to read old Ed Burke, because *I* have the time, because *I* am on a voyage to nowhere, and in no hurry to get there neither.

Bird! says Declan aloud, startling the gull surfing effortlessly above the stern, are you in this for the long haul? Because if so I'll have to edit the crew manifest, and we'll have to talk about shares of the proceeds and stuff like that. Hey, can you calculate sight reduction tables?

*

The Peaceful Sea, Fernão de Magalhães called the Pacific, when he wandered into it for the first time in 1520, in his ship the *Trinidad*—a caravel, a two-masted ship. The South Sea, Vasco Núñez de Balboa called it when he saw it for the first time, in 1513 (and promptly asserted ownership of the entire ocean and all lands encroaching upon it). The Panthalassic Ocean, scholars call the Pacific's predecessor, the ocean of the world when the world was young. The Endless, some early and brave travelers called it, people who sailed by the stars. The Mother, other old cultures called it, in their various languages. It is the biggest ocean on earth and perhaps in the universe. It is about half of the wildernesses we call oceans on this planet. It composes about a third of the surface of the earth. Some parts of it are more than six miles deep. On average it is about two miles deep. It weighs about eighty quintillion tons, an idea represented by an eight followed by eighteen zeroes. In the hundred thousand years or so that human beings have been exploring the Endless, we have discovered some two hundred thousand species of animals and plants living and working in it, which some of us believe to be perhaps a tenth of the actual animals and plants in it, the rest of those beings not having revealed themselves to us as yet. If it is true that human beings in our current form rose in Africa, and then ambled briskly into the rest of the world, there must have been a moment when one human being, probably a curious and mischievous child, peeked through a fringe of forest, perhaps on a high hill, and saw the biggest blue thing on earth and perhaps in the universe. Imagine that scene for a moment: the child's gape, the thrumming roar of the ocean, the child's thrill and terror, the shock and allure of encountering a thing far bigger than the imagination had previously stretched. Imagine that child's wide eyes and sizzling brain. Imagine the message imparted to his mother by the fire that night. Imagine *that*.

*

On this voyage, this particular jaunt, this epic adventure, this bedraggled expedition, this foolish flight, this sea-shamble, this muddled maundering, this aimless amble on the glee of the sea, we will navigate not by what's *in* the ocean, which is elemental but really *in*cidental if you take the long view, but by the wilderness of the bottom, which is . . . fundamental, so to speak, says Declan to the floating gull, who appears to be paying close attention. In my view the *water* of the ocean is essentially fascist, trying to dictate all life and action by weight and violence, whereas what is beneath it, the bones, the skeleton, the actual warm skin of the planet, is generally unremarked, unsung, unknown, but, as a population is the foundation for a government, the bedrock, the necessary and patient mattress for what sprawls upon it, so to speak. So a real journey into the Pacific ought to steer by the mountains below; and wouldn't that show more respect for the planet we are actually *on,* rather than steering by the light of stars we will never actually see? Are you with me here, bird? Why should water have the last word, you know what I mean? Let's take the long view. Let's forget the past and keep an eye on the horizon. Let's think of this as an expedition of inquiry, during which a man, let us say a former dairyman and sometime fisherman, sails west and then west, curious about seamounts and fracture zones, and vast epic valleys into which light has never penetrated since the dawn of time, and caves and intricate wildernesses in which reside creatures never seen by the eye of man or gull, and soaring mountains on which live ancient eels and squid the size of ships, and he conducts experiments into fauna and flora as such opportunities present themselves, and earns his protein with his longlines, dipping into ship's stores only for the occasional lime, doing his best to avoid demon alcohol which has never served him well, and keeping an eye on the shape of his sanity, such as it is, or was, and leery of such things as talking freely to gulls, for example, which may be a sign of incipient something or other. You with me here, bird?

*

Neither the *Plover* nor its master had the slightest initial experience with sails and masts and rigging and wind management, but Declan, having dreamed of a footloose voyage on the ocean since he was the boy who tripped over a ratty rug in the library and fell facefirst into *Kon-Tiki:*

Across the Pacific in a Raft, by Thor Heyerdahl (followed in dizzying succession by Robert Gibbings's *Over the Reefs* and *Coconut Island,* and James Norman Hall's *Faery Lands of the South Seas* and *Under a Thatched Roof,* and Jack London's *South Sea Tales,* and Robert Louis Stevenson's *In the South Seas,* and Joseph Conrad's *Typhoon* and *Youth,* and *The Journals of Captain James Cook,* and Captain David Porter's *Journal of a Cruise Made to the Pacific Ocean,* and Richard Maury's *The Saga of Cimba,* and Herman Melville's *Typee,* and Edward Frederick Knight's *The Cruise of the Falcon,* and *The Venturesome Voyages of Captain Voss,* and then literally hundreds of books about the islands west and south of his muddy tense pained angry lonely home in the rain), had bought the old trawler when he was seventeen, from an old man who built it half-size because he had half the money he needed half his life ago and only used it half the time now that he was half the man he used to be. Declan then used it for fishing the near coast, generally for salmon and halibut; but always in the back of the back of his mind, tucked away beyond conscious thought, was the irrepressible idea of someday heading west and then west, for no particular reason, just to see what he could see; and so he had edited and amended the boat slowly and idiosyncratically over the years, adding a mast and standing and running rigging so as to use the wind wherever and whenever possible, thus saving gobs of fuel, and becoming familiar with such mysterious and obdurate words as batten and clew, and luff and leech, and toggle and tang, and reaching and running, although the *Plover* did not do overmuch reaching and running, more like shuffling and shambling, as Declan said, not without a deep affection for the old cedar creature. He built a simple hoist for the engine, and a cedar weather box for the engine to sleep in, for when the *Plover* had sails on, in winds that looked like they might last; and when razzed by other fishermen, and by the weekend sailors in Newport and Depoe Bay who laughed aloud at the little trawler with its mast like a grade-school flagpole and its sails made of old kitchen towels, as a wit from Waldport sneered, Declan thought happily of all the fuel he was not expending, and gave everyone the cheerful finger; his usual digitous discourse.

★

And no *thinking* on this trip, either, he said to the gull floating over the stern. No recriminations and ruminations. No logs and journals and literary pretensions neither. Thinking can only, like the boat, proceed forward. We can only think west. Sweet blessed Jesus. Four days out and I am already talking to a fecking gull. Why are you here, exactly, bird? What's in it for you? Because there's not a whole lot of food available here, my friend. This is a working boat. Everyone on or over the boat has to work for a living. That's why I am fishing for my supper, and no, you cannot have half, although yes, you can have the head and tail and innards. Did you *want* to be going west and then west? Because that is where we are going until further notice. And what are *you* doing on behalf of the boat, may I ask? Are you providing some rudderly service that I am as yet not aware of? Are you protecting the boat in some mysterious capacity? And don't give me any of this spiritual crap. And don't get all literary on me either, talismans and metaphors and symbols and crap like that. You are most definitely not a metaphor, my friend. *You* are a herring gull and this is a boat and I am the guy on the boat. It's that simple. You are no albatross and I am no ancient mariner. I read my classics. In fact I vow that if an albatross ever hangs in exactly the same position you are hanging in right now I will strike myself three times on the breast and intone prayers and imprecations. This I swear. You are welcome to hang there as long as you want but don't steal anything. I cast no aspersions on gull people. I am just laying out the rules. Maybe you are unlike all the other gulls who ever lived and you are the first one who won't steal whatever he or she can at the drop of a fecking hat. In which case we will get along fine. If that is not the case and you steal anything from the boat I will catch your raggedy ass and cut you into filets and savor each and every gullicious bite. Are we clear here? On this boat there are no gray areas. There are no misunderstandings. There are no misapprehensions. There are no infinitesimal gradations of emotions and feelings. No one makes mistakes as regards anyone else. There *is* no anyone else. There's no past and there's no future. We are stripping it all down here, my friend. No man is an island, my ass. *This* is an island and I am that very man. *You* are a guest nine feet in the air over *my* island. Are we clear here? You can visit any time you like, but don't expect anything from me. We are all islands, my friend. We are all playing it straight for a change on this island. I expect nothing and you should expect nothing. The rules are simple here, bird. No emotional complications can ensue if we lay it out clear as day in advance. We can crash, sink, burst into flames, get smashed by a huge squid or a whale or a cyclone or pirates, or I can die in any number of interesting ways and the boat goes on by itself skipperless, but that's the sum total of possibility, understand? We are stripping things down to the bones here. No more expectations and illusions. No more analysis and explications. We are going to live a real simple life here, my friend, and deal with what is, rather than what seems to be. We have wind and fuel, we have food and water, and we have the biggest fecking ocean on the planet in which to putter around, and we are damn well going to putter around until further notice, is that clear? Are you with me here, bird? Hey?

*

In the first four days alone Declan saw so much stuff bobbing in the ocean that he started keeping a list with a pencil: sneakers, hockey gloves, the top of a coffin, a poem in Japanese carved into a maple plank, half a bottle of wine, a plastic turtle, two dolls' heads taped together with a huge tangle of duct tape, lots of seeds of various species, what looked like the keel of a fishing boat, three oars, most of a fishing net, an enormous root ball from what Declan judged to be a Sitka spruce, the tiny skull of a sea lion child, two life buoys, a very old basketball on which every hint of nub had been eroded so that the ball shone like a dark sun when he scooped it up with a net, ropes of every sort of shape and color many of which he salvaged just in case, a ukulele he thought about salvaging but recovered his sanity, every sort of tampon ever made on this blue earth, a cassette tape that he carefully dried and rewound and tried to play in the boom box in the cabin to no avail and the shrill awful screeching of it made the gull launch shocked off the cabin roof, all sorts and shapes of seaweed, seven dead murre chicks, and what certainly *looked* like a muscular squid tentacle about twenty feet long, although he saw it from a distance at last light, so it *could* have been a whip of bull kelp, or God knows what else, though probably bull kelp, probably.

Probably bull kelp, he said to the gull, who was staring at it too, looking nervous. Don't you think that's bull kelp? Bull kelp gets to be like a hundred feet long, you know. Grows like a bastard. Grows a hundred feet in three months, that's *a foot a day*, that's just disturbing. Imagine if *you* grew a foot a day, pretty soon you would be an albatross, and then where would you be? Albatrosst, albalost. Sure that's bull kelp. It just *looks* like a tentacle. And tentacles don't travel solo, you know. So it has to be bull kelp. Sure it does. Well, hey, full dark, *I* am just going to step into the cabin here and buckle up, might be weather coming, better tether the old ball to the old chain, you know what I'm saying? If a squid bigger than the boat comes for you just give me a holler. Squawk three times so I'll know it's you. Or do that disgusting barf thing I love so much when you do it on the roof of the cabin. A truly endearing habit, barfing up fish guts. Is that what your mama taught you for manners, barfing on other people's property? Because that is not what my mama taught *me*. Ah, you ask, what *did* my mama teach me? And the answer is my mama taught me jack shit, because she wasn't around much longer than it took to pop out four kids and drag the old suitcase down the old driveway and leave the old man and the four ducklings, but she taught me *that,* bird, yes she did, she taught me there's times to cut and run. Taught me that good, yes she did.

★

Why did I name the *Plover* the *Plover,* you ask? says Declan to the gull, who had not asked. I'll tell you. Listen close now, because I have not explained this before and will not again. Far too much repetition in life altogether. We should say things once and let them just shimmer there in the air and fade away or not, as the case may be. The golden plover of the Pacific, the Pacific Golden Plover, is a serious traveler. It wanders, it wends where it will. It is a slight thing, easily overlooked, but it is a heroic migrant, sailing annually from the top of Pacifica to the bottom. It forages, it eats what it can find. It talks while it travels and those who have heard it say it has a mournful yet eager sound. This seems exactly right to me, mournful yet eager. We regret, yet we push on. We chew the past but we hunger for the future. So I developed an affection and respect for the plover. It's a little thing the size of your fist, other than those long pencilly legs for sprinting after grasshoppers and crabs and such, but it can fly ten thousand miles across an ocean itching to eat plovers and reaching for plovers with storms and winds and jaegers and such. You have to admire the pluck of the plover. It doesn't show off and it isn't pretty and you hardly even notice it, but it's a tough little bird doing amazing things. Also it really likes berries, which appeals to me. Most of them fly from Siberia or Alaska to Australia and New Guinea and Borneo and such but some of them camp out awhile in Hawaii and just cruise around in the long grass in the sun eating and dozing. This appeals to me. So when it came time to name a little drab boat that wasn't dashing and didn't weigh much and no one notices much, but that gets a lot of work done quietly and could if it wanted to sail off and go as far as it wanted way farther than anyone could ever imagine such a little drab thing could do, that might pause here and there at an island so as to allow a guy to eat and doze in the grass, well, that's why we are the *Plover*. So now you know. Don't keep badgering me with questions.

★

On the seventh day there arose a tempest such as man nor bird had never seen and the *Plover* was tossed hither and thither as if by a vast and furious hand not unlike an idiot boy in a bathtub slamming the water with his fool flipper because he can, the cretin!, shouts Declan at the gull. The Pacific never being particularly pacific, the storm raged for two days, and was followed by another day of immense uneasy swells; Declan, who had never been seasick in his life, threw up every hour on the hour as if he were a broken alarm clock, and by the time the swell finally eased he was as limp and pale as a rag in the rain. Then the *Plover* came within yards of being crushed by a vast grim oil tanker at four in the morning, at exactly eight bells, as Declan realized with a shiver, the traditional nautical slang for death; and had he not been clipped onto the boat's jackline, the safety rope he rigged before a storm, the savage bucking of the boat would have tossed him into the endless fog. Then it began to rain, not hard but steadily, for days and days; then he discovered that one of the extra fuel tanks aft had broken off and been lost some-time during the last few days; then he hooked, fought, and lost a tremendous bluefin tuna that would have been glorious eating for a week and lovely dried salted savories for a month; then the rudder fouled on what appeared to be the biggest fecking gill net in the history of the uni-verse where no one but a fecking idiot would set a fecking net; and then, on the first dry hint of sunny morning in weeks, Declan realized the gull was gone.

*

And flooding in upon him, to his absolute astonishment, was a black sadness and loneliness and despair so sudden and thorough that he sat down heavily on the deck and wept as he had never wept before in all his life. He was overwhelmed, inundated, swept away by it, his usual salty confidence shredded and tattered so that who he had thought himself to be was completely shattered and he was merely a being in a boat, alone and foolish, running away from everything that had ever meant anything to him, a coward and a joke, utterly alone, unloved and un-loving. The sun strengthened by the minute and the boat steamed so remarkably than an observer might have mis-taken it for smoke; but there was no man or woman or child for hundreds of miles around, and Declan felt the absence of his kind like a new hole in his flinty soul. He sobbed amid the steam, his face in his hands, until he was empty, a shell in the stern; and finally he fell asleep, his arms wrapped over his head like a shroud. There was the faintest of swells in the sea and the *Plover* rocked gently, carried west and southwest by the current, no sails set, the engine asleep in its little cedar house. Two young humpback whales slid by silently big and blue and black, on their way south, but they did not remark the boat, being intent on each other and their own vast literature, and Declan slept on through the warming morning. Tuna arrowed beneath the boat, and bonito, and marlin, and cod six feet long, headed east to eat a ton or so of the smaller residents of the continental shelf; and a mile below, as Declan slept, the *Plover* drifted over a vent in the ocean floor around which gathered blind crabs as white as snow, and nameless fish with transparent heads, and creatures never seen yet by the eyes of man; but we have seen them in our deepest dreams, looming out of the dark, with eyes like fire.

★

Consider, for a moment, the Pacific Ocean not as a vast waterway, not as a capacious basin for liquid salinity and the uncountable beings therein, nor as a scatter of islands still to this day delightfully not fully and accurately counted, but as a country in and of itself, dressed in bluer clothes than the other illusory entities we call countries, that word being mere epithet and label at best, and occasion and excuse for murder at worst; rather consider the Pacific a tidal continent, some ten thousand miles long and ten thousand miles wide, bordered by ice at its head and feet, by steaming Peru and Palau at its waist; on this continent are the deepest caves, the highest mountains, the loneliest prospects, the emptiest aspects, the densest populations, the most unmarked graves, the least imprint of the greedy primary ape; in this continent are dissolved beings beyond count, their shells and ships and fins and grins; so that the continent, ever in motion, drinks the dead as it sprouts new life; the intimacy of this closer and more blunt and naked in Pacifica than anywhere else, by volume; volume being an apt and suitable word to apply to that which is finally neither ocean nor continent but story always in flow, narrative that never pauses, endless ebb and flow, wax and wane, a book with no beginning and no end; from it emerged the first fundament and unto it shall return the shatter of the world that was, the stretch between a page or two of the unimaginable story; but while we are on this page we set forth on journeys, on it and in it, steering by the stars, hoping for something we cannot explain; for thousands of years we said gold and food and land and power and freedom and knowledge and none of those were true even as all were true, as shallow waters; we sail on it and in it because we are starving for story, our greatest hunger, our greatest terror; and we love most what we must have but can never have; and so on we go, west and then west.

★

Sweet Jesus, it's just a bird, and just a gull at that, the bilge rats of the air, a quarrelsome greedy race that eats their own, said Declan aloud to where the gull used to be. It's not like you were an albatross or some such gentry. Good riddance. No one barfing on my roof anymore. None of your foul and disgusting squirts and pellets raining on the boat from above, none of your toenail scratches in my lovely cedar finish, no having to notice your awful rubber feet like a fecking flying lizard, and that damned red dot on your bill. Out out, damned dot! How does it go, the Scottish play? I remember performing it in the gym, in school, the candles in the dark, the wild wind, the constant rain, all rain all day all night all winter, no one else could remember the lines: *I have many nights watched with you, and seen you rise. A great perturbation in nature! Out, damned spot! out, I say! Hell is murky! No more o' that, my lord, no more o' that. Heaven knows what she has known. What's done cannot be undone. God forgive us all! I think, but dare not speak. . . .* Exactly so. That's what I'll do. I'll think but not speak. No family, no friends, no girls, no gulls, no destination, no beer, no talking. Silently scuttling on the ceiling of the sea.

★

Consider, for a moment, that the longest chain of mountains and volcanoes and hills and guyots and cliffs and sheering walls on the face of the earth is invisible to the eye, unless you are plunged into the blue realm of Pacifica, which houses the Emperor Seamounts, which stretch nearly four thousand miles across the wild ocean like the longest grin there is; and consider further that only the very tail of this endless ridge, this vast vaulting, peers above the surface, and is christened Hawaii; and consider further that there are more volcanoes along that line of mountains than anyone has yet counted, let alone mountains; and let your mind wander along that line, in and out of ravines, a wilderness beyond the reach of man, a wilderness that thrashed and throbbed for millions of years without a single witness of our kind; how very many stories those mountains and valleys have hosted, battles and loves, heroes and cruelties, beings who changed the ways of their kind, last survivors of their races, ancient kings and queens, blind bards and tiny warriors, creatures beyond counting who left neither fin nor fossil, and are remembered perhaps only by whatever it is that forces fire through volcanic vent, and heats the bottom of the sea; caves and passages beyond number and explorers far beyond that numberless number; literatures and languages, songs and singers, villains and visionaries we can only dimly begin to imagine, even their shapes and sizes and colors endless and mutable; and over all this, for thousands of years, we floated in boats, utterly unaware of what was below, a wilderness beyond all reckoning or robbing; so what was it we were so sure we knew? We do not even know what it is we do not know, and what we do know passeth speedily away, inundated by what we do not know; yet on we go through the ravines, gaping as we go; having come from salted water and all headed home again; leaving behind neither fin nor fossil, but stories and voices, tales and music, shreds of memory, faint wakes of words in the water.

★

Late in the afternoon of his twelfth day out Declan saw a ship. He hove to, hungry for talk. The ship was big and rusty and silent. A hail from the railing ten feet above him.

You American?

Yes.

Fishing?

Yes.

Selling fish?

No.

My name is Enrique, said the man at the railing, suddenly expansive. I am this boat. She is mine. We are fishing also. Who says there are no fish? They are liars. Fish jump in our boat. You want beer?

No, thanks.

If you try to rob us we will shoot you. There's no one out here.

Okay.

You American?

I am still American, yes.

You are the Navy?

No.

You have drugs to sell?

No.

Maybe we will shoot you and take your boat.

Not much to take.

No fish to sell?

Still no fish to sell.

Okay, fuck you then, says Enrique cheerfully. Good luck.

Same to you, friend.

As the bigger boat sheered off southeast, Declan noted its name, in red letters three feet high, poorly painted: *Tanets*. Isn't that a Russian word, *tanets*? he said aloud to the gull, before realizing that the gull still wasn't floating nine feet above the stern. Why would a Russian trawler have a guy named Enrique running the boat? Fecking Wild West out here, man.

★

On the *Tanets* Enrique strolled back to the pilot house calculating odds and percentages. Odds were that the

American was a thief of some sort—why would a fisherman be so far out in such a small trawler, without a crew? And what kind of trawler was also rigged for sails? Odds were that the American was also a crazy man, in which case boarding him and taking whatever was useful would be ultimately a service to society, teaching the man that foolishness is punishable, especially at sea. But a man alone in a small boat this far out could also be some sort of agent. Probably this was some sort of subtle and complicated trap, best avoided altogether. Odds were also that the little trawler had nothing worth stealing, and violence for its own sake was poor business, usually punished somehow; Enrique was a passionate believer in retribution, not in religious terms but in general universal judicial reckoning. Not to say he was a moral man in any known sense of the term, no; he had done more than his share of illicitry, and the business affairs of the *Tanets* were complicated beyond the grasp of the most assiduous lawyer or accountant, not to mention customs agent, police officer, or harbormaster; but Enrique, while cheerfully and even eagerly flouting the laws of nations and international entities, measured odds and percentages meticulously, and was as wary as any man alive of arrogance and overconfidence, hubris and carelessly free behavior, especially in the matter of violence; violence was a tool, a means of effecting circumstances, and should be used with great care, he believed; and also simply the *possibility* of it, the prospect, the aura, the suggestion, he had learned, was better than actual execution, the former almost always serving to achieve the end desired, whereas the latter almost always led to

unforeseen consequences and complexities; and the unforeseen was Enrique's worst nightmare, the thing he fought
most bitterly to avoid. Thus he left the *Plover* to herself, and
the *Tanets* lumbered southeast, Enrique silently comparing
charts with his pilot.

*

The problem with the ocean, Declan considered, was that
it was so *wet;* otherwise it might be a sort of lovely billowing playground, a place where you could fall and not be
hurt, make a mistake and be forgiven. But no, here nothing was forgiven, you paid thoroughly for the slightest
mistake, darkness fell not like a mercy but like a hammer,
and this was where moist went to heaven. Everything was
moist beyond reclamation, the fish, the birds, the bedraggled garbage floating on the surface, even everything above
the surface, like the mist that some days never could haul
itself fully up into being a self-respecting cloud. It was in-
conceivable that anything whatsoever on the boat would
ever be dry ever again. Even his tiny bunk below, which
he had built meticulously fitting the boards together in
endless overlay and overlap, to keep out any hint of spray
and fog, now smelled like a sleeping bag left in a dank
basement for a long winter, and felt like a cold coffin rather
than the cheery redolent cedar study he had envisioned.
His books were beginning to swell, his skin itched from
moist clothes and grating salt, his crackers wilted, his spirits flagged. Also while we are on the subject of general
complaints about the ocean, he thought, the colors are
nothing to write home about. The ocean blue, my butt.

Mostly it's puke gray, when it's not evil green or some shade of foul charcoal that gives you the seasick willies if you stare at it too long. Now, if the thing were *transparent,* that would be cool, you would be fascinated all day and knocked out all night by the light show. Who designed this thing? Where do I file my complaints? Who's in charge here? You can see why so many people who lived out here were nuts and mystics. The thing's *designed* to make you crazy. There's no pattern to it, no organizational principle. Whatever you are sure of is sure to not be at all what you were sure it is. People imagined seeing islands and vast monsters. You can see why the old people thought it was the end of the earth; it *is* the end of the earth. It's not even really part of the earth. I don't see no earth out here. You see any earth? he asked the gull, out of force of habit, but realized, again with a pang, that not even the gull had stayed with him, and he was inarguably and utterly alone. Darkness having fallen suddenly like a fist, he urinated copiously over the stern and went to bed.

*

In the morning he went over his charts carefully and realized that he was approximately at the edge of what he had always thought was the wetter half of Oregon, if you considered Oregon in the larger sense, which is to say not merely the four-hundred-mile-wide dry part with mountains and wolverines and settlements, but also the four-hundred-mile-wide wet part adjacent, also with mountains and major predators and settlements; and this is not even to mention the four-hundred-mile-deep part, which he called Subterroregon, or the four-hundred-mile-high part, which he named Atmosphoregon, although he had sometimes daydreamed of voyaging to the peak of Atmosphoregon, to the physical boundary called the critical level of escape, after which you have essentially left behind planet, air, and time; an idea that appealed greatly to Declan, although he would have to steal a rocket to make the trip, an idea that did not appeal to him. Whereas the wetter half of Oregon, the four hundred miles of impacific ocean adjacent to the four hundred miles of dirt Oregon, appealed deeply; he even had topographic charts of it, labeled Wettern Oregon, which an oceanographer friend of his had drawn in exchange for fifty pounds of fresh halibut. This guy, remembered Declan with a grin, was a kick—he had legally changed his name for a while to an adjective, he played the flügelhorn in a jazz band that deliberately played only such events as weddings between Lutherans and Presbyterians and baptisms of babies named for animals, and he had once flensed a whale by himself, over the course of three weeks, on the beach, living in a tiny blue tent above the high tide line. He was one of those guys who seemed electrified by everyone and everything, the kind of guy who totally lit up when he saw a sparrowhawk helicoptering over a corn shock, the kind of guy who liked every kid he ever met and every kid liked him, the kind of guy that dogs leaned against so as to get their bellies and ears rubbed at the same time as only dog people know how to do properly so that the dog makes that crooning mooing moaning humming thrumming sound of Delighted, the kind of guy who liked all kinds of music and liked finding new music even more than digging the music he already loved, the kind of guy who when he walked down the street in a foreign city the old sour grandmothers shuffled out in the street to pinch his cheek and scold him affectionately for his silver earrings and braided beard like the beard of a goat in a jazz band. But he had been wounded by a storm, this guy, his little daughter hit by a bus driver when she was five years old waiting for the kindergarten bus, and his light was dimmed, and by now no one thought he would ever get it back. Declan had often asked him to come for a long voyage on the *Plover,* man, let's go fish for salmon in Alaska! let's go surf the Island of All the Saints off Mexico! let's steal a rocket and shoot for Venus! But now his friend was the kind of guy who said quietly *nah* and went to go give his daughter a bath, which took a long time and was best done with aforethought, so as to get her safely cantilevered in and out of the tub, her huge gray eyes staring hungrily at everything, her close-cropped hair starting to turn white despite her youth.

About midday the lurking mist finally burned off completely and it became the single most beautiful day he had ever spent at sea, and Declan had spent a thousand days afloat; *this* day, though—this day was ridiculously beautiful, embarrassingly beautiful, egregiously beautiful, as if the ocean were preening, or apologizing, or waking slowly, naked in the perfect light, and stretching luxuriously, showing off its glorious parts, giving the spotless sky a half-hooded come-hither smile; the water grew bluer than the bluest blue, bluer than Oregon's Crater Lake ever even *imagined,* a glittering translucent limpid lucid pristine generous blue that gave you the happy willies just staring at it, my *God* what a world, to dream up a color like *that*!

The quietest and steadiest of breezes aft; sea ducks in meticulous geometric triangles and rhombi; flying fish fully a foot long sailing glittering for fifty yards and more; the first storm petrels he had seen, flying so low over the placid sea that they seemed to be running on it; the first shearwaters he had seen, sailing effortlessly along and suddenly slicing down for fish, and once for a bright orange squid, wriggling wildly for an instant before it was shredded, what in heaven's name was a squid doing at the surface, did squid rise to savor such days also? And whales, taking turns as if their pods were on parade or procession; a raft of sperm whales and calves, sighing through the extraordinary water as big as buses; two humpback whales who slid along the sides of the *Plover* to port and starboard, lifting it inches higher for a moment, perhaps a quiet cetacean joke; and by far the biggest sunfish he had ever seen, easily seven feet long and a thousand pounds, dozing on the surface, and looking uncommonly like a small dance floor, or the wall of a cabin. The fisherman in Declan, which was a lot of him after long years of plowing the sea for meat, stared hungrily at all that placid toothless food, so easily caught as it basked; but something else rose in him to trump the hunter, and he hove to for a while alongside the creature, to simply gaze in wonder at the thing, until finally it woke with a start, snapping awake just like a child in the last row of math class first period on a muggy hot day, and slid effortlessly away into the deep.

★

If an ocean, thought Declan, is the sum of all the rivers pouring into it, then we are on various braided rivers, really, rather than the sea, and this thought occupied him for quite a while. He dug his charts out and counted the fattest rivers surrendering themselves to Pacifica—the Columbia, the mighty river of the West, the Father of Rivers; the Stickeen, the great Canadian river cloudy with the sperm of salmon in the old days; the roaring Fraser and Yukon and Skeena, all ice and silted melt from mountains so remote no one knew some of them; the poor Colorado, with so many names over the years, the River Red, the River of Embers, the River of Good Hope, draining the vast American desert, giving itself away to everyone, and finishing as an exhausted trickle; the Mekong, the Xi Jiang, the San Joaquin, the Shinano, the Rio Grande de Santiago, all diving headlong finally into the greatest of waters, losing their names as they joined their brothers and sisters in their mother and father, from which they would again rise into mist and cloud and be reborn as rain and river; and then there were the even larger rivers called seas bellying into Pacifica, noted Declan, checking them off with his nubbed pencil: the Sulu and the Coral, the Celebes and the Tasman, the Seas of Japan and China; not seas at all, really, but only fists and fingers of the mother of seas, poking and lapping and dissolving the placid land. Everything was in motion all the time, he thought, the water dissolving the land, the land rising and falling, the sky slurping the sea, the seas trading places, the rivers sprinting as fast as they could go to their wild dissolution; tall mountains were slowly melting as others were thrusting up to be born, and beings beyond count or calculation also arose and melted, were born and dissolved, their shells and husks sliding finally back into the ocean; so that everyone and everything was a boat, he thought; but none of them as dashing as the *Plover,* with its deep green paint the color of shadowed cedar groves, and its bright red sailcloth the color of salmon on their way to sex and death.

★

Declan's buddy, the guy with the daughter who got hit by the kindergarten bus, had lots of names. People called him all sorts of things. People kept *giving* him new names, for reasons they couldn't articulate. The easy explanation was the urge to nicknamery, especially from men, who use names as handles and jokes and forms of glancing affection and respect; but women did it too, and more than the pet names lovers give each other. Something about him invited christening, perhaps, in the way that people have the irrepressible urge to name mountains and pets; perhaps naming is a grappling to understand, or a way to assert control, or an attempt to manage mystery; if something has a label, a name, a category, a definition, the beginning of an explanation, it's not so wild and inchoate anymore, even if the name applied is a total misnomer, like the Pacific Ocean, which isn't. So Paco, Peco, Polo, Pavel, Placido, Pomo, and Piko he was variously labeled, the only nomenclatural consistency being that initial *pop*—which is what his daughter had called him, before she stopped speaking, after the bus stop. Popa and Pipa, they had called each other when she was little, and the way she had told the story to her friends in kindergarten, with the absolute conviction of someone who had spent *five whole years* on this planet and knew the score, was that they gave each other those names when she was *little,* she used to produce spit-bubbles to make her dad laugh, and he would do the same, the two of them sprawled in the warm country of the quilt, bubbling and snorting and giggling and slobbering, until her mother his wife their hero came in pretending to be annoyed but sometimes brandishing the spit-slurping mop in their faces which only made them laugh all the harder, which was the best time of all because then we would all be tangled up like a big vine on the bed, she would say, those were the best times *ever,* better than *any* other times *any*one ever had, even times that you would *think* would be the best times ever couldn't be even *half* as good as the times we were all laughing and tangled up like a big knot in the big bed in the little house. Those were the best times *ever.* If you were a brand-*new* time, she would say, and you wanted to be a *great* time when you grew up to be an older time, *those* would be the times you would try to be like. Those were the best times *ever.*

★

Just after the sun melted into the sea and dusk slid into the boat there was a silence so absolute and profound that Declan sat in the stern to listen. Is it listening if there's no sound, does that make sense? A great silence is an enormous thing, a positive negative, the full null, he thought. You could actually *hear* a really deep silence; it was like a held note on a musical scale so big some of the notes didn't have names yet. The sea was glass, so there was none of the usual lapping and yammering and slapping of water on wood; not a being to be seen, no splish of fish or whir of wing; the engine at rest in its tiny wooden house; even the boat, usually a mansion of creaks and groans and thumps and clanks, of tools falling and freight jostling, of weights shifting with a sigh, of the mast making squeaking love to the cabin, was as silent as an empty crib. He remembered a line from watery old Herman Melville: *all profound things and emotions of things are preceded and attended by Silence, and Silence is the general consecration of the universe.* Hmmm. A melvillacious line, that. So very many silences, and kinds of silence: chapels and churches and confessionals, glades and gorges, pregnant pauses and searing lovemaking; the stifling stifled brooding silence just before a thunderstorm unleashes itself wild on the world; the silence of space, the vast of vista; the crucial silences between notes, without which there could be no music; no yes without no. Perhaps silence was the ocean and sounds be boats upon the deep, he thought. Perhaps silence was the mother and sounds her yearning children. Do we not yearn for silence at the deepest level, and merely distract ourselves with stammer and yammer? Isn't that why I am out in the middle of nowhere? The ceiling of the silent sea. The silent She.

★

But after midnight the weather grew worse and the ocean swelled and roiled so furiously that Declan finally made his way up to the cabin, clipped onto the jackline, and went over his charts with a flicker of fear. The *Plover* was roughly at 45 degrees north and 140 degrees west, and if he stayed on the 45th parallel, as had been his vague disgruntled plan, he would be driving right into the belly of the North Pacific's winter storm season, which no sane man would do unless he had a much bigger ship and the smell of serious money in his nose. He could turn south, and ride down the 140-degree-longitude line along California and Mexico, but coasting meant Coast Guard and traffic and pirates and drug smugglers and harbormasters asking questions. He could turn north, and ride along the much wilder emptier coasts of British Columbia and Alaska, where the fishing was better but the weather, let's face it, was horrendous, and somehow the last thing he wanted right now was the prospect of ice; his soul felt like ice as it was, and even the thought of a long black cold winter in some dank dark inlet crammed to the gills with dripping spruce and cedar and pale moist silent people smelling like fish and last night's lurching drunk made him shiver. He went over the charts carefully again as the boat bucked and shimmied. I'll be good and damned, he finally said aloud, to where the gull used to be. I'll be damned good and fine. We have to go fecking south. Damn my eyes. I don't believe this. The fecking South Seas. This is a joke. What is this, an eighteenth-century novel? Is this some weakass movie where we sail into a lagoon and are greeted with flowers and songs? Fecking fecking feck. I don't believe this. I just want to get lost, is all. The fecking islands of the South Seas. God help me. Can't a guy just sail west without issues and problems? What have I ever done to deserve this? Hey, Ocean, I killed some of your fish, all right? But they would have died eventually anyway, you know that, I just borrowed the ends of their lives, is all. Is that so bad that you have to drown me? I didn't add any garbage to your fecking pristine waters. I just tried to eke out a living, is all, and feck all a living it was. I thought we had an agreement. I thought we were silent partners. I never took more than I needed. I didn't shoot your seals or flay your whales. I didn't catch that fecking sunfish the other day you showed me. I was respectful. I returned fish parts I didn't need to your cleaning crews. We had a deal. You didn't kill me and I didn't foul you. And now this. Jesus fecking Christmas. You're forcing this decision on me. I don't want to make decisions. That was the whole point. No decisions, no thinking, just go. But no. Now I have to make a fecking decision. The whole point of the thing is shot. Fecking *fine*. South and west. Unbelievable. Fecking feck.

He wrenched the wheel 45 degrees to the left. Instantly the storm abated so noticeably that he stopped cursing and listened intently; and after a few minutes he locked the wheel in position and went back to bed, sleeping far past dawn.

II

24° NORTH, 159° WEST

BUT ONCE IN VIEW of the islands of the archipelago, Declan found himself leery of land, and for reasons he could not explain he hove to, north of the last and loneliest island, and plunged into his collected Edmund Burke. The sun shone, the sea murmured gently, birds he had never seen circled curiously, and he sat in the stern reading and eating the last of his shriveled oranges, the pips like faded juicy leather. Old Ed gave a terrific speech sort of about ships, did he not? He flipped through his green volumes until he found Burke's speech in Parliament after the Americans, sick of being bullied from afar, calmly ransacked the British ships *Dartmouth, Eleanor,* and *Griffin,* and he read it aloud to the fork-tailed terns sailing around the *Plover* like huge butterflies: *You wish to condemn the accused without a hearing,* shouted old Ed to his snarling countrymen, *to punish indiscriminately the innocent with the guilty! You will thus irrevocably alienate their hearts. . . . They cannot, by such means, be made to bow to authority; on the contrary, you will find their obstinacy confirmed and their fury exasperated. . . .* Rip it, Edmund my boy! No flies on old Ed! Exactly right too. Authority cannot be assumed, it must be earned, and earned by example, not by force; or authority could be conferred if you sailed alone, captain of the absent crew, the untenanted berth, the empty manifest; better that a man sail alone than that he sail in tumult and confusion, subject to the various winds of others; indeed men *were* islands, John Donne was an idiot, and the wise man owned up to this cold reality, shipping alone, leaning on no one, no one leaning on him, wary of shoals and reefs, disappointing no one, and proffering no false harbors to friend or lover. Such a man, sailing alone, encumbering none, would in fact be a benefit to the common good, if there are those who believe in such an ephemera, by removing widows and former wives and former lovers and dependent children from the general tumult; Burke himself says *a man that breeds a family without competent means of maintenance, encumbers other men with his children,* and who am I to add to the maelstrom of the gene pool, already a trackless ocean producing more valleys than peaks, am I right? Better to sail alone, and let the battered vessel wander where it will. The only honest course. Assume nothing, trust no one, encumber not and be not encumbered, make your own way, steer your own ship and none other, exactly so. Besides, what do I know? *Whoever undertakes to set himself up as a judge of truth and knowledge is shipwrecked by the laughter of the gods,* says old Ed. Which is exactly so. No flies on old Edmund B.

★

But he was lower on fuel than he expected after the two terrific storms, not to mention losing a tank overboard, and the island he could see all green and wreathed in mist was filled with fruit beyond calculation—he could smell it even miles offshore—and despite his powerful reluctance to land at all, let alone speak to anyone, he determined to slip in after dusk, tie up somewhere for the night, and refit as necessary; he also found that having seen land he suddenly had a powerful thirst for beer, and beer made him dream of meat, and meat of wine, and wine of cigars, and by dusk he was so addled thinking of the sensuous pleasure of a cigar that he hauled his sea anchor and headed toward a crescent bay he could see opening like a smile as he approached the redolent island in the sifting dark. The engine chortled quietly. I'll just tie up to a jetty for the night, there's no marina or anything, get a steak and a cigar, stash some fruit, and away we go, no big deal, no permits and all, no one needs to know, cold hard cash, maybe a box of cigars to go, and just as he sighed luxuriously thinking of the dark pleasure of a mouthful of smoke, a quiet voice spoke to starboard.

Ahoy the boat.

Jesus blessed Christ. Who are you?

The *'Ili'ili.*

What?

'Ili'ili, river rocks.

What the hell do you want?

35

Are you the *Plover*?

Who wants to know?

I have a letter for you if you are the *Plover*.

Show me.

A light went on and Declan saw a muscular young man with long black hair in a narrow wooden canoe painted bright blue. The word *'Ili'ili* was carved into the bow and the prow was carved into the head of a hawk. Beautifully carved, too—Declan admired the extraordinary craft of it for an instant before he snapped back to attention.

Who the hell are you?

Who the hell are *you*? the young man answered; was he smiling?

They stared at each other for a moment, and Declan quietly reached for the baseball bat he kept tucked under the stern railing.

I might be the *Plover*. Who wants to know?

I have a letter from a friend of yours.

What friend?

You call him Piko.

Piko's here? No way. Not possible.

Possible. He's on the island with his daughter.

He . . . what? Why are they here?

Here's his letter.

Cautiously suspiciously reluctantly Declan reached for the letter, a papery gleam against the dark sea. The young man stood, hand on his hawk, and handed it up.

Thank you, *'Ili'ili*.

You're welcome, *Plover*.

Do you know Piko?

We have other names for him.

We?

He has many friends here.

Where is here?

Makana.

Makana is this island?

Makana is a mountain on the island where some of us live.

Who are you?

A friend.

Are they okay?

Better read the letter.

Come aboard if you like—I have lots of almonds.

Thank you, no. I have children to watch. I appreciate the offer.

Thanks for your help. Piko is a good friend of mine and I love his kid.

Piko is a greater man than he knows, and the girl is a . . . gift, said the young man, again with what looked to be a smile, although it was hard to tell in the dark. He spun the canoe effortlessly, with just a shrug of his shoulder, and it slid away silently through the dark like a long blue knife.

Dear Dec: This letter will come as a surprise. But when I heard you were gone from Neawanaka I figured you would eventually drift this way. Remember how you used to ask me to take a long trip to go fishing or surfing or whatever? The time has come, man. The tide came for us. *Ma'i 'a'ai*, the cancer came for Elly and just ate her up day by day. Every day she lost a pound. She got smaller and smaller as we watched. Eventually she weighed about fifty pounds and all that was left of her was translucent skin stretched on sharp bones. You could basically see through her. Her skin was like the most incredible paper. She never complained. Her hair turned brown and then silver, and then it left. She just lay in bed with Pipa all day. Pipa got smaller too. She stopped eating too. The two of them got to be as small as sparrows. I could pick them up with one hand. On the last day Elly just sang quietly in bed all day with Pipa. I was in the bed too. It was lovely outside, all wild light coming down through the knuckles of the trees. There was wild light all over the bed. Elly just stopped breathing and all the Ellyness went out of her just like that. It was the weirdest thing. We buried her ourselves out by the big cedar on the hill. So she could have a decent view. That's the one place where you can see the ocean. I made the coffin. Pipa helped by watching. She did a very good job of watching. But she kept on getting smaller after Elly died and it was time for us to leave. There was too much not-Elly for us to be there. Everywhere you looked there was a hole exactly the size of Elly. So I sold everything and quit the job and we came here to wait for you. We knew you would come this way. Dec, it's a big thing to ask, but I have to ask it— can we go with you? I have money, I can help with the boat, I have all my charts and equipment, we can take whatever you think you can use, I'll take care of Pipa. I don't know where you are headed but that's where we are going. It's a lot to ask, man, but I have to ask it. We're ready whenever you are. Pipa's a lot easier to carry now that she's the size of a sparrow. We will be on the beach whenever. Come on up to the mountain if you want or we can come down. If you don't want to come ashore just wait for my friend Kono and he can carry messages. You can trust him. Up here I am throwing fire. I kid you not. It's a long story. I'll explain when we see you. Dec, I really appreciate this, man. I can't explain why I know this is the right thing but I know it's the right thing. Trust me. Yrs Piko

But getting the girl down from the mountain was no small feat, because she did not actually weigh as much as a sparrow, she mewled in terror when anyone other than her dad carried her, and the tiny community where Piko and Pipa had taken refuge was a lot farther up a twisting tangled trail than you would think, gazing at the unprepossessing mountain from the shore. Declan and Piko, smoking cigars, contemplated the problem from the wooden tower on the edge of the village. This tower was an odd structure altogether, some forty feet high with a carved wooden platform on top, something like a small theater stage, and a waist-high railing around it carved with all sorts of flowers but only one kind of bird—the fairy tern, Piko explained, *manuoku,* a shy gentle creature that lived everywhere on the mountain and laid its eggs aloft, unlike its tern cousins, who camped down in the duff with their buddies the albatrosses.

How'd you get her up here? said Declan, still trying to get his land legs, spooked by his sudden waterlessness.

Carried her, said Piko, puffing happily. Man, this is a good cigar.

Took a while?

Days. You wouldn't believe how steep and twisted that trail is.

Sure I would. I just walked it.

Imagine walking it with a nine-year-old kid on your back. Walked an hour, rested an hour. Turned out to be kind of a pilgrimage. We camped out along the way. My back still hurts.

I druther not wait days. I druther get going. I am getting wiggy on land these days. Druther be on the water.

Ah.

It's actually not that big a mountain. From here to the beach is a pretty straight shot. Whyn't we rig a slide?

Like a zip line?

Alls we need is good rope. I got plenty of rope.

We could do that.

We could most certainly do that.

Let's do that.

Could we just sling Pip? Do we have to sling you, too? She's tiny and you're huge.

I think we can just do her. It'll go so fast she won't have time to be scared.

We could do that.

We could most certainly do that.

They did that, and in remarkable shipshape fashion, too; Declan was, if nothing else, as he said, handyish, and Piko was one of those long thin guys made out of steel wire, ten times stronger than you would ever imagine looking at the skinny sinewy of him. Other people chipped in and Declan plotted the rigging but mostly the labor was Piko, wearing his usual baggy silver pajama pants, shirtless as usual, barefoot as usual, silver earrings swaying and clinking, his silvering ponytail plastered against his sweat-soaked back, his braided salt-and-pepper goatee sopped against his chest. He had started growing that goatee—his third armpit, Declan called it—when he was sixteen, and somehow never did get around to shaving it off, and now it hung down nearly to his waist, thin and cheerful, braided anew every morning, and sometimes featuring feathers and coins and religious medals; Pipa used to braid notes and drawings into it when she was little. Man, Declan would say, it looks like you got a kelp whip growing out of your face, which is disturbing, but it's your own ugly, and besides maybe that's an oceanographer thing, having seaweed on your chin, or whatever. Your call, brother.

By late afternoon the sling line was set and tested twice, Piko tucked his daughter into an air chair made of pillowcases and fishnets, Kono waited patiently with her, and Piko and Declan ran down the trail as fast as they could go to receive the holy package. Pipa flew like a tiny pale bird, squeaking and fluttering, into her father's arms, and rather than tears or terror on her face, Declan noticed, there was the hint of a hint of a smile. He didn't say anything to Piko about that, though, and soon they were all three aboard the *Plover,* headed north by west; Declan thoroughly relieved to be at sea again, at some deep level that surprised him; he had been uncomfortable on the island, wary, itching to be back on the boat. Man, he thought, you never loved the sea, and now you get wiggy on land, where the hell else is there? Do I have to live on the wing like a blessed albatross?

★

Where to actually bunk the kid was a problem, though, a conundrum made harder to solve by a blizzard of fairy terns around the boat. Jesus Christmas, said Declan, it's not like we are fishing and there are scraps of fish to be had, what's the deal? There were really an amazing number of terns, more than they could count, and they whirled and spun and fluttered and thrilled and chattered and made their creaking gentle music like a hundred wagon wheels. Sweet mother of the mother of the lord, said Declan, do we have to go below to get a word in here? Which we have to do anyways to figure where to stash your progeny, brother. Better get to that now. To bed at dark and up at dawn on this boat, captain's law. Whyn't we put your little fairy tern in my bunk, and you and I can camp out alongside? You can open these sliding panels, see, so she's right there, she can see you and you can see her and no one has to look at old Declan, but she's tight as a tick in there, she can't bounce out no matter what the weather. Fair enough? Jesus Christmas, Piko, when are you going to cut that goat testicle off? Pretty soon it'll be getting tangled up in your private parts, *that'll* be hard to explain to a doctor. She's all square in there? All tucked in? Good night, little pumpkin seed. So you to port and me to starboard, brother. You are left wing and me right wing. We'll figure it out. Just move that stuff up front a little. We'll balance it out tomorrow. Let's get some sleep. No weather tonight. You want an orange? Jesus blessed Christmas. I don't believe you're finally on the boat. Jesus, what a crew. I can't believe I have a crew. I am awful sorry about Elly, man. Real sorry. She was a peach. I sure liked her. Why she married you is a mystery to me, but strange things happen, is what I think, and hey, you got the pip out of the deal, so you totally win. You don't see some beauty marrying *me* and then presenting me with the world's coolest kid. Nope. Old Declan O Donnell, a solo mio, solo sailing the silent She. Say that three times fast, brother. Good night, crew! Long day. We'll figure it out. Good night, Pipsqueak. Sleep tight. Shipshape sailing the silent sea. You guys want an orange?

★

Nihoa and Nalukakala, Kauo and Kanemiloha'i, Punahou and Kapoho and Pihemanu, Mokumanamana and Mokupapapa, ah, the Leeward Islands, the dots and rocks and sand spits and atolls and coral outcrops west and north of the populated tail of the Emperor Seamounts, that vast chain of mountains beneath the sea, that tremendous fence amidst the Endless; a scatter of souls lived there now, intent scientists and stoner caretakers and such, though in the old days there were tiny villages and tiny terrace gardens and beaches and cliffs used only for prayers and sacraments; but the little islands were covered by incalculable

43

numbers of birds of every shape and size, tiny finches to
epic frigate birds, little golden ducks with piercing eyes,
albatrosses by the thousands of thousands, and most of all,
it seemed, the same brilliant bright white terns that had
followed them since they left Makana. The terns were so
used to the *Plover* now that dozens of them perched cheerfully on the rigging, and one particularly brassy specimen
sat comfortably on the cabin roof exactly where the gull
used to reside. Every time the wind surged or changed
direction the feathers of the terns ruffled and riffled with
an audible fliffle and Pipa rustled in response, sitting in
the throne they'd rigged for her in the stern; Declan had
tinkered his fishing chair to fit her like a huge cotton
glove, and they could spin her in any direction for stimulus and sightseeing. Declan spent most of one afternoon
ostensibly puttering around the boat fixing things but actually gauging the pip, while Piko snorkeled and fished
the brilliant shallow waters of what appeared to be Disap-
pearing Island, if my charts are right, said Declan, be careful, man, if the island vanishes come on back to the boat,
we're not going anywhere today, it's housecleaning day.
And indeed he draped everything adamantly moist on the
cabin and rigging to dry, shooing away the terns for a moment, and oiling the engine, and triple-checking sails and
backup sails, and wading around the *Plover* in his battered
high-top sneakers scraping off the biggest of the freeload-
ing barnacles, and airing out bedding, and opening all
hatches and doors, and counting and recounting fists of
garlic, and again discovering that he was shipping a huge

cedar bow and some fifty arrows, I do *not* remember
stashing arrows, that is totally weird, although now I can
actually shoot fish, if ever there was a place to shoot huge
strapping fish this would be the place, man, as even when
wading around the boat with scrapers in hand he had seen
snapper, jacks, grouper, tangs, surgeonfish, squirrelfish,
parrotfish, goatfish, butterflyfish, eels, and lean gray reef
sharks fast as whippets, not to mention gleaming friendly
dolphins and seals as fat and sleepy as uncles on Sundays.
Place is a fecking paradise, he thought. You could live here
for a year eating fish and never seeing a blessed soul.
Doesn't sound half-bad. Onions and limes and grouper.
Dry out in the sun. A thousand miles from anywhere anyone anyhow. *Peace is always in our power,* says old Ed Burke,
although what did he know, all tumult and struggle and
hated because he was right, the poor old Irish goat. Boy, it's
bright. I better cover up the pipsqueak before she turns red.
Poor little parrotfish. What does she think in there?

★

Birds! she is thinking. Birds come back! And as if called or
lured and drawn to something riveting or masterful or
beloved the terns did come back, by the dozens and then
the hundreds, this time lining not just the cabin and the
rigging but the railings and indeed every open space on
the boat big enough for their strong gray feet and dainty
black claws; they mewed and mewled and stared at Pipa as
if waiting for something to be said, a lesson to be delivered, a message conveyed; but she only sat there under
her fluttering white hat, her hands fluttering like wings,

wearing a hint of a hint of a smile. And not only the terns were drawn to the *Plover* as if to a home they did not know they had—boobies, sanderlings, shearwaters, petrels, ducks, curlews, plovers, gulls, hawks, and a dozen tiny bright birds of every color and many names swirled over and around the boat as if they were trying to write a complex story in the brilliant air, all of them talking at once in their myriad languages, their sounds their names, *io* and *ulili* and *hoio* and *ao* and *uau* and *koloa* and *ewaewa* and *ukeke;* but above them all, like a dark god, soared *iwa,* the frigate bird, king of thieves; and when his shadow passed over the birds below they scattered, his shade slicing through them like a knife. Even Pipa was frightened and she mewled so loudly that Declan ran up on deck from below to see if she was okay. She stared at him, fluttering her hands like wings, and she did not calm down until Piko heaved himself over the side, dripping, and put the braid of his beard in her hand so she could feel the rope that bound her to him. Mess of fish in a mesh bag there, Dec, he said quietly, and Declan spent the next hour cleaning the fish, salting some for the road and soaking some filets in lime juice to cure; just as he finished, tossing the detritus overboard for the cleaning crews, he noticed the horizon darkening to the north. Nuts, he said to Piko. I thought we could dry out here awhile but we better get some water under us before the hammer drops. Don't want to be around these shoals in serious weather. You might want to buckle down the pipsqueak. That's a storm with hair on it, I think. Nuts. I was looking forward to doing a lot of nothing in the sun for a while. I haven't seen the sun since I was a little kid the size of your baby girl. I heard *rumors* of it, sure, big hot thing people worshipped and all, but it's new to me. Don't know what to do in a world without mud and moss, brother. I was really looking forward to some dry time. Nuts. Always the way it is, whatever it is. Inordinate expectations, says old Ed Burke. Lovely phrase. I agree with old Ed. All expectations are doomed to die. So I expect nothing and then whatever good happens is good, you know? And whatever bad happens is normal. That's the way it is. Tie everything down, yes. You want to double-lash those boxes, yes. That's fuel, we need the fuel, can't lose the fuel. Ready? Haul up anchor. Let's run west by south and beat this thing if we can. You got the pip tucked in tight? Let's gun it a little and beat this thing. Where did all the birds go? Man, a minute ago we had a crew of a thousand and now it's just us again. Here we go. Hang on, brother.

★

The *Tanets* was registered in Liberia as the *Tanets,* or the dance. It was also registered in Oman as the *Volchitsa* (the she-wolf), in the Maldives as the *Cherypaha* (the turtle), and in Indonesia as the *Sokol* (the hawk). In all cases the boat was listed as having a Russian owner, a crew of four, and papers to ship lumber from one side of the ocean to the other; in actuality the *Tanets* had not carried timber for years, since Enrique had taken possession of the boat from its late owner, and it carried a crew of three: Enrique, the pilot, and a massive impassive crewman with no name at all. In actuality the *Tanets* was a fishing vessel, in a manner of speaking; a nomadic enterprise, a commercial entity with the widest possible definition of commerce, or, as Enrique had once phrased it, hunting and gathering in the most ancient and traditional manner. In actuality the *Tanets* had no fixed abode or port of call, and rove at will. It was not a pirate ship, having never sunk another ship; it was not a merchant, as it did not sell nor buy in any orthodox manner; it carried cargo only briefly, as the general rule imposed by its master was immediate consumption or exchange; it was not a gunship, although there were guns aboard; and it belonged to no navy or nation, despite its plethora of identification papers of various nationalities, produced as situations demanded. In actuality the *Tanets* was nothing that it seemed to be, and something of a shadow in legal and maritime terms; as soon as it was reported to be seen in the east it was gone into the west, and many people who were sure they had spotted it from ship or shore almost immediately doubted themselves when no record of a rusted dark gray mystery ship could be easily found. Also Enrique preferred to move at dusk, when the boat blended into the sift and shawl of darkness, and on moonless nights, when the *Tanets* would emerge silently from the lees of islands, or the shoulders of lonely jetties, or the tangled mouths of isolated rivers, and slide quietly into the long dark sea like a shark. From long practice each of the three members of the crew held the same position when they set out to hunt and gather—the pilot in the cabin, Enrique behind him with charts and binoculars, and the impassive crewman in the stern, making sure no one saw them leave.

The *Plover* ran. The storm was boiling from the north and northeast at a terrifying rate, and Declan knew from painful experience that the savage wind and mammoth swells would hit at the same time, so they ran, all sails set, engine at full roar. Make sure the leeboard in her bunk is up! he shouted at Piko. What? The leeboard! keeps her from bouncing around! The ship tore through the water faster than he could ever remember the old bird whipping before. The water grew gray and then black. Clip yourself on the jackline! he shouted at Piko. What? The jackline! this rope! it'll save your ass! The storm loomed and brooded and filled the world. For an instant Declan thrilled in the speed and flow of the boat and then he knew they could never outrun the storm and they were utterly and thoroughly screwed. Sea anchor! he shouted at Piko. What? The drogue, the chute! This they had actually practiced setting once, and now Piko flung it off the bow perfectly just as Declan slewed the boat around to face the hungry storm. They whipped down everything but a storm sail so Declan would have steerage if necessary, paid out line to the drogue chute, and stared at each other. The wind hit first and then a series of swells so big even Declan felt bile in his throat. Let's go below! he yelled, but no voice could outshout this storm, and he grabbed Piko's elbow and gestured.

Down below Pipa was mewling in terror.

Stay with her unless I call you. Put your life jackets on. She's in there tight. I can help, Dec.

Nothing to do. We either ride it or sink. If it sinks, stay together.

You staying down here?

Yup. I'll check the chute here and there.

Can we ride it out?

We can't run away fast enough. The only thing to do is face into it. If we try to run we'll get pitchpoled for sure. The chute should hold us facing into it. If we go sideways we sink. If we get rolled we sink. This is a serious bitch and we basically just have to endure it. The boat will float if we stay facing the storm.

How long will it last?

Hours. And it'll get worse than this.

Nothing I can do?

Stay with the pip. If I need you I'll call. The wind will start to scream and she'll be really scared. Just stay with her unless I call you.

Okay.

Isn't this great, Piko? Happy you came?

Sort of.

The bucolic South Seas, said Declan. Serene and tranquil vistas that please the eye and calm the roiling soul.

The wind started to scream. Declan estimated forty knots, maybe fifty. It went on and on and on and on and on and on and on and on. Pipa puked on Piko. Declan went up three times to check the chute the first hour and four times the next hour. The swells grew to ten feet, fifteen. The thrash and smash of water were such that he wore his snorkeling mask on deck. On and on and on and on and on and on. The wind snapped the rigging like a bowstring, a thread, a strand of web. On and on and on. The mast snapped with a crack like a cannon explosion. Piko leapt up from the bunk and ran on deck. No no no! shouted Declan. Go below! The pip, the pip! But all Piko heard was the last word and he slid back down the stairs to her bunk just as the ocean punched a hole in the hull to starboard and water shot howling through as if from a fire hose. He grabbed Pipa and ran on deck. No no no! shouted Declan, horrified to see the girl, and in the worst nightmare imaginable he watched as Piko reached for the jackline, lost his grip on his child as a tremendous wave hit them like a hammer, and Pipa rode the froth of the seething wave over the bow and into the maw of the sea.

★

Piko dove for her instantly an incredible leap from the top of the stairs his head crashing against the railing with a terrible crack but he had her foot he caught her foot! and Declan dove for him and grabbed his clip just as Piko washed thrashing over the rail but Declan snapped the clip to the railing just in time the line went cruelly taut he saw Pipa's wild face in the water her hands fluttering madly he saw Piko gagging but Piko would go to the bottom of the *sea* with that foot in his hand he would *never* let go and Declan hauled with all his might o god o god pull jesus blessed jesus he saw Piko's braided beard whip in the seethe like a fish tail and he grabbed it with his left hand and hauled on both rope and beard with all his might and both Pipa and Piko came thrashing gagging puking over the railing he left Piko clipped to the railing and grabbed Pipa and ran down the stairs to her bunk shouting all right! okay! stay here! I'll get your dad! don't move! As if she could move the poor busted kid and he leapt back up for Piko who was a streaming gray huddle and sag on the deck. Unclipped him from the railing shoved him down the stairs. Piko! Stay here! Do not come on deck! Do you hear me? Stay here! It'll blow over soon. One more hour. Piko! Listen to me. Stay here. I'll take care of it. I'll take care of things. You take care of her. Can you hear me, man? Piko!

A soggy mumble: Dec.

Jesus, man. You all right?

Pip?

She's all right. Stay awake. Don't come up. She's okay. Jesus, Piko. Stay here.

And none of the three moved again for what seemed like hours, as the storm raged away to the west; the wind shrinking from shriek to howl to roar to shout to thrum to sigh, though the swells remained mountainous far longer; the birds returning to the world, although now they were jaegers, the dark falcons of the sea; and finally when the swells began to subside he hauled in the drogue, his arms heavy and burning. He examined the hole in the hull, the size of his fist, and plugged it with plywood and epoxy enough to keep the water out; he'd fix it better when he had time. The mast was a loss. Nothing to be done now. Cut and stored rigging for splicing and rerigging later. Both pumps going strong. Piko and Pipa asleep. He rolled them both out of their wet clothes and wrapped them in layers of blankets. Poor little pipsqueak. Course south by west. He could not turn into the still-powerful swells and beat back to the little islands, not with the muscular current and insistent mounds of water behind him; he would have to ride the current south and west and hope to hit Wake Island or the Marshall Islands, and stop there for repairs and refitting. Nothing to be done. *Our patience will achieve more than our force.* Burke. I don't think I have ever been this tired, and Christ I been tired. They didn't drown. Boy. They didn't drown. Heck of a day. The Pacific Ocean, my butt. Total misnomer. They sure didn't drown, though. *Great* day. Best day ever. I got to sleep a little. Just an hour. How come suddenly there's no terns, why is that? Jaegers'll eat your eyeballs. Wonder where that gull went? Abandoned ship. Absent without weave. *Heck* of a day. Just a little nap. Just.

*

Two days of warm sun and gentle breeze and work around the boat drying things and stitching things and repairing things and doubling the patch in the hull and splicing and rigging rope and fixing one of the pumps which gagged and gave out, waterlogged, and praising the other as the greatest tough little pump that ever was, *you* are going to pump heaven, little man, *you* are my favorite pump ever, we'll make a little pump crown for you and have a ceremony when you are done returning the ocean to whence it came, my good little pump brother.

Late on the second day they rested, all sprawled in the merciful sun, Pipa asleep.

Tell me about the pip, Piko.

Not much to tell.

What works?

Her hands, pretty much.

That's it?

All her *parts* work. I mean, she eats and grows and stuff, but she's sort of trapped in there. She makes that cat sound but she can't really talk. There's days I think she's making some tiny progress but then the next day I know she's not. She got nailed by that bus, Dec. Hammered her head against the highway. She broke some bones but that's not what's broken anymore. The her of her broke, I think. I wonder sometimes if the her of her is in there or not. I don't know which would be worse, her being all there and trapped inside or her not being there anymore and just her outside keeps going.

Can she make a comeback?

I don't think so, Dec. Been four years. Doctors said no.

I thought I saw her smile a couple times.

Me too. I don't know if it's for real, though.

Her eyes work, right? She knows what's going on.

Maybe.

I don't know anything about kids but I think so.

Didn't you take care of your kid brothers?

They took care of themselves. We weren't that kind of family. You and Elly were that kind of family. Not us. We were on our own from the start. Like fish eggs. Probably why I am stuck at sea.

Speaking of which, when are you going home?

Not. This is home now.

You're going to spend your life on the boat?

I don't know, man. I am just sort of winging it here.

Destination?

Unknown.

Agenda?

Don't sink.

That's it? Don't sink?

Yup. Ambition can creep as well as soar, says old Ed Burke.

What?

Edmund Burke, man. Ed is like the patron saint of the *Plover.*

You are a nut.

Yeh.

Are we ever going to land?

You in a hurry?

No.

Well.

I guess we are at sea too.

Yeh.

Sorry to poke, Dec.

No, man, it's a pleasure to have you here. And I really like the pip. I never told you how sorry I am about her and Elly. I am really sorry, man. Maybe the boat will be good for the pip. She's already had wild adventures on the *Plover,* right? So maybe that's good. Maybe excitement is good for the little peanut. Get her jazzed up, am I right? That could be.

That could be.

That could most certainly be.

Later, lazily:

What was this fire-throwing stuff you mentioned back on the island? What was that all about?

Oahi, it's called. You really and truly throw burning logs out over the ocean. You wouldn't believe how far some guys can throw those things, like a *mile.*

What's the point?

Old tradition. Kind of a holy thing. Ceremonial, celebratory. I just got fascinated by it and got really absorbed and who knows why. We came to the island after Elly died and something about *oahi* just was . . . healthy. I can't explain it very well. Pipa liked sitting in the dark and watching the firesticks go flying out over the water. The wind hits the mountain there and rises and if you get your feet set and throw right your fire just floats out there forever. It's the wildest thing. You wouldn't believe someone can throw a burning log a mile and it just hangs there traveling slowly on the wind until it finally hits and sizzles. Incredible.

Any wood'll do?

Best is *papala* or *hau,* real light dry woods. Papala you can light one end and throw it like a javelin and the fire burns through it as it's in the air. Hau mostly you would light both ends and whip it so it spins end over end. It's hard to learn to do it right and it's no picnic climbing up the mountain carrying wood but when you see it done well, or even better when you occasionally *do* it well, there was some powerful magic in it, man. The people who really get it don't talk about it much. They taught me because I respected it and didn't talk about it, and because they saw what it meant to Pipa. She would be down on the beach wrapped in blankets with the aunties and they told me she peeped all night long like a chick hatching. They sure liked Pipa. They called her Peepa. One of the aunties told me the pip was learning how to use her new eyes and ears, which I don't know what she meant but it felt good to hear something other than *poor kid* and *cripple*.

You get good at throwing fire? We could use you in battle.

I was decent. It's not strength as much as balance, is what they taught me. I am not the strongest guy but I did okay. It's not for fighting, though, you know. More like praying, I guess.

Huh.

We spent a lot of nights there, Pipa and me, Pipa on the beach with the aunties and me up on the mountain with the throwers. Good guys. We'd make a fire and tell stories and then throw. Sometimes people would be out there in boats trying to catch the sticks as they fell. In the old days it was the height of cool to catch a stick and mark yourself with it, that was heavy medicine. One friend of mine, he was a master at gauging the wind, and he'd shoot over in his canoe and grab the burning stick just before it hit the water. Incredible hands. You met him—he was the guy who delivered the letter. Kono. Excellent guy. There's a lot of stories about that guy, and he's a great storyteller himself, he's like the storycatcher in his town.

Tell me one.

There was a kid named Nou who wanted to be a fire-thrower so bad he could taste it, but he was a little kid, and back then only the top men were allowed to do the deed. Nou sneaks up the mountain anyway one night, but it's a hell of a climb, as you know, and he's beat, and stops to rest, and he hears a small voice calling for help. It's a *menehune,* like a wood elf, and Nou, a decent kid, frees the elf from the rock that trapped the guy. The *menehune,* also a decent sort, says he will help Nou throw his fire the farthest that night. So Nou gets up to the top of the mountain, but the older guys are furious that he's there against the rules, and they want to toss him overboard, but Nou makes them a bet that he can throw the farthest, if he loses they can throw him over. Okay, fine, they say, probably snarling, you know, like in the movies, and he whips his log, but it's his first time, and he's little, so his log just falls straight down toward the forest below—but the *menehune* is on task, and he asks the wind for a little help, and the wind catches Nou's stick and sails it so far out it looks like a star on the horizon. New world champion of firethrowing: Nou.

That's a good story. What happens to Nou later?

Oh, they killed him later anyway. But his friend the *menehune* cursed his murderers' feet for that, and they could never climb the mountain again, the end.

When bad men combine, the good must associate, said Declan, else they will fall, one by one, an unpitied sacrifice in a contemptible struggle. Old Ed Burke.

Man, what is your deal with old Ed Burke?

Brilliant Irish guy, said Declan cheerfully. One of those guys everyone thinks they know what he said but hardly anyone actually reads what he actually said. I just dig the guy. No one reads him anymore and I feel bad for him so I figure *I'll* read him, at least. Keep the man alive. So at least one regular person in the world is reading him for fun rather than to chew some obscure detail to death like they do in colleges. Did you know he would give a speech first and then sit down and try to write down what he said? Incredible. Who does that anymore?

You are a nut.

A guy throwing burning sticks into the ocean from a mountain is calling *me* a nut.

Just trying to learn a useful trade.

Haw. Let's eat. You better wake the pip or she'll miss dinner.

This is good, being here, Dec. Thank you.

No worries.

It's real generous.

I needed a crew. You were the first two that applied.

Thanks, man.

No worries.

★

But he did worry, in his bunk, at night. How was this going to work? What about food and fuel and repairs? What if Pipa got worse and needed a doctor? And not to be overly selfish about the whole thing, but this was not the plan. This was a solo voyage. Now there's three of us. I wasn't looking for company. Not having company was the point. Company just expects things from you. Other people are kind of fences, aren't they? Assumptions and expectations. I don't want anybody expecting anything from me ever again. I was just going to float. Now we have to go somewhere and do something. But they are rootless too. They are flying solo. What are we going to do for money? What do I do when Piko finally says it's time for them to go home? He'll have to land her at some point. She'll need wheelchairs and ramps and machines and visiting nurses and stuff and he'll have to get a suit job to pay for that. Poor kid. That kid is a cripple forever, I bet. No mother, no house, no voice. Poor little fish. Jesus Christmas. Almost lost that kid. Shouldn't have her on board. Irresponsible. Probably illegal. No permit for that. Jesus blessed Christmas.

And thinking of Christmas Declan suddenly got a wash of old old memory from when he was maybe ten years old and his sister Grace was maybe eight and the boys were little crawlers, this was before their mom left dragging her suitcase down the driveway and never came back, before the old man froze up inside totally and hated everyone and everything, and he was sitting by the fire, a roaring winter fire of cedar and oak, a frozen mist like a blanket outside weighing down the spruce trees, the cows all huddled together for warmth in the barn, the radio playing something deep and gentle, some cello thing like deep voices humming, and Grace was half-asleep with her head on his feet in a little castle of pillows they had built by the fire, and the little brothers were tipped over like bowling pins asleep on each other on the huge dark couch, and his mom didn't hate his dad yet, and his dad was listening to her at the pine table, she was carving something in the air with her hands like golden birds in the gentle light from the kitchen, and his dad had his face propped in his hands like a pear in a bowl, and maybe he was even smiling, the old goat. A Christmas night long long ago. No tree, no presents, no special dinner, but no punching or screaming or cursing either; and everyone together. Best Christmas *ever.*

*

The *Tanets* survived the storm also, with less damage, being bigger, but at the height of the storm the pilot, smoking a cigarette, had stepped out of the cabin to relieve himself and been swept overboard so fast that Enrique, sitting in the cabin poring over his charts, shouted at him to close the door! before he realized there was no one there to do so. He leapt for the thrashing door but knew it was too late even before he gauged the rage of the water. He had expected this, in a sense. He had expected to lose his pilot somehow, in the same way he would eventually lose his massive impassive crewman; pilots and crew came and went, died or fled, stole and ran; it was the nature of people to die or flee, it was their natural end, the spin of the wheel. He made an effort to remember the name of the pilot but could come up with nothing more than the end of his first or last name, he couldn't remember which: ivić? Something Somethingivić. Nor could he remember quite when the pilot had joined the crew. Probably Vladivostok, when they had to leave in such a hurry and he grabbed the first man who could read a maritime chart. The wordless crewman was different; he had come aboard on the blackest night Enrique could ever remember, many miles south and west of Hawaii, where there was no land for hundreds of miles. The man must have had a boat, but there was no boat or canoe to be seen near the *Tanets* when Enrique and the pilot found him standing silently in the stern, wrapped in red cloth from his armpits to his knees. Even with a pistol in his face he would say nothing more than *taromauri,* his quiet answer to every question, and Enrique, who ultimately could not care less about origin and explanation, put him to work; he was immensely strong, seemed to know his way around ships, and ate like a bird despite his mountainous size. For a few weeks Enrique kept his pistol at hand, wary of the man's strength and sudden mysterious appearance, but after some months neither he nor the pilot even noticed the crewman much. He ate alone, always sitting cross-legged in the stern, and always wore his vast red cloth, and when not working seemed content to sit calmly in the stern, eyes closed, either sleeping or plotting savagery, as Something Somethingivić said with a leer. He and Enrique called the crewman Taro, after what seemed to be the only word in his vocabulary, and had even stopped speculating idly about Taro's sins and crimes a few weeks before the pilot stepped out of the cabin to relieve himself and never came back.

★

But the *Tanets* now needed a pilot. Enrique could maneuver and navigate a bit, but if he was busy piloting, the *Tanets* had no brain, and brains led to money, and the whole point of the *Tanets* was money, and the impassive crewman appeared to have no piloting or navigating skills whatsoever, so Enrique contemplated where he could get a pilot in a hurry. He sat in the pilot house, smoking the cigarettes

Something Somethingivić had left behind on the chart table in a crumpled golden packet. He could go down to the Line Islands, half of which had the advantage of not being American and so were less chained by rules and regulations, and there hire or borrow or steal a pilot. He could go west and south to Tungaru or the Marshall Islands, also small entities with less fanfare about laws and papers, and there hire or borrow or steal a pilot. Or he could press a pilot into service off the first boat he saw; the best plan, he thought, as it entailed less travel, an infinitesimal chance of police interference, and a minimum of witnesses. Come to think of it, he remembered, that was how Something Somethingivić had come aboard in Vladivostok; Enrique had made an arrangement having to do with boxes he had picked up one night in the disputed islands near Japan, and Something Somethingivić had awoken at sea, displeased but not especially surprised to find himself suddenly the pilot of a boat of changing nationalities and identities depending on situations. This sort of thing had happened to him many times, beginning at age fifteen, when he sold himself to an army for the price of his younger brother being shoved stumbling into an icy forest at night to make his way across a border, which he might well have done, despite his tender years; even at twelve years old the younger brother, quick and silent, knew how to find the eggs of wild birds, how to trap fish, how to wait in the snow by schools in the morning and steal food from smaller children. Something Somethingivić in fact had drifted over the years toward coastal cities like Magadan and Vladivostok for the express purpose of finding little Danilo, certainly little no more, if he was alive at all; the rough chaos of land's end, where many men and memories crossed paths, was where a man might find news, a clue, a trail to follow; so that suddenly finding himself at sea, in a tramp boat bent on commerce of any shade of legality, was not so bad a way to listen more widely for news of a missing man. He would be in his twenties now, Danilo—probably tall, like all their tribe, and probably not a drinking man, given the demons that had savaged so many of their clansmen, and probably alluring to women, given his heavenly voice. Even at the age of eight, when Danilo opened his mouth and began to sing, people stopped in the street, people pulled cars and trucks to the side of the road to listen, people wept as his voice strummed the joy and pain and memory in the hollows of their bones.

★

Fixit Day on the *Plover,* by command of the captain. Declan and Piko repatched the hole in the hull, repacked supplies, dried spare sails, set lines for fish, swam with Pipa. They repaired the mast as well as they could, which wasn't very well, but it will have to blessed Jesus do for the moment, said Declan. We have enough fuel to make Tungaru and we can use the mast if the wind stays easy. Time for your tutorial in sight reduction tables, spherical trigonometry, observed latitudes, celestial declinations, and computation of the azimuth! Time for you to undertake considerable things, as old Ed Burke says! You're an oceanographer, don't you already know this stuff?

Nope. I know more about what's in the water than what's

on it. We always had taxi drivers when we did research projects. Guys like you.

Tall handsome guys?

Trolls with tattoos.

I only have the one tattoo. Don't lie in front of the kid.

Got it when you were drunk?

Nope. Birthday present for my sister. I told Grace I would do one crazy thing for her, whatever she asked, and she thought about it for a couple days, and she decided we should both get tattoos, and I said tattoos are stupid waaay beyond the usual stupid, paying people to punch holes in your body is nuts, but she insisted, although she wanted both of us to get *is fearr bás ná náire,* death before shame, but that's nuts, so I got this one, *misneach.*

Meaning?

Stay afloat. Don't drown. Don't quit. Stay with the boat.

Lot of meanings for one word.

Big word.

Let's go over charts and navigation, Dec. I feel like I am not really helping much as a crewman. Wouldn't it be best if I steered and you could fix things?

Yeh. We can take turns. I think we can make Tungaru in three days if the weather stays clean. We can refit there and make some decisions.

Like?

Piko, what are you going to do with the pip? You can't stay out here forever.

Says the guy who is going to stay out here forever.

C'mon. She needs nurses and stuff. How are you going

to pay for that? You want to go back to Makana? Oregon? You got to get a job somewhere, counting whale peckers or whatever it was you did.

Actually I studied oceanic dead zones. Hypoxia. Low oxygen in the water.

I'm serious, man. You got to work and the pip needs a crew.

I'll figure it, Dec. Thanks.

You're blowing me off here, Piko.

I'm not, Dec. I hear you, man. It's just that I don't know what to do yet. It's just me and Pipa and I don't quite know how to work it. I leaned on Elly more than I knew. She was the glue. She wouldn't let them put Pipa in the cripple house. I wanted to let them do it, Dec. I couldn't stand it anymore. I fought as hard as anyone in the first couple years but then every time I saw Pipa it burned me for who she could have been and never will be. The kid we had died on the road by the bus stop. That kid is dead. I couldn't take it anymore. That sounds scummy but it got real dark for me. I never told anyone. Elly knew. Pipa knew too. I think it burns her inside somewhere that I was the scummy dad who would have said yes to the cripple house and probably hardly visited her there. I used to think I was a good guy, Dec. I was a good guy before something hard came along to test me and I failed totally. Then Elly got sick and she got smaller and smaller and you could see through her and she died holding Pipa in her arms, Pipa making that bird sound and me sobbing like a baby. Pipa kept making that bird sound for weeks afterwards and it drove me insane, Dec. I had to hide in the shed outside sometimes because she would just lie there chirping and mewling and I knew she was crying for her mama and not for me. I never told anyone any of this and it burns me even telling you but I am so lost at sea that being lost at sea for real is not so bad. I don't know where to go. I want to be the best dad ever and I was the worst. So what happens next, I don't know. Maybe it's on your charts. Sorry I popped a gasket here. I miss Elly. I miss Pipa. I guess I miss the me I thought I was but wasn't. What's an azimuth?

★

Pipa knew. She remembered how her dad stopped rocking her in his arms every night, stopped sitting in the beanbag chair making up stories about foxes, stopped washing her slowly in the afternoon with old soft towels. He didn't stop all at once; he just did one less gentle thing a day. He continued to do the hard things, the dutiful things, the awkward things, but the thousand tiny quiet other things—the unconscious braiding of her hair while they watched basketball, the eggs flipped for exactly thirteen seconds as they had together determined was exactly the exact right number of seconds to get eggs exactly over easy, the notes left for her at the breakfast table, notes written on whatever he could find, sometimes oak galls, sometimes maple leaves, once the carapace of an enormous beetle—those things slid away silently, one per day. She knew. She watched the little gentle things he used to do leave the house, padding away into the moist forest, the branches shivering from their passage. But she could not speak and she could not write and she could not catch his eye in such a way that he knew she knew; and she discovered she did not want to catch his eye that way, for fear he *would* know she knew, and be pained by his own retreat; to hurt him was unthinkable, incomprehensible, unimaginable, it hurt to even *think* about hurting him; but she missed those towels more than anything in the world. A thousand times those towels had wicked up water from her shimmering skin, and sacrificed their nubs to her, and become so incredibly thin you really could see through them when they billowed in the yard like small sails in a salty wind; but no words fit their softness anymore, they were way beyond soft, they were a sort of skin themselves when her mom ever so gently rubbed her with them after a bath; but Pipa remembered her father's hands behind those towels like sweet bones under the skin, and remembered the day he only used two towels instead of three, and then one instead of two, and then none instead of one. She knew.

★

She also knew more than anyone knew she knew. She knew how to call to birds in ways no one heard but the birds. She knew how to see inside dark places without using your eyes. She knew how to sleep with her eyes open and how to be awake in some parts of you and asleep in others. She was learning how to call to fish although whales and porpoises were as yet a mystery. She knew which trees were the friendliest near the house they used to have. She could hear what people meant when they said things they didn't mean. She could hear people coming from a long way away. Miles and miles. People were much larger than their bodies, is how she would have tried to explain it if she could talk again. People are a lot longer and thicker than they think they are. People jostle with more things than they know they do. We don't have any words yet for how this happens but this happens, is what she would try to say. Our bigger selves are always bumping into each other and into other things. Only things that are alive have this big thing around them. Some people and some living things, when we jostle and bump them it's comfortable, it's like when Dad would dry me off with the towel gentle and rough, it's good to be rubbed like that, or like when Dad bumped shoulders with his brothers and they would laugh, but some people and some things, when your bigger self bumps against their bigger self, it feels uncomfortable, or it even hurts. And some big selves don't forget that hurt. The hurting stays like a scar. Like your big self remembers things that you don't. But only living things, or things that used to be alive. And your big self stays alive for a while after your body stops. Like it's always looking for the smaller person that used to be in the middle of it. And other people's big selves are looking for that missing person too. But the missing person isn't there anymore so the big self gets smaller and thinner and it cries as it fades. I heard Mama's big self crying all the time afterwards. Crying for the person it used to have inside it. Her big self, it used to go around the house looking for Mama and crying and crying, and Daddy would say what *is* that noise, Pip, it sounds like a cat is stuck under the house, I better go see if there are raccoon kits down cellar or what, and I would want to shout Daddy it is Mama's big self! don't you feel Mama's big self? But he didn't feel it. Or maybe he did but he didn't say. His big self is quiet now. It didn't used to be so quiet! His big self was the loudest funniest self you ever saw! It would rub against any other big selves and that would be so funny! Like that time with all those whales on the beach, there were so many big laughing selves I kept getting knocked down on the beach when they laughed and we were all laughing so hard! Those were the biggest selves I ever saw until now. Daddy sent them back. His big self rubbed them all back in the water. Now there are some big selves below us that are so big I can't even feel the edges of them and I don't know how to call to them yet but I will. Some of the small fish say that you cannot talk to the biggest selves down there at all but I think you can.

*

Late in the afternoon they slid past an unmarked atoll so crammed and bubbling with terns that it appeared to be a seething white raft in the brilliant blue sea, and they paused for a bit to stare at the sudden profligacy. Declan was interested, Piko was fascinated, but Pipa was mewling and flapping her hands wildly with that hint of a hint of a smile, and sure enough hundreds of terns were soon lining the rigging and railings again, a tern perched on every open square inch of the boat, staring fixedly at Pipa.

What is she, queen of the birds or something?

Got me. Birds at home didn't do that.

Even with hundreds of the little white creatures on the boat there seemed to be thousands on the atoll, and Piko and Declan watched for a while as some rose and hovered effortlessly over their nests like spirits, and others circled over the little island like sentinels, and others bobbed in the lagoon like boats in a children's pool.

Manuoku, the fairy tern, said Piko. Lovely bird, gentle, not much for harrying.

You know your birds?

Some. Spend enough time out here and you get to know some of what's out here.

You liked working out at sea?

Loved it. It's the last great wilderness. There's medicines and foods and amazing secrets down there more than anyone could ever count. Might be the future.

What, the ocean?

Yep.

Ocean's a killer, man. Trust me.

So are we, Dec.

At least we feel bad about it sometimes.

Maybe the ocean does too.

Nah. Trust me. It just kills and eats and moves along. The best you can do is work out a truce. I thought we had a deal, I harvested and she let me plow the waters, but there were some incidents and misunderstandings, and I am not sure where we stand now, me and the old blue beast. Old murder mother.

Pipa mewled loudly and a whole line of terns shot into the air as if commanded, just before a dark gray bird shot over the boat like a bullet.

Jesus blessed Christ. What's that?

Jaeger. Looks like a gull but acts like a hawk.

71

The jaeger now plunged headlong into the seething mass of terns on the atoll and emerged with a struggling chick in its razor beak; and then suddenly there were two more jaegers falling like arrows, and ten more and twenty more, and the atoll was suddenly a battlefield of screams and shrieks and shredded terns. Pipa flipped and fluttered and mewled and Piko gathered her into his arms to bring her below away from the carnage as Declan set the *Plover* south and west. Down below Pipa went silent but her eyes were open. Piko rocked her silently. The last Declan saw of the atoll was a single tern rising to battle the jaegers as they stooped again to the slaughter; but as he watched the tern was torn limb from limb, shreds of it raining down on the darkening sea, where lean fish flashed suddenly like knives.

★

Night was blacker than black. Moonless starless. Declan in the cabin dozing. No light anywhere in the world except a faint luminescence in the *Plover*'s wake. Suddenly a wall is alongside and a grappling hook flung down like a huge talon. Declan storms out of the cabin and runs into a shotgun aimed at his eyes. A huge shadow slides past him silently and goes below. Piko comes up with Pipa in his arms. The huge shadow stands behind them. A voice behind the shotgun says quietly you come with us or he comes with us. Choose. Declan uses foul and abusive language. The grim shotgun barrels touch his forehead. The voice says okay fine we will take the other guy. Declan says no fecking way over my dead body who the feck are you get off my fecking boat. The voice says your dead body is fine but then who will care for the child? Piko says easy Dec easy. The square shadow behind Piko and Pipa doesn't say anything. Piko says easy Dec easy we will figure it out. The voice behind the shotgun says go. Pipa doesn't say anything but everyone sees her shocking eyes. Piko says easy Dec easy now be easy. He hands Pipa to Declan. Piko says we don't have a choice right now so you take care of the pip and we'll figure it out easy now. The voice behind the gun says go. Piko clambers up the wall into the darker darkness above. The voice behind the gun says remember to forget this. The voice behind the gun and the huge shadow vanish up the sudden wall into the darker darkness above. Declan stands there seething and shaking. Pipa stares up where her dad went. The darker darkness slides away south. Declan makes a strangled sound. He sits down with Pipa in her chair in the stern and kisses her awkwardly on the head and says listen pipsqueak I don't know who those guys are but we are going to find your daddy and make everything right, okay? I *will* fix this. You trust me and I will trust you, okay? They went south so we will go south too. They won't hurt your dad, okay? Your dad will be okay. I will square this you bet. Anybody home? Can you hear me in there? Pretty soon you and your dad will be sitting together looking at the birds, okay? Stuff happens and you fix it. That's the way stuff is. No worries, Pippish. We will figure it out, okay? We'll work together like a good crew does. You and me, okay? No worries. Can you actually talk to birds and stuff? If you can talk to the birds tell them to keep an eye on that ship for us, okay? Like scouting parties. We could use scouts.

Jesus fecking Christmas. Okay. This is like a bad storm and we will just stay with the boat and stay cool and work through stuff and make it out on the other side and everything will be okay. Okay? Jesus. Okay?

III

1° NORTH, 173° EAST

DAYS OF EPIC RAIN. Declan talked to the Tungaru Police Service. The rain was incessant. He talked to the commander of the coast guard, which consisted of a single patrol boat. The rain fell sideways and backwards and from several directions at once. He talked to the minister for fisheries and marine resources. Sometimes you couldn't tell the rain from the ocean. He talked to the minister for foreign affairs, who was the same minister as the minister for fisheries and marine resources. People talked about the rain as if it were a person. He talked to the attorney general. Old man rain is sure angry today! they said. He talked to a man who knew a man who would know the men who would steal a man. One man in a store suggested that they sacrifice dogs to the rain as they used to in the old times. He raged and sulked and shouted and filed complaints and filed reports and waited in steaming anterooms and offered bribes and roared and accused and challenged and waited behind huts for messages that would surely come but did not no matter how much he raged and promised and bribed. A small girl on the island of Beru drowned when she caught her foot in a rain barrel and the barrel slowly filled with water and next day someone noticed her pigtails floating in the barrel. Our patience will achieve more than our force, said Declan quietly to Pipa in the bunk, after three fruitless days in Tungaru harbor. That's old Ed Burke and we are going to steer by old Ed here. No passion so effectually robs the mind of all its powers of acting and reasoning as fear. So we are going to stay cool and figure this out. We will get your daddy back and make the thief pay. O yes. We will work during our despair, as old Ed says. O yes. Stay with the boat, Pip. *Misneach.* We don't know each other very well but we are going to work together here. We're a good crew. There's three of us now and we are going to stay three of us. *Misneach a ghlacadh,* arm the boat. Our antagonist is our helper, says old Ed. He that wrestles with us strengthens our nerves and sharpens our skill. I can do some things and you can do some things and we will get some things done. I think you are awake in there and there's ways to get you out. Maybe old Ed will help us. Old Ed was a tough old bastard. His enemies hated his guts and he laughed at them for their clumsy attempts at his destruction. I know you can hear me, Pip. You stay with the boat and we will get somewhere. I didn't expect a crew and I didn't want a crew but now we *are* a crew and that's good. Maybe I was wrong to not want a crew. There. I said it. Don't go blabbing that to everyone. Keep it to yourself. A good crew keeps its own counsel. Old Ed didn't say that but he should have. He was an islander, you know. I bet you *do* know. You know more about everything than I do, that's for sure. I see you smiling, Pip. I see you in there.

★

On the *Tanets* Piko was immediately put to work as the pilot. He explained to Enrique that he was not actually a pilot and Enrique replied firmly that indeed he was now the pilot and becoming a good pilot as fast as possible was the best way to avoid major accidents to his former shipmates, for example a sudden fire. You would be surprised how many accidents of that sort happen to small boats this far out in the open ocean. It is not unusual to find small boats floating rudderless with no one on board and no sign of what happened to the captain and crew. The ocean is a wilderness and there are all sorts of accidents in the wilderness. You would be surprised. Piko was not surprised. He bided his time. He calculated percentages. He examined his situation. He banked his fires and shut down the roar in his heart. He wrote Pipa's name on a piece of paper and fingered the paper all day long to keep sane. He approached his situation in a scientific manner. He tried to stay calm with middling success. He gathered information and was alert to pattern. He sifted through facts and gauged possible courses of action.

He could flee; a poor choice, given the lack of means by which to flee and lack of knowledge as regards the location of the *Plover.*

He could overcome his assailants; another poor choice, as they were armed and he was not, and the impassive crewman was so enormous that even Piko, with a healthy ego and male confidence in his own strength, dismissed the thought of winning *that* fight.

He could attempt to cripple the *Tanets;* an idea that appealed to him, and that he filed away for further action pending more information.

He could appeal to passing vessels for assistance; probably a dangerous idea, not to mention there weren't any passing boats.

He tried to stay calm and think that the best thing he could do for Pipa was to return to her in good shape and as fast as possible, which would take guile, not power. He tried to stay focused. He tried to absorb as much as he could as fast as he could about the *Tanets* and Enrique and the impassive crewman. Information is weaponry. The more he knew the better he would be able to solve the problem. Despite the drama, and the undeniable danger, the problem was essentially simple: he was in the wrong place, and he needed to return to the right place. There would come a moment when he could set things in motion to solve the problem. That moment was not now. Therefore he would gather as much information as he could in order to be prepared when the moment came. Information wins wars. He tried not to think of Elly. Sadness was a weight he could not afford to carry. He took every opportunity to explore the ship, such as it was; for all that it seemed so much bigger than the *Plover,* most of it was cargo space. He could not discover what the cargo was. The hold was locked twice over and the impassive crewman was always nearby, watching silently. He tried to talk to the crewman but the crewman never replied nor smiled. There was never a moment when Piko was awake that the crewman or Enrique or both were not in sight, and even if they did not seem to be aware of him he knew they were; and when he turned in at night they locked his door from the outside. That first night, when he lay in the heaving dark in his reeking bunk, so frightened for Pipa that his chest burned, and he heard the cold snick of the lock, a rage and fear rose in him like a roaring tide; but he quelled it deliberately, coldly, and calmed his breathing, and bided his time. A moment would come. That moment was not now. Therefore he would wait until the moment was now.

★

The problem, said the minister for fisheries and marine resources and foreign affairs, is jurisdictory first and geographory second. The rain had stopped and the palm trees seethed and bristled in the onshore wind. The incident occurred outside our territorial waters. It is a matter of the high seas. The high seas are not adequately policed in my opinion. This is why for example we have a smuggling problem. I hope you will keep these remarks in confidence. I hope to expand our police presence in the near future but our budgetory expectations are necessorily low given the lack of income sources. Additionally the other boat involved in the incident is geographorally unknown at present. We can and have issued information to our Police Service boat but as you know they have not seen the culprit and there is only the one boat at present. I hope to expand the number of boats in the near future but that is a matter of subtle negotiation with our Australian friends who do not at present see the matter with the same urgency as we do. So you see our ability to assist you further in this matter is limited even if our willingness to do so is not. I am a father myself and can well imagine the feelings of the man in question. Also I am an uncle as you are and I can imagine the pressures of your worries as regards stewardship and care of the child. I would be happy to make arrangements for the temporary care of the child as a guest of the republic under my aegis if that is what you choose to do. Also I can alert our citizens to your plight and ask them to report sightings of the other ship as a matter of public service to a guest. I speak with confidence for our citizens when I say that they would make every effort to assist you in finding the father of the child. Unfortunately we are not in a position to offer financial assistance at the present time but you would be surprised how far goodwill and sharp eyes at sea go especially when the matter at hand is a saddened child. Our citizens are much on the sea, given the geographoric nature of the republic, and if the other boat is anywhere within a hundred miles I would be surprised if it is not soon seen.

The minister stood and bowed and Declan stood and for an instant, as he reached to shake hands with the man, ten thoughts ran through his head at once, so that his head thrilled and sizzled: what a wry kindhearted soul, this minister; why would he bother to be so helpful to a stranger; how sensible it would be to put Pipa in a home for a few days; how good to have someone smart and professional care for the kid; how much easier it would be to chase that bastard and get Piko back if I didn't have to worry about the kid; how can a country even a small one possess only one fecking police boat; what can I trade from the *Plover* for a serious gun; how did I get into this anyways; all I wanted with this trip was to just be left alone for a long while; no way I can leave the pip. No way. I got a kid now. How funny is that? Never even had a serious girlfriend and now I have a kid. Fecking miracle.

Most sincere thanks for the offer of help, sir, but I must keep the child with me. I promised her father. But the eyes of your citizens for that ship, yes sir, I would be most grateful if as many eyes as possible were hungry for that ship. Yes sir. Most grateful indeed.

★

Declan had never bathed a child. He had never wiped a child's bottom. He had never fed a child with a spoon. He had never held a child in his arms and rocked her to sleep. He had never held a child with his left arm and positioned a barf bucket with his right arm and thought that his left arm was going to absolutely fall *off* after a few minutes. He had never recited the names of every bird he had ever seen to a child. He had never cut a child's toenails and fingernails. He had never cut a child's hair. He had never run sections of rigging through a child's hands while explaining the various sizes and shapes of rope necessary for conduct through this vale of tears and fears. He had never placed a wriggling bright green fish in the startled hands of a child. He had never tucked a child into her bed by running his hands along the outside of the blanket like a lawn edger to make sure the kid was tucked in tight as a tick in the rick of the bunk. He had never stared at a child's face after she fell asleep and gently moved a tangle of hair to the side of her face ostensibly so she could breathe better but really so he could see the incredible miracle of her herness. He had never taken some scatters of old canvas and stitched them together into the shape of a Fairy Tern, complete with jet-black eyes and beak, and stuffed it with handfuls of coconut hair, and stitched it shut so tightly and beautifully that a seamstress would have been awed, and tucked it into a child's arm so that when she awoke in the morning she would make the most amazed bird trills and mews he had ever heard which he heard from the cabin where he was as he would admit if he was an honest man waiting for her to wake up and discover the tern.

But he did all these things with Pipa.

★

The bus that smashed Pipa was driven by a man named Kinch. He was a school-bus driver. Yes, he had heard all the jokes from the kids on the bus. Klinch, Klutch, Klench, Klutz. Sure he heard them. He didn't mind, much. He liked the kids, mostly. Only once in a while did he stop the bus, or get out of his seat silently, or step off the bus to have a word with the mom or dad or grandma or neighbor who was there to retrieve their kid. Only once had he ever furiously followed a driver who blew past the bus even with the stop sign blinking, and even that one time he was so startled at his own rage that he had to calm down for an hour before he called the cops with the license plate number which he had scratched on the dashboard of the bus with his ignition key to be sure he got it right; those six numbers remained on the plastic skin of the bus ever after, and he would run his fingers over them sometimes like a blind man reading a terrifying story. Them numbers never did heal, he said once to another driver, who looked at him oddly. After the accident he didn't drive anymore. He just stopped. He walked in the next morning and put his letter on the dispatcher's desk and walked down the hall to the supervisor's office and sat down to wait. His buddy took his route. He went to work for the town doing other things. For a while he worked at the library but there were too many people who when they saw him turned and looked away like they hadn't seen him. For a while he worked at the police station as a night dispatcher but there were too many kids getting hammered or worse. For a while he worked at the docks checking registrations and bills of lading and safety equipment and permits and load limits but then a guy from a new boat asked him isn't this the town where a bus hit a kid waiting for the bus, Jesus, can you imagine such a thing? Finally he worked fixing trucks and buses for the town but then he started fussing over the buses too much and had to quit. By then his wife's pension package was mature and she quit and cashed in and took the same job on contract and he didn't have to work but he had nothing else that interested him so he quietly went crazy. He got religion for a while but that didn't work and he got into art for a while but that didn't work and finally he built a canoe with a little cabin in which he could camp out for a couple or three days on the islands off the coast. More and more he took to taking his canoe and vanishing for a few days into the islands where he counted the little foxes who lived there and drew maps of their trails and watched as they caught mice and eagles caught them. He knew it was only normal and natural that eagles caught fox kits but the first time he saw it happen with the kit mewing and struggling in those inarguable talons he lost his temper so thoroughly his nose bled, so the second time he saw an eagle stoop on a kit waiting for its dad by a bush he leapt up and roared and danced and the kit dove to safety and the eagle sheered off grim and furious, and Kinch laughed so hard that he wept.

*

Dusk on the *Plover*. Pipa asleep. Hatches battened, ropes coiled, pots washed and stored. The boat rocked gently. He saw a dark gray heron picking its way silently along the beach. My kingdom for a Jesus blessed Christ cigar. But suddenly a wash of memory and regret, a terrible brilliant flash of images and sounds all at once: young crows moaning in the trees in summer at home, the dusty-old-raspberry flavor of thimbleberries in August, the hilarious stench of skunk cabbage in March, the waddling sprint of ground squirrels in summer, the ubiquity of wild cucumber vines, the layers of blue mist like veils and tendrils in the morning over the green hills, the hills arranged like breasts and fists. The oily clay, the crumbling sandstone, the cougar prints as big as dinner plates along rivulets high in the hemlock hills where no one ever logged. The tunnels in the trees up there where only deer went easily and even old man bear thrashed and lumbered, too big for the deer roads. The way when you really wanted to eradicate wild cucumber you had to track down the man-root deep in the loam, never where you wanted it to be for easy access, and get your brothers and buddies to shovel down after it with you, and when you found it finally it really was as big as a man, with arms and legs and everything, and you had to haul it out of the dark, heavy as sin, before you could kill it.

★

Dawn like an eye opening. The *Plover* rocking gently. A pregnant silence, a deep silence filled with waiting, the invisible musicians with their transparent hands poised over their evanescent instruments; and then a lorikeet whistles in the woods; and then the inquisitive quizzical koels ask their quiet questions, and then a sea of warblers all at once as if by command, by signal, by the descent of a baton only they can see; and then the deluge, pigeons and doves, noddies and tattlers, godwits and turnstones, curlews and pipers, teal and widgeon, boobies and petrels, whimbrels and phalarope, and o my little terns! says Pipa in her spirit voice from the dark of her coffin bunk to the first terns coming to her call, gliding into the rigging like brilliant prayers; and with the blinding white terns now come bigger gray terns, and cocky terns with dashing black crests, and terns with black masks, and a tiny tern with a call like a creaking door. They line the railings and cover the cabin and shuffle scratchily aside only to admit a single large gull, which appears silently like a dream and takes up its familiar spot on the lip of the roof of the cabin, right above the doorway. And who might you be? asks Pipa with her big-soul voice, her spirit voice, the voice that goes with her bigger-than-her-body self. The gull explains, in her creaky raspy rusty-hinge voice, her travels and travails; she does so at elephantine length, the gulls being a garrulous race. Pipa explains the situation and the gull says she will have to ponder the matter. The terns, rippling on the rail, express general skepticism; when have gulls ever looked out for anyone other than themselves? Pipa opens herself to all birds in the harbor. The gray herons on the beach are startled by the touch of her spirit; they have never been spoken to in this way before, with a voice they cannot hear with their ears. They rustle and burble uncomfortably, stalking stiff-legged around in the shallows like tall stern old professors, and Pipa says gently perhaps you should have something to eat before we continue this discussion; the herons are a peckish race. She and the terns discuss the danger of jaegers and skuas in the open sea. We think you should approach *iwa,* the frigate birds, say the terns. They are afraid of nothing. What about the albatrosses? asks Pipa. The terns go silent; they can find no way to comprehend her question. The albatrosses are the albatrosses, say the terns finally in their small white voices. We cannot talk to the albatrosses. They live forever and they have no enemies. No one eats them and they eat none of us. We do not see them except at sea. When they come to land they keep to themselves, singing in their forest, until their new children are ready to live forever also. The albatrosses are the albatrosses. They are much older than we are. In the beginning of the world there were no islands and the albatrosses were the only birds because they could fly forever. All the world came from the albatrosses. Their droppings became all the islands. We do not know how they came to be or what happens to them when they die. They are the oldest of birds. They are not unfriendly but they have no companions among the birds. No one speaks to them and they do not speak to us although they sing among themselves. The albatrosses are the albatrosses. We cannot speak of them because we do not speak to them. Even the gulls cannot speak to them and the gulls speak to everyone all the time. Perhaps *you* can speak to them. What kind of being are you, to speak to us? Are you a bird with useless wings?

★

Declan emerged scratching his belly and urinating over the stern and then gaping at the troops of terns before noticing the gull. He laughed aloud.

Sweet blessed Jesus Christmas. Welcome back, bird. Could use another hand around here. Things are intense. Lots of work to be done. Hard work. Messy. You're a messy race, you'll be comfortable. We are going to go fishing. Fishing for men as old blessed Jesus Christmas said.

Trawling for trawlers. Harvesting a man. Adding to the crew. Which reminds me we have a kid on board. Her name is Pipa. She's a pipsqueak. You wouldn't know the word. You'll like her. She don't say much. Quiet kid. Add her to the manifest. That's three of us now with you and we will go get our fourth back. His name's Piko. You'll like him. Looks like a tall skinny goat. Good guy. He got borrowed but we are going to borrow him back. O yes. I bet today is the day.

Indeed today is the day. The minister for fisheries and marine resources and foreign affairs sends a message that a rusty gray trawler has been seen to the northwest, near the atolls the fishermen call Anewetak. There are so many atolls and islets there that no one is quite sure how many there are. Some of them have no names. He, the minister, has enclosed charts and graphs for the *Plover*'s progress. He, the minister, cautions caution in those waters, as even the charts and graphs enclosed are not perhaps fully accurate, and the shifting sands and tides in that wilderness of atolls and islets, not to mention the effects of storms, make caution the watchword of the wise. He, the minister, wishes that he could be of more direct assistance in the matter at hand, but he trusts that the recipient understands the press of ministerial duties, and the vagaries of communal responsibilities undertaken by the undersigned by virtue of his appointment to the ministry, a signal honor, which he, the minister, wishes to discharge with every iota of his energy and passion for that which we hope someday, by the grace of Atua who made all things, will someday be a republic, not unlike, perhaps, that from which the *Plover* came, and by the grace of Atua shall safely return. Also we enclose ten shillings as a gift for the child.

★

Moonless night. Overcast. A thorough and incredible dark, as if the concept of light had never been invented. The only hint of light other than the boat's running lights is the *Plover*'s wake, a bioluminescent furl. Pipa had been buckled into her chair in the stern but she mewled so plaintively that Declan finally picked her up and grumbling carted her around the boat until she indicated where she wanted to be; to his amazement, she wanted to sit at the very tip of the stern. This is a particularly and remarkably poor idea, Pippish, said Declan, but she was so weirdly insistent to be exactly *there* and nowhere else that he finally surrendered, muttering darkly, and he arranged her sitting up, facing forward, and strapped her down with every scrap of rope and line he could find; I may never get you *un*strapped, he murmured, and you will forever be the figurehead of the *Plover,* every ship no matter how small should have a figurehead, isn't that right, you know what a figurehead is? Heck, sure you know what a figurehead is, you are probably some kind of raw genius and just can't get your genius out your windows anymore. She stared at him with those eyes like pools like seas like windows. It was so dark he could see only the faintest outline of her head, although her hands seemed to glow gently. The terns that had been with them all day as they roared northwest had faded away as dusk fell, but the gull was again silently floating exactly nine feet above the stern, last he noticed, at sunset.

Back in the cabin he slows the boat to a crawl and stares into the murk. Never despair, but if you do, work on in despair, said old Ed Burke. Exactly so. *Misneach.* No way I can see the bastard's ship, can I? But he can't see us either. So I'll *smell* him. Old shitbucket smelling like rust and oil and dead things. He must be stopped for the night. No one can navigate in this. Should have told the pip to maintain total pip silence. As he thinks this he notices her hands waving madly; is she waving at him to stop? He shuts the engine off. Blacker than the blackest black. The tiniest of lapping wavelets ticking against the boat. She flaps her right hand. Is she signaling? Can she signal? Jesus. He peers and squints; nothing; but there is the faintest whiff of diesel fuel. Isn't there? Is there? There is. He shuts off all lights. It is the darkest night in the history of the world. How can I still see her hand? How is her hand lit up? Weird. He slips up to the stern. Her eyes are wild. He bends down to whisper directly into her ear. Pipa, don't move. Don't make a sound, okay? I'll be right back. Everything will be okay. I am going to get your dad and we will be back in about ten minutes, okay? We'll come up the stern as quiet as we can. Don't make a sound when you see him, okay? It's real important that you don't make a sound. Don't let any of your birds make a sound either if they are around, okay? I'll be right back. He slips back to the stern and strips down to his black shirt and shorts and eases over the side and vanishes into the darkest night in the history of the world. For a moment Pipa sees a shiver of biolumi-nescence opening like a fan behind Declan and then the dark closes in again like a tide.

Beneath the boat there are fish so tiny no eye can see them. There are fish bigger than the boat. There are mammals and mollusks and cetaceans and crustaceans. Far below sprawled at an awkward angle as if its neck was broken by the fall there is a warship so covered with mud and kelp that its name and numbers are lost. Barracuda swim through its corridors. Fifty feet away there is another warship from another country. It too is now a reef. Once it was designed for death and now it is a nursery. The two ships sank together one evening. It took all day for them to sink. Men rode them down through the darkening water. On one ship there was a boy of fourteen. He was tall for his age and had learned that if he did not speak when questioned but only nodded assent his interlocutors assumed he was older than he was. He had loved the sea ever since he could remember and probably before. He first heard it when his father carried him down to the shore when he was two years old. They lived in an apartment in the city and his mother and father borrowed a car and they drove down to the sea with the boy and his sister. His sister was afraid of the sea. He could not imagine how that could be so. He ran to it like it was waiting for him. It thrummed and seethed in his dreams. He wanted to be in it and of it and on it and under it. At age ten he ran away from home and tried to go to sea and his father was desperate and searched the docks all night and found him just before dawn huddled near a crab boat. At age twelve he ran away again and boarded a freighter and was loading cargo until the bosun discovered him and put him ashore.

At fourteen he stood as tall as he could and nodded silent assent to questions and the navy took him and he had been at sea one month and one day when his ship sank. The ship was terribly damaged in the morning and the bow half sank first and then the stern half. The bow sank in the morning and the stern sank at dusk. The boy huddled in a room alone as the ship sank. He could see his sister's face and hear his mother weeping and feel his father's hand on his shoulder. His father had lean long hands as hard as wood but they had never touched the boy with anything other than the most gentle and tender affection. Everywhere else in the stern as it sank there was roaring and rending but in the room where the boy was the sea whispered in ever so politely and slowly. The boy kept his head above water for as long as he could not from duty but from love, because he loved his mother and father and sister and wanted to see their amused faces and feel his father's hand on his shoulder, but finally he closed his eyes and opened his mouth and sank to the bottom of the room and the last thing he heard was the thrumming and seething of the sea just as he had heard it in his dreams when he was small.

The *Tanets* is stopped for the night. Enrique in the pilot house, smoking a cigarette, absorbed in charts. Piko in the stern. The impassive crewman amidships, watching Piko. The silence of a darkened stage just before the play begins. Enrique thinking of Something Somethingivić. A loss is a loss. Men have been lost before. Many men. The way of the world. The song of the sea. We all lose what we start with. The nature of the beast. It happened to me. It happens to everyone. An excellent pilot. He had a brother. The brother who sang like an angel. I had brothers. Not one of us could sing, however. Mama told us that! It comes time to leave and you leave. The way of the world. The nature of the beast. The world is a beast. You make your way. You leave and you do not come back. What is there to go back for? An ocean of dust. I made my way. I have a boat. I go where I want. The laws do not apply to me. What laws? I take what I like. Who is to say no to me? They will not come for me. They will not take anything of *mine*. I am the shark now. I go where I want. I take what I want. They think the law will protect them but there is no law. There are only people who believe in law. If you do not believe in law there is no law. I am the law. I teach them the true law. The true law is that there are sharks and there are the things that sharks eat. That is the law. If I want fish I take fish. If I want timber I take timber. If I want guns I take guns. If you can take something, take it. That is the law. So much talk about the law. What is there to talk about? Talk talk talk. My papa talk talk talk about the law and they came for him and said they were the law and so much for his talk talk talk about the law, where was the law then? There is no law. The law is I am the law. If I want a pilot I take a pilot. This pilot is not so good as Something Somethingivić. Perhaps he will be lost too. A loss is a loss. His child will learn the law. The small child. Better to learn the lesson young, like I did. I am doing his child a great service. The shark is a great teacher.

Pipa hears everything there is to hear. Fish sliding beneath the boat. Spirits overhead. Stars singing. The boat groaning gently in its oaken voice. The rigging keening. The engine box yearning for the engine. An albatross, very low, a foot above the surface, waiting for that one moment in a thousand when a fish has risen too close to the glittering night. The flitter of water against the boat. The keel yearning for motion. The infinitesimal shifting of stale almonds in their hidden bags and corners. The keen atomic whine of the steel belts with which she is belted in place. Her mother's gasp as her father made love to his wife slowly silently slowly in their room down the hall which they did not think she heard but yes she did and knew it for a rich ancient sound, not fearful but densely mysterious, a summer night forest sound, thick and moist. The sigh of their grizzled dog by the fire. The plummeting of woodcocks in love. The probing tongues of flickers. The thump of an owl against a vole. The shimmer of snakes. The roil of squid far beneath the boat. The infinitesimal dissolution of the pages of Declan's six-volume set of sight reduction tables. The shimmer and slosh of fuel in the tanks. The clench of barnacles against the hull. The shriveling of the last oranges and lemons and limes. The infinitesimal rocking of Piko's cigars in their redolent box. The sizzle of the match he used to light his cigars on their porch in the woods at the end of the day when he sat barefoot and weary with Pipa on his lap and told her stories of the seethe of the sea. The plop of her mother's tears on the furl of ferns as she hung the laundry after she knew she would die during the summer the osprey came and sat every night in the trees outside Pipa's window which osprey never do Papa said so but they did that time. The hiss of a cigar doused by the sea; two splashes deep in the dark not far from the *Plover;* and then a third splash, quieter but more thorough, as if something larger but more familiar with water had entered the sea; something that knew the sea and the sea knew that something; something that spoke the language of the sea and knew what song to sing on entering; so that the sea accepted it gently, and knew it as a native child with salt in the blood.

★

The *Plover* slides away through the epic dark. Piko dripping in the bow with Pipa in his arms. Declan steering, one eye on his charts, one ear for any hint of a hint of pursuit. Wavelets murmuring lapping licking the boat. Boy, it is *dark*. Thank God it's so dark. No one can find us if we stay quiet and slide out of the picture. South by west. Am I bleeding? Feck. Fecking feck. Don't bleed on the charts. All right. Minor hole. A dent in Dec. Had worse holes. A hole man. Holistic. All right. No stars no moon no fecking comets we might just make this. We might just pull this off. Jesus blessed Christmas. Assault and fecking battery on the high seas. Kidnapping. Armed kidnapping. Jesus. A guy sets out on his boat for a little solo voyage and it turns into a fecking adventure novel. All right. Check charts again. There's a glob of little tiny islands and atolls and such southwest of here, Declan had explained that morning to the gull on the roof, who looked interested but noncommittal. We could get good and lost in there if we pull this off. We get Piko back, we slide away into the endless, we're golden. No bigger boat will ever find us if we just stay low. There's a million little islands out here. We could hide out awhile. We get good and lost and then slide east. He doesn't know which direction we went and we get lost and then cut east. You with me? North we hit weather we don't want, west we hit countries we don't want to hit, south we hit countries we don't want to hit, east is good, man. East is water followed by water. Water is the country we want. You with me here, bird? You know, if you were a *good* traveling companion, you would *say* something sometimes. Didn't you ever read books where birds can talk and things like that? Maybe the pip can talk to you. Maybe she can talk to birds. Are gulls like the silent punks of the bird world? Are you guys all in a gang or what? Is that the deal with the red dots on your beaks? Like tattoos? Man, you can talk to me—I won't tell anyone you squealed. No? Yes? No.

*

They ran all night, Declan at the wheel; he wanted to be as far away as far away could be when the sun came up. If it came up. You never know about the sun, you know. People get all cocky about the sun coming up tomorrow, *I* don't get cocky about the sun coming up. The sun comes up, *then* you can say the sun came up, but don't be getting all expectatious about it, one thing I have learned is to have no expectations and assumptions, man, that's the road to hell. Whatever you are sure of, don't be. Can't be crushed if you never expected anything. Vote for the man who promises least; he'll be the least disappointing, says old Ed. *There's* a guy who never expected anything. Born on one island, died on another. That's what I'll expect, to die on an island. Some tiny island out here in the endless friendless. Bleached bones a harbor for coconut crabs. That's about right. Something will use me for shelter. So I'll be useful at last. The old man told me enough fecking times I would never be useful but how wrong he was, the old shark. I caught a lot of fish from old mother ocean, didn't I, and I own the fecking boat free and clear, and no one owes me a penny, and I owe no one, and we got Piko back on the boat, and I am so tired I couldn't spit if you gave me the spit and a running head start.

Toward dawn he saw dimly ahead what he so wanted to see, a welter of tiny islets and atolls, some baked naked and some dense with low trees and bush; he eased the boat into a particularly bushy one, slid into a tiny inlet, and tied into some trees. He was so weary he could not move, and he stood there, head hanging, unable to even run through the automatic closing-up-shop checklist in his head, the one he had run through every night for years, depthtideanchorsenginehousedpee. For an awed moment nothing moved, not the sift of the sea beyond the inlet, not a leaf, not a grain of sand, not a crab on the beach; and then everything moved gently all at once, a swirl of sand, a crash of surf, a clash of crab, a quiver in the thicket of trees; Declan shivered awake from his standing sleep, and gaped as a bird with a titanic wingspan floated silently across the mouth of the inlet; gray above and white below, wings easily six feet wide, a pink bill, hooked at the very tip; an albatross! But it was gone as quickly as it had appeared. Declan turned to go below, but turned again to see if the gull was still sitting there on the roof; and there it was, wide awake, startled, staring at the air where the albatross had been.

IV

IN HIS OFFICE on Tungaru the minister for fisheries and marine resources and foreign affairs is being interviewed by the editors of the three largest newspapers in the islands; both radio stations are also represented, and there is a man with a stylus drawing pictures of the event in wax for reproduction on cloth and paper, and there is the single television station's single television camera, operated by a man standing on a box that once contained bullets, and there is a man with an ancient camera that may or may not be loaded with film, and there is such a crowd of clerks and secretaries and shopkeepers and burbling children in the building that the staircase outside his open office door groans with the weight of their quiet dreams. The minister for fisheries and marine resources and foreign affairs is today announcing his candidacy for first minister, minister of *all* affairs, minister to whom all other ministers must report and apply, and his announcement is remarkable news for many reasons; he is respected and liked by everyone, and so all would wish him well no matter what he wished to achieve; he is attempting to leap, in one electoral day, from the populous third tier of the ministry to the lonely pinnacle of the first, disregarding the tradition of years spent in the Kabuki theater of the second, where ministers pose and preen and take mistresses and conduct quietly savage campaigns against one another as they jockey for the final prize; and he is announcing not only his candidacy, which is a surprise but not a shock, but his platform, which is stunning.

I wish to make all the poverties die, he says, to the scratchy music of skittering pens and slowly revolving ceiling fans. I wish to establish a republic of free people beholding to no fading empire or nation or country at all. I wish to establish a republic where every tenth person, male or female, young or old, is chosen a National Dreamer. I wish to catch every drop of rain that falls on every island in such a manner that we do not ever again have to purchase water or pay for other nations to construct factories for the cleaning of the water of the sea which is our mother. I wish to teach every child to read and write starting at the age of one, and have annual competitions for the most amazing stories written by children between the ages of one and nine. I wish to make the use of automobilities in the islands an enterprise so burdened with onerous taxes that eventually automobilities are used only for a national taxi service. I wish to file judicial cases in the courts of various former empires and nations and countries for the repayment of one-fifth of the profits accrued by commercial endeavors over the last three centuries, such funds, if collected, to be stored untouchably in the National Dreamer Bank until further notice, the other four-fifths of the profits acknowledged to be our contributions to the health of their children over the last three centuries, our best wishes. I wish to establish a new ministerial position, the ministry for children, such position to be held by a child between the ages of seven and eleven. I wish to establish a police force with two boats for every island of whatever size or nature, including atolls. I wish to establish an army of thinkers who will imagine and execute ways for the republic to borrow the energy of the sea which is our mother. We *can* use our mother's muscle; that is *not* silly talk. Do we not each of us use our mother's energies every moment of our lives? Are we not in fact made by and shaped by and consist of the energy of our mothers? Well, then. I wish to establish many more things, gently and respectfully, without guns or shouting. I think we are all children even if we have old bodies and we should make a republic that runs on the wonder of children whether we are old or young children. I think because we are poor and tiny that we are out of the way of war finally and so we can invent new ways to live that bigger countries cannot invent yet because they still are in the way of war. I think we could be such an amazing place that people all over the world will come to see what we became. I think many people who live here agree with me in the chapels of their hearts. The symbol of my candidacy is the lorikeet, which as you know is a most beautiful little bird, friendly and gentle, which used to be everywhere here but was wiped out, but now there are a few living here again, and if Atua is gracious to us, and we work hard and gentle together, the lorikeets will come back and be everywhere here in the trees like they used to be. We will be like the lorikeets, almost dead but coming back amazing! That is all I have to say this afternoon. Thank you for the gift of your ears. As my gift to you, we have water here for anyone who is thirsty. *Ti abu,* farewell.

★

Enrique heard all this, from the bottom of the stairs; he had come to the ministry to make inquiries about this and that, in particular if anyone had seen a green fishing boat with red sails, and been caught in the crush of people cramming onto the staircase to hear the minister's announcement. He had quietly wandered the halls listening for news of potential crew members, union halls, shipments he might be able to be of assistance with as they perhaps languished between inspections and licenses and stamps of approval; one thing he had learned in his maritime career was to drift productively on land as well as at sea; a man could hear a great deal by wandering purposefully with his ears open and his mouth shut. Another thing he had learned on land was to dress well and stand up straight and walk briskly and speak clearly and ask friendly questions and then just listen with a smile; people would tell you much more than they expected to if you were generically presentable and left silence next to them like a friendly stranger; it was like they were waiting for some friendly silence so they could fill it up with words; and words were useful, words were hints and intimations, words were fingers pointed in certain directions, if you listened carefully; more than once he had listened carefully to clouds and thickets of words in offices and agencies and stations and union halls and old sailors' homes and hotel lobbies and bars and then set his course toward where he was sure money was hiding. And money was hiding everywhere; in words, in numbers, in the way people said things that meant other things; sometimes Enrique thought that the larger the lie the more likely there was money hidden nearby. And you could change money into any form you could imagine. It could be changed into sand, fish, wood, cloth, houses, boats, animals, books, machines, even people; one thing he had learned was that you could actually buy and sell people, despite all the laws that said you could not do so; and indeed everyone, if you looked at it from the right angle, sold himself or bought someone else; and the people who were most vociferous about freedom and rights and independence were often the ones who were quietly buying and selling the most people. So he listened carefully to the minister for fisheries and marine resources and foreign affairs announcing his candidacy for first minister, and did not believe a word he heard; but he saw the thrilled faces on the staircase, the sheen of their excitement, the throb of their collective dreaming; and he concluded that there must be a very great deal of money hidden behind all this, which he resolved to find.

★

Piko is dreaming of Elly. She is a young osprey along the river by their house. She is a wriggling flash of something in the sea. She is a scatter of late leaves from the alders along the road. She is a pine marten sliding like furry liquid through spruce branches. She is screaming as she gives birth to Pipa. She tried and tried and tried to emit Pipa but finally the doctors cut a thin door in her belly for Pipa to emerge and Piko ever after thought of it as a smile on her skin. She is singing behind the house. She is singing to her patients in the hospital. She was a nurse. She became a nurse because she had a dream one night in which she was singing to a woman who was about to die but was delighted to die because she said she saw her second son in a clearing waiting for her with his face as bright as the sun in summer. She was a nurse for seven years. She said she would be a nurse until the day she died and maybe after that who knows? They drew signs and symbols by which to speak to each other after she died. They did this at the beach one day. This was when Elly weighed so little that Piko could carry her with one arm and a picnic basket with the other. This will be me, said Elly, drawing an osprey. See the crooked wings? And I'll whistle, like ospreys do. So look and listen for me. This will be me, said Piko, drawing a frigate bird. See the crazy throat sac? And I won't say anything. You'll just see a graceful thing that suddenly looks like a clown with red balloon, and that will be me. Wait for me, okay? And then we will wait for the pip, okay? And maybe the pip will have kids of her own then, so we will wait for her kids, maybe there will be four or five of them, wouldn't that be funny, but then he noticed that Elly was weeping, and in his dream he stopped talking and laughing about the grandchildren they did not have and would never have now and took Elly in his arms and kissed her all over her head and face including the gleaming moist dome where her hair used to be, and in his dream he called to Pipa, and in his dream the pip darted over to her parents like a minnow, and licked her mother's tears away like a puppy, and Elly started laughing so hard she got the hiccups and couldn't stop hiccupping until Pipa said Mama I have to pee more than *two* horses, which arrested her hiccups but started her laughing again.

The inimitable seaside brightness of the air, said the minister for fisheries and marine resources and foreign affairs to his interviewer, the brine and the iodine, the lap of the billows among the weedy reefs, the sudden springing up of a great run of dashing surf along the seafront of the isle, to quote our friend Robert Louis Stevenson in full eloquentery; is that what you were thinking when you first saw these islands? Because while these things are so, other things are also so, for example parents who get so drunk they beat their children bloody, and young men who have no prospect of any other work than legal or illegal theft, and young women with no prospects except to marry a man who is working in legal or illegal theft, those are also things that are so here. Not to denify our friend Robert Louis Stevenson, who was honest about what he saw in

Pacifica, and he saw a good deal of our blue continent, the Îles Marquises, Tahiti, Hawaii, the Îles Samoa, and he was here also in these islands, although his sojournery here was not as pleasant as one would wish, as many residents in the first place he arrived were inebriated, the king wandering the streets in his pajamas, and the king of the second place he arrived wearing a top hat and using sewing machines as anchors for his fishing boats, which is not something we do on a regular basis now, although there is a good deal of using things designed for one purpose for another purpose altogether. In my view this is the essence of creativery, rather than something shaggy and raggy. You must remember that here there is a great deal of sea and air and rain, but essentially little of everything else, even island material itself. I find it instructory to consider the islands as they actually are, the tiny tips of mountains in the sea, and it seems to me also, if we take the long view, which I think we should, that mother sea has loaned us these islands for a while, and might well take them back at her leisure or fury; so that the whole idea of *owning* slices of islands is silly talk. The sea owns them and we reside at her pleasure, and we can all too soon unreside; and of course this has happened again and again in the islands, for all sorts of reasons, hurricanes and tsunamis and the ravages of disease, and other reasons lost now to understanding; even myself, the least travelest of men, I know of villages standing empty, their stones slumped, their thatch dissolved, their hearth fires long covered with sand. To live here you must be comfortable with the idea of not living here at all. Do you see what I mean? The

way to reside is to visit every day. This is one of the ideas
I would very much like the National Dreamers to take up
when I am elected, so that we can be clear about this with
our children and grandchildren. We cannot leave them
slices of land, as we do not actually own the land, and we
cannot leave them money, as we do not generally have
money, but we *can* leave them charts for living, in a manner
of speaking. We can leave them good stories like compasses
that point toward true things. We can do *that,* at least, if
we cannot do much more than that.

★

Pipa woke first. Hints and intimations of dawn, intuitions
and premonitions of dawn; and then dawn pouring infinitesimally into the boat as if from a vast sifter filled
with grains of light; and then full dawn, quietly, shyly,
coming from nowhere and everywhere, the boat bright-
ening slowly as if someone were turning on a vast lamp.
Pipa, half-awake, sent her larger soul aloft, groggily, the
spirit scratching and yawning; but just as she sensed the
gull on the cabin roof, and the crabs on the beach, and
the lorikeets burbling sleepily in the trees, she also sensed a
new being on the boat. She snapped awake and mewed
and flittered her hands at her father, her right hand almost
at his cheek, and she *yearned* with all her soul to send her
fingers that final inch between them, that awful inch, the
inch she could not span, the inch she never would span
again; but he sensed her hand like a wing by his cheek
and he snapped awake, saying what? what? are you okay?
She tried with every cell of her extraordinary body and
soul and itch and urge to form a word but she could only

mew and gibber, and she wanted to shriek with rage, but she could not even scream; but he knew what she wanted to say, and he leapt up, wide awake. He crouched by the ladder for a second, listening, and Pipa had a startling flash of insight into her father's beings, his total selves, all of him at once, all the hymn of him, just for an instant, an epiphany so powerful that she sagged back in her bed as if from a shock of light; his long arms like wiry ropes, his muscular patience, the black box deep in his soul in which he locked his memories of her so that they did not shred him like tiny razors; his fear that he was forgetting his wife's face, now that she was ash and scattered to the wind; his fear of his own selfishness, his desire for love he would not admit he wanted; his silvering ponytail like a dorsal fin against the broad seethe of his back as he crouched alert in the shadow; the infinitesimal swinging of his braided goatee nearly brushing the floor as he tensed like an arrow; his beard weighted at the end by the brilliant coin he had stitched into it yesterday to amuse his daughter, whose tiny fingers had a thousand times stitched into it feathers and coins, leaves and twigs, songs and prayers, wishes and dreams, kisses and tears, once the talons of an osprey.

Piko crept silently back to Pipa and kissed her and motioned her quiet and woke Declan silently. More gestures. Declan found his bow. They crouched by the ladder; two men almost thirty, in the fullness of their strength, seasoned by rage and pain, yet open to adventure and liable to joy, neither man hungry for money or power, each thirsty for something deeper he could not name but only feel it

missing; two lean arrows grim in defense of the child behind them; and then they shot up the ladder so fast it was
as if one man with two heads and four arms burst onto the
deck and instantly split apart, greedy for violence.

★

The intruder was enormous. The intruder sat cross-legged
in the stern. The intruder's hands were placed flat on the
deck, palms up. The intruder wore a vast red cloth from
armpits to knees. The intruder had very short very black
hair that stood forth like thin young trees starving for the
sun. The intruder was barefoot and wore no earring nor
adornment of any kind nor mark of any kind except vast
blue tattoos covering both shoulders, a muscular sea of
ink. The intruder was calm in the face of an arrow aimed
at the place on a neck where your thumb fits neat as a pin.

Jesus, said Piko. It's the crewman from the slime boat.
Taro.

I am not a man, said the intruder.

What?

I am a woman.

What?

Nor is my name Taro.

All the rest of his life Piko would remember the oddest
things about the next minute: the absolute unshatterable
stillness of the three human beings in the stern, as if
painted against the boat; the rusted staggered echo of her
voice, as if the speaker had not used it in a year; the faint
clatter of crabs on the beach, the lick of wavelets against
the boat, the breath of breeze in the bush; the flick of the
wind that set his goatee swinging again, with the bright

coin like a pendulum weight at the bottom; and then Declan lowering his bow, though he did not retract the razored arrow.

Jesus blessed Christmas, said Declan. Who the hell are you and what are you doing on my fecking boat? And there better be a good answer or I stick this arrow through your fecking neck. Keep your hands where I can see them. Jesus.

I have had many names, said the intruder calmly. The last name I had of weight was Maraia, which means one who is accursed.

Where is the *Tanets*? said Piko, finding his voice.

I do not know.

Where is the captain of the *Tanets*?

I do not know.

How did you get here? said Declan, the bow still taut.

I came with you last night when you came for your friend.

You been aboard all night long?

Yes.

Where?

Here. It was dark.

Another remarkable instant of absolute stillness.

Piko? said Declan quietly.

Jesus, said Piko. Jesus. It could be. He—she—I don't know. He never was pals with the other guy and he, she, was friendly enough to me. It was the other guy who made decisions. The slimeball. This one just did the work. Jesus. A woman. Why did you leave the *Tanets*?

I was finished, said the intruder.

Finished with what?

It was time to be finished.

Jesus, said Declan, what is this shit? Answer the question straight or I'll stick an arrow in your ass. You don't crawl onto someone's boat at night and talk mystic crap in the morning, especially if you were party to a kidnapping. I got enough trouble without fecking kidnapper hitchhikers. Answer straight or fecking swim home.

Allow me to stand, please, said the intruder, standing. Piko stepped back and Declan raised the bow again.

She stood up, her tremendous arms loose by her sides, and then with a curious gesture she brought her folded hands together and said quietly, My people are albatross people. I had a baby girl. She came to me on the beach. I thought she would be a great traveler. She lived her first three days in a house of spirits. We welcomed her with a great feast and a dance that went on all night long, the longest dance anyone could remember. We thought she would be a wonder among us. She was a most attentive girl. She would point to the ocean and then we would notice a school of fish. She would point to the sky and then we would notice flocks of birds. It seemed that she could see ahead both in miles and days. It seemed that she knew things also which no child could know; the place in the ocean where flying fish flew in pairs, the place where the mottled sharks give birth, the place where people suddenly had two shadows, the place where *teuu* the giant fish would eat boats, the place where even turtles jump out of the sea. How could she know these places? Yet she knew them. She knew everything there was to know about the sea without ever spending years upon it like the old men who knew the most. The old men were skeptical of my daughter in the beginning but then they discovered she had true knowledge and then they took her everywhere with them, even to the place where the waves run backward, and the place where the porpoises tell you how to go farther safely, and the secret places of the terns. We thought she was a gift and she would always be among us but one day she dove into the sea and never came up. I was on another boat there when this happened. This was near the *betia,* the sea-mark, of the terns. We had seen the first terns flying to-gether, one spinning circles around the other as they do in that place, when my daughter suddenly stood up, as if she had been summoned or called, and she cried out to me, as I was sitting in the other boat, and her face was shining, and she dove into the sea, and she vanished. We waited there a very long time, and I dove down to find her, and many of us dove down to find her, but we never found her. So it was said that she had died, and a great sadness came upon our people, and I left that place, and went in search of her, tak-ing service on whatever ship would take me, no matter what the service; but now that time is finished, and so I have come here, to this moment, with you.

*

There are times, said Declan much later, supposedly in another context but maybe not, when you just take a flyer on things. People make too much of facts. Also people make too much of gut feelings. Gut feelings probably mean food poisoning. Most of the time you try to be sensible but sensible is just as overrated as intuition. Both of them are just calculated gambles. So sometimes you deliberately gamble the *other* way, you know what I'm saying? You do the thing that isn't sensible, because sensible is just a percentage. In a sense you are being *extra* sensible by playing the odds *against* sensible, sometimes. Do you have any idea what I'm saying? You gamble backward, which sometimes is the most sensible play. You throw the odds into a tizzy. You throw them off their game. You rattle their fecking cages. Odds are ultimately prediction devices, so if you reverse them sometimes, for no particular reason, then everything's all swizzled and incalculable again. Which is good. You see what I'm saying? That's just fair all around. If no one acts exactly how they are always supposed to act, that's good. See what I mean? That's just normal, also. That's how things really are. We are all prediction and expectation junkies and it's all nuts. If a girl, say, is always leaning on her intuition, she's always making decisions based on what she feels in her guts, then she's always making one *kind* of decision, so the odds stack up against her, you see what I'm saying? Same with a guy who is always being sensible and making the right play based on what he thinks are facts. The guy himself becomes a factor because he's a fact nut. This is not even to get into how mostly what you think is fact isn't. But if you make a decision sometimes that's completely the other *direction* from facts, the odds are that you made exactly the right decision a certain percentage of the time, you know what I mean? So who doesn't want to be exactly right a certain percentage of the time? Not me. Like on the *Plover* that time with the woman we thought was a man but she wasn't. That's a good example. Ask Piko about that time. He knows what I mean. He knows *exactly* what I mean. That is the greatest fecking example ever. You ask Piko.

★

It took Something Somethingivić seven minutes to drown, the night he stepped out of the cabin of the *Tanets* to relieve himself and was swept into the roiling ocean: the seven longest minutes of his life. He knew he was going to drown; maybe he always had known he would drown; but he decided to drown slowly, to drown with intent, to drown in his own good time. If he stayed calm and kept his head above water until he was exhausted and sank, he could live another two or three minutes, he thought, and that would be a kind of victory, a kind of epitaph, a kind of something. If he stayed calm and did not thrash and did not drink the sea he could drown at his own pace. He leaned his head back and closed his mouth and tried to breathe through his nose. He tried to close his eyes but they would not close. The storm roared above him but the waves were so large they acted like windbreaks. He watched them loom and tower with a curious lack of fear; he was so intent on breathing calmly and steadily and deeply that he thought of nothing else but breathing for the first minute. Calm calm calm. He made no effort to swim or move at all, not even kicking his feet; his whole existence was intent on floating and breathing through his nose. Calm calm. He pried his shoes off with his toes. The huge wave he was in carried him up to meet another huge wave and as he rose from the trough the wind shrieked and the top of the next wave blew into his face so hard his head snapped back and his mouth opened; but he instantly shut his mouth and swallowed the sea he had eaten. Better in the belly than the lungs. The water was warm. In the forest with Danilo they were free to roam for miles. Danilo knew where there were nests with eggs and berries you could eat and trees with small sleepy birds you could eat. He knew those things. How did he know those things? The woods went on forever. Danilo was easy in the woods even when he was little. When he was lost as a child he was never lost. He might have made it through the woods. If anyone could make it through the woods in the winter he could. It would have been nice to meet him as a man. He would be tall and smiling. He would smile and ask what song do you want, brother? They would sit somewhere near the woods. They would not even eat. They would just look at each other and smile. Remember this other song, brother? Another tremendous jolt of water snapped his head back again and this time he swallowed a lot of it and he was terrified. He tried not to cough but he could not help coughing and another wave hit him as he coughed and he whirled his arms to keep the water off and he felt suddenly utterly exhausted and heavy and sad. What last song do you want, brother? The light in the woods late in the afternoon as they walked home on subtle trails only Danilo could see. The way Danilo held a spruce branch for a second so it did not thrash back and strike his brother. The way Danilo sang quietly, a few feet ahead, so that all you could hear, walking behind him in the last green light, was a bolt of song floating over his shoulder, and then it was gone. The weight of the whole ocean was upon him now. What last song do you want, brother? And he closed his eyes, and opened his mouth to sing, and a wave like a wall crashed upon him, and he sank into the long green light, breathing the sea, his hands rising to cup his brother's face.

What *did* happen to Danilo Somethingivić?

He did survive in the frozen forest. He was not caught and raped and shot and buried under the snowpack by two poachers hunting tigers in the woods. He did watch from high in a red spruce tree as a tiger, a vast grim ghost, stalked and killed and ate one of the poachers. He did not travel during the day but only late at night when only animals and drunkards and thieves used the trails and roads through the epic snows. He did learn to vanish into the woods quick as a sable when he heard the slightest noise at night. He was not caught and held for identification and repatriation by unending layers of authority and assumed authority. He did make his way east through the forest and along the outer edges of towns and cities, occasionally joining school yards and children gathered in knots for games and events, occasions he used for the theft of food in any form whatsoever, and so eating carp and pike, deer and mushrooms, herring and rabbit, potatoes in every conceivable form, even thin salted slices of bear once, a treat so tasty he filled his pockets with bear until he found himself trailed into the woods by slavering dogs. He did not speak for months, afraid that a single word could betray him. He did arrive finally at the shore of the endless ocean which seemed to him very like the endless forest except that it was gray not green. He did not wish to stay in the frigid city in which he found himself and so he slipped aboard a tanker late one night when only animals and drunkards and thieves were awake. He did by chance choose a tanker heading south past Japan and Korea and China. He did not hesitate to slip aboard a tugboat and then a trawler and then a cargo ship, the ships in toto bringing him south and then east. He did get caught twice along the way but once he lied so eloquently and movingly about who what where how that the bosun laughed and let him go (this was the trawler, off Mindanao) and once he was being frog-marched to the bridge by a grinning deckhand who reeked of marijuana when he saw how close the cargo ship was to its destination islands and he stumbled deliberately and tripped the gaping deckhand and whirled out of his molasses grasp and dove into the bosom of the sea. He was fourteen years old. The deckhand was going to report the stowaway but then realized that losing the boy was probably bad news to deliver and then he forgot about the stowaway altogether when he realized the ship was about to dock and he was not in the hold where he was supposed to be. Danilo swam underwater for as long as he could, delighting in the warmth, and in ten minutes he was hidden among dense mangroves where no one could find him and he could once again reinvent himself, perhaps this time as a young sailor weary of the sea and hoping to find work. A week later he was loading and unloading trucks at the tiny airport, singing in a church choir at night, and soaking up the local languages, beginning with the name of the island: Babelthuap.

★

Fixit Day and Meet the New Kid Day on the *Plover,* by command of the captain. General examination of equipment in toto especially gudgeons, pintles, rudder, turnbuckles, shrouds (upper *and* lower), sails, propeller, engine, water tanks, *both* bilge pumps, all aspects of the restroom facilities, winches, flashlights, diving mask and fins, slickers, and an audit of food supplies remaining especially almonds, a man cannot have enough almonds, as old Ed Burke should have said but didn't. Serious work on the hole punched by the storm. Repainting as necessary. Actual no kidding holystoning of the decks, on general naval principle. Airing of bedding. Soaking of the pip in the billows of the sea and hosing off thereafter to general laughter, sweet blessed Jesus, did you ever see such a bedraggled slip of a pip as that one? But it was Taromauri who asked quietly if she might dry off the pipsqueak with a towel in each hand. The towels looked like handkerchiefs in her enormous hands. The first time she touched Pipa with a towel Pipa made a sharp sound like the whistle of a flute; but then she mewled happily and fluttered her hands as soon as they were free of the sea of the towel. Taromauri dried Pipa's hands first, gently, slowly, and then her arms, and then her face and hair, and then her back and chest, and then her legs and feet, using both towels at the same time somehow, as Pipa piped and burbled. Declan and Piko had both stopped what they were not doing anyway to watch. Somehow the world maundered along around them as the four of them stood on deck, each alert to the mountain of the moment; Pipa almost smiling as the two towels gently but thoroughly dried every millimeter of her holy pelt; Taromauri silent and intent and immense; Declan amused but amazed, and still, down deep, suspicious; Piko moved, frightened, roiled, saddened, thrilled. The first woman to touch her since. The towels the bath. I used to dry her off like that. In the yard. Under the cedars. The sharp red smell of duff. Flittering into her hair. Braiding her hair. Make my hair a *rope* again Papa! Make *two* ropes today! Remember the time we made *ten* ropes in my hair Papa, and Mama laughed so hard her coffee came out her nose which made her sneeze so hard she *peed,* remember that Papa? That was the funniest day in the history of *ever,* remember that Papa? Papa?

★

Late in the afternoon Declan calls a halt to Fixit Day so everyone can go for a swim, and he appoints Piko captain of the *Plover* for one hour exactly, and Piko as his first act of command commands that everyone get *off* the boat for a while, onto the beach, and tell stories, but the stories cannot be about yourself, he says, smiling, they have to be about other people, we are getting all solipsistic and narcissistic on the boat and stories are the antidote, okay, I'll go first. The second girlfriend I ever had was totally into otters and all she ever wanted to do was study otters and swim with otters and make recordings of otters and listen to otters and watch otters and measure the mudslides that otters made and visit museums to study otter artifacts and read about otters and dream about otters, and this was a lot of fun in the beginning because I like otters too, man, I mean who *doesn't* like otters, otters are the tough burly clowns of the animal world, no one messes with otters, but they are total goofballs, probably because no one messes with them, and they can catch and eat whatever they want whenever they want, I mean that's a pretty good life when you think about it, no one messing with you and eating anything you want and playing in the mud, but after a while things started to pall a little because it was pretty much all otters all the time which did not leave a whole lot of room for dessert if you know what I mean which I know you do. Dec?

Ahhh, let me think a minute. Does it have to be girl-friends? What's a girlfriend?

Liar.

I had a girlfriend in like sixth grade, man. After that it was . . . acquaintances.

Liar.

Except maybe the one.

Lia— Tell it.

I kid you not, her name was Wanda Kiwanda. A name she couldn't stand. Pinned on her by her mother and grandmother and great-grandmother all the way back like eighty generations to whatever cave it was in Russia they lived in when the glaciers melted. Her thing was reinvent-ing herself by reinventing her name over and over again. She would be Wendy for a week and act like she thought a Wendy would act and then the next week she would be Gail and act Gailic and so on like that. She would switch names every Sunday night so as to be a new person bright and early Monday morning. You would think this would drive you nuts as a boyfriend but actually it was a kick because you had a new girlfriend every Monday morning regular as clockwork. It was kind of stimulating, if dizzying.

What happened to you and . . . Wendy?

Wanda. Eventually she figured out that another way to be a new person all the time was to leave. So she left.

Did you miss her?

You know, weirdly, yeh, I did. She was a sweet girl. She was like an excitement junkie, that girl. *Everything* totally made her day. You never saw anyone so delighted by a cup of coffee, for example. She was *appreciative,* you know? Panappreciative. She was a sweet kid. I haven't thought about her for a long time. I think to be honest I was sort of hurt that I wasn't exciting enough for her to stay so I deliberately forgot her. My family was real good at deliberately forgetting stuff.

Why is that?

Ah, who cares. Next.

Taromauri stood up, her epic arms loose by her sides.

You don't have to stand up, you know, said Declan. This isn't church.

But Taromauri brought her hands together in that same odd gesture, as if her hands were meeting for the first time, and she said, I will tell you about the husband I used to have. He was a good and gentle man. His name was

Kekenu, and his people were the turtle people. The thing he was very good at was catching someone's last breath and saving it to blow on the next child who came into that family. He was *very* good at that. He had the quickest hands, and he could catch that last breath coming out and save it in a little bone jar. He could catch last words and songs also. Not everyone can do that but he could and he became famous for it. But then he changed when our daughter went down in the ocean and didn't come back up. He forgot how to catch last breaths and songs and words. But that was his work and he wasn't good at any other work. He started writing letters to our daughter and leaving them on the beach at low tide for the ocean to take to her. Every day he wrote a letter and staked it to the sand and every day the ocean came and took it. But he never got a letter back from her. He thought maybe she had become an eel and was living in a reef somewhere. He thought maybe the eels had called to her that day on the boat and that's why she went down to see what they wanted. He thought that if she read his letters she would understand that we understood what she had done but that we loved her and would be very happy if she would leave the eel people and come back and be our daughter again. He thought you just had to ask politely and it could happen. You couldn't go fight the eels over what had happened, of course, but you could just explain calmly how *you* were seeing things, and perhaps they would explain how *they* saw things, and an agreement could be worked out, like perhaps our daughter would be a woman sometimes and an eel other times. Things like that happen. But we never got a letter back from our daughter, and the eels never said anything either, and after a while Kekenu stopped writing letters. When he stopped writing letters and leaving them in the surf he stopped being Kekenu. He had been a good and gentle man, and I loved him, and our daughter loved him, but when he stopped being Kekenu he stopped being good and gentle, and so our time was finished.

*

The gull heard all this, of course. Sure she did. And she figured that since Pipa never spoke, *she* would tell a story, which she did, with the usual rough glee of the gulls, and her story went like this.

We have saints and criminals too, you know. Did you think you were the only people with saints and criminals? Every people has saints and criminals. Sometimes in the same person. Sometimes saints are criminals who were awakened. That is the story I am telling. There was a gull who was a great thief. He was the biggest and strongest and fastest and smartest gull anyone had seen in as many years as the oldest of us was. Because he could do whatever he wanted he did so. He took whatever food he wanted and mated with anyone he wanted and killed anyone he wanted. Sometimes he plucked the eyes of sharks and spit them back at the sharks. Sometimes he mated with a gull and then killed her and ate her. Sometimes he stole jaeger chicks and dropped them screaming into the fires of people. There were many worse things he did. I do not want to have those things in my mouth. But one day something happened to him. We do not know what it was and he could not explain it himself. He went another way. He shared food. He fought only jaegers. There were many other things that he did. No one can remember all the other things that he did. No one knows why he went another way. Not even he knows. But he went another way. That is the story I am telling you. Now I am finished with my story!

*

On the beach they had watched openmouthed as the gull squawked and warbled and bobbed, finishing with a little hop and bow, and Piko laughed so hard he got the hiccups. Sweet blessed Jesus, said Declan, who *is* that bird and what is he going on about? But he calls us to order, shipmates. Away to the billowing sea! And set the fishing lines because we are out of fresh fish and I am starving and if I see another blessed almond on this trip I will throw you all overboard. Batten the hatches and ready the sail. Hoist the anchor and feed the gull. All hands on deck. Strap in the pip and let's get ready to hit the road. We leave at dusk on the button. East, my hearties! One hour of all sails and then bare poles and low motor. Away to the impacific Pacific! Away to the mother of all mothers! Away to the hatchery of most of the fish in the galaxy! Away to the ocean that eats people! Away to storms that make you puke and wonder why in heaven's name you are not at home by the fire in a house with a lock to keep the wind out! Away to wind funnels that make you pee in your pantaloons and wonder why you are not living in the desert where no water can find you and drown you and melt your skin and dissolve your bones! Away to the ocean wherein are animals no man nor woman has ever seen or probably will ever see no matter how cool our coolest instruments! Away to the ocean wherein lie bones uncountable from beings uncountable of species uncountable! Away and avast, two men and a woman and a child and a gull! Avast and away, four hominids and an avian and whatever else we have on board I do not yet know about! Awast and avay!

★

The minister for fisheries and marine resources and foreign affairs had no wife. He had no children. He had many friends but he was peripatetic personally and professionally and no one friend or colleague ever knew where he was at every blessed moment so that when he vanished it was some hours before his vanishment was noticed. His secretary searched the ministry offices for him and then searched the adjoining streets and then searched the beachfront and then called the secretaries and staffers in the offices of the other ministers none of whom nor their spouses nor lovers nor friends nor sycophants nor lobbyists nor bagmen nor counselors nor lawyers nor children nor neighbors had seen him for some hours either. The hours in which no one saw him lengthened. The police searched for him and volunteers combed the beaches and woods and streets and the police boat set out into the wet wilderness in search of him. But he could not be found. His name was spoken by every fifth mouth, his face pinned and posted and mailed and nailed on walls and boats and poles and palms, but soon he became a memory, a cold case, a rumor. An interim minister was appointed, who made sure he did not have a profile or portfolio as popular as his predecessor; reports were

filed, eulogies and elegies sung and spoken; a formal ceremony of remembrance was held in the ministry, again fill-
ing the stairs with the rapt men and women and children
who had heard the minister speak, and had felt a shiver and
shimmer and hunger and spark inside themselves at his
words, a yearning to believe him, an urge and itch to live
in the world he spoke about, a cousinship of dreams, a
companionship of convictions about what life could be like
not only in their islands but across all islands, across the
whole wild sweep of Pacifica, the huge blue continent that
could maybe be a new kind of country; but the canoe in
the rotunda of the ministry, the canoe filled to overflowing
with notes and flowers, the canoe past which thousands of
mourners filed all night long after the ceremony of remembrance, was missing the minister. Long past dawn the next
day there were still people in line on the steps of the ministry, waiting to approach the canoe, drop a flower or a letter
into it, run their hands along the *kanawa* wood, and whisper prayers for the soul of the departed, that his spirit may
evade the watchers in the woods, and walk freely along the
beach, and embark upon the sea of the stars from which we
all have come and to which we must return. When, finally,
just after noon, the last of the mourners had gone and the
custodial staff was removing the flowers and boxing up the
mountain of notes and letters, a sudden brief shower of rain
thrummed the building. *Wan te mate,* one old janitor said
quietly to another, that is the canoe of the dead, come for
him; and the second janitor, who had been morose and silent, smiled and said *be bon roko raoi wana,* his canoe certainly arrived promptly.

5° SOUTH, 160° EAST

MAYBE THE OCEAN THINKS. How do we know? Maybe the ocean licks its islands every night like mothers lick their cubs. This could be. Maybe it chants their names in its many languages in the morning and makes them rise again toward the sun: Aotearoa, Aranuka, Pukapuka, Tuamotu. Maybe it touches fingers with the other oceans at night just to be sure they are all still there and not drawn away finally by the thirsty void after mere billions of years. Maybe the ocean remembers the old days when the worlds were just made and there was naught upon the waters but storms upon the sea; the ocean's wild and tumultuous youth. Maybe all the smaller seas and oceans are the children of the mother of oceans, and Pacifica dreams of its swaddlings Coral and Weddell and Bering and Ross and Tasman and Okhotsk. Maybe Atlantica wishes to someday be Pacifica and that is why it gnaws and chews at Holland and Haiti. Maybe not a fishlet falls to the bottom of the sea without the ocean knowing. Maybe the ocean remembers every soul who sank beneath the billows and fell to the floor and slept there for years and finally sifted into the bones of other beings. This could be. Maybe the ocean feels every boat like a scar on its skin and only permits them to pass so that its knowledge of men deepens. Maybe the ocean is made furious by the untrustworthy sky from which come lashes and flashes. Maybe the ocean throws islands at the sky as vengeance, as prayer, as a joke, a shout or song of lava and coral. Maybe the ocean invented the languages spoken over it these thousands of years. Maybe the ocean remembers the ancient oceans that once were and are no more: Iapetus, Tethys, Mirovia, Panthalassa. Maybe the ocean stares at the stars and yearns for the oceans on other worlds: Titan, Callisto, Enceladus, Io. Maybe the ocean remembers the story Atlantica tells, of the man on the shore long ago who stared out and formed the word *okeanos* in the holy cave of his mouth, naming the mother of all things, finding her name with his tongue, telling his brothers and sisters; but maybe that is only one name for the mother, and there are thousands of thousands beyond thousands of her names; maybe those names are the names of the beings who live below her belly; maybe if we spoke those names we would sail home in some amazing unimaginable new way; this could be. How do we know?

★

Piko and Declan in the cabin.

Where are we going, Dec?

I am thinking of some little atolls east and north. American territories. Islands where only scientists stop by here and there to count albatross peckers or whatever. You'll fit in there.

Populated?

Usually not, I think, but little atolls like that sometimes have doctors and naval observers and construction guys living there on and off, fixing landing strips and lighthouse beacons and stuff like that. There's a few islands there that have little villages of fifty people or so. Be good places to just camp out and stretch a little. I'd like to get out of town for a while, maybe haul out the boat and go through everything, clean the bottom, do some fishing. There's reefs around those atolls so crammed with fish we can probably just ask them politely to jump in the boat. The pip can probably talk to fish like she talks to birds, right?

She sure does have a thing for birds.

Birds have a thing for her, man. Have you noticed the terns? I mean, we are tern central ever since she joined the crew. I never saw so many terns in one place in all the years I have been on the boat and now we are a tern ferry or tern bait or something. Weird. Was she always like that with the birds?

Pretty much, yes, now that I think about it. Walking with her was always a kick, you would be walking down a moist silent street first thing in the morning on the way to the bus or to go fishing and you would swear there wasn't a bird awake for a hundred miles and as soon as the pip stepped out her front door, *boom,* bird symphony. Like traveling with a bird rock star. I was always shocked they didn't break out their little tiny cameras and autograph pads, you know? Especially the little birds. You know all the little brown guys, the dusky sparrows and juncos and wrens and bushtits and finches and all those little brown ones the size of your thumb that you can't tell apart one from another? They loved her best, I think. Maybe because she was their size. But even when she was a baby she would just sit in the grass and birds would come bubbling out of the bushes and run to her like she was dwarf Jesus or something. She would just laugh and they would all be burbling and whistling and hopping up and down like someone poured joy juice in the grass and everything was happy bonkers. Man, it was hilarious. I haven't thought of that in years. Boy. There were days when the birds got so excited they would climb up on her shoulders and perch in her hair and she would be wearing the birds like a singing jacket and of course they were so excited they couldn't totally control themselves and I would have to hose her off after a while. Man, that was funny. Even *that* made her laugh. You never saw a kid so happy to have birds poop on her head. Man.

★

Of course it was crowded on the *Plover* now. Sure it was. Pipa in her pipibunk, her tiny cabin, her tiny wooden boat, and Declan and Piko sleeping to her east and west; Taromauri, after some experimentation with her weight and the balance of the boat, slept in the stern, in a sort of tent Piko invented from tarpaulin and rigging; you could furl and unfurl the tent like a sail off the stern railing, and, with a second ingenious rope, pull it close against the body of the sleeper like a coat. Piko was inordinately proud of his invention and crowed about it for a while until Declan swore not only the gull but Pipa was snickering.

And there was the gull, the fifth passenger, who sometimes surfed behind the boat, exactly nine feet above the stern, smiling and silent; and there were two young island rats, *kiore,* the sixth and seventh passengers, which had boarded the boat in the harbor, drawn by the sweet smell of almonds, and were now shyly exploring the hold, which, having held many tons of salmon and halibut and crab and scallops, smelled and tasted and reeked of *kiore* heaven; and there was a tiny warbler, *bokikokiko,* the eighth passenger, who had been flying past the boat in the deeps of the night and had struck the mast a glancing blow and fallen unconscious to the deck and rolled under a water tank and upon waking found itself sore ill and bruised, and so stayed hidden under the trammeled waters until further developments unfurled; and there were several snails, comprising the ninth through twelfth passengers, and there were a scatter of seeds of the screw pine, which could be considered incipient or prospective passengers, of the numbers thirteen through nineteen; and there were the barnacles who rode below, in troops beyond number, whose allegiance to the ship was so firm that it would be severed only by violence; and also beyond counting were the clans of kelp and the tribes of weed, which fixed themselves in and among the barnacles, and so built a tiny wilderness, some twenty feet long by ten feet wide along the keel, around which teemed a vast populace of tiny fish of a hundred species, who came and went as they pleased, treating the boat like a country on the move, from which they emigrated and rejoined as tides fondle and flee a beach. So the *Plover* carried not four beings but a dozen, a hundred, a thousand passengers at any one moment; and no man not even the captain knew the number, or the sweet shape of their days, but only that they traveled together, not one among them sure of their final harbor. It is the nature of all greatness not to be exact, said old Ed Burke, who knew whereof he spoke.

★

One morning Pipa, sitting with Taromauri in the bow, her fingers fluttering like feathers, signaled to Declan that there was some sort of island ahead. Declan hove to, puzzled; he had scoured his charts for any land whatsoever in the days to come, and there was no record of even vanished atolls or reefs of any kind. But indeed the pip was right; ahead lay a long flat low island where no island officially could be. They drifted closer, puzzled.

It's . . . rippling, said Piko. Is that normal?

No.

What kind of island is that?

I don't know, man. There's no island on the charts.

Wae, said Taromauri suddenly. *Inai.* A mat of used things.

And indeed it was, as they soon saw; a mat of garbage maybe a mile wide, garbage as far as the eye could see, jostling and rippling and clinking, gathered by wind and weather and current into a vast blanket of shards and shreds, a shawl of tattered things: bottles, tampons, bags, sneakers, diapers, toothbrushes, fishing line, fishing nets, plastic bags, straws, packing pellets, toy scraps, gloves, syringes, cups, packing crates, boxes of every size and description, glass balls, logs, jackets, boots, shoes, slickers, bobbing oil drums, and even something that looked like a huge refrigerator, all baked by the sun to the desiccated color of a desert.

They rocked at the edge of the plastic island for a while and stared. Turtles slid in and out of the shadows beneath the mass; terns and gulls hovered above it; and Taromauri was sure she saw crabs skittering through the bright chaos of the island's landscape. It was like a small city, thought Piko, all jumbled and brilliant and faded and fouled, but lit with life; and Taromauri, realizing that a reef of even this breathtaking falsity, an anti-reef, would be a haven for the small and hunting ground for the large, broke out the fishing gear and caught two large trevallies before they turned and headed east. Inside one of the fish, when she opened it, was a pink plastic bow tie on which was stamped, in ink fading but still visible, entwined wedding rings.

*

A long gray calm gray moist gray day; everyone slept in late; there was no particular rush to get anywhere; it's like a parenthesis in a sentence, noted Piko drowsily; and even Declan, who usually turned becalmings instantly into Fixit Days by command of the captain, even unto buffing the deck, forbore to issue orders, and instead started talking about buffing the deck, one time with bless me a fecking holystone some British imperialist slavemaster fish-tourist left on the boat after he and his jolly mates chartered me for halibut one time, o God that was funny, they were as rollicking courteous johnbully as you can imagine and they had no fecking idea what to say at all when I gave them the old man's stump speech about how the fecking British enslaved the Irish worse than they ever enslaved any of their possessions elsewhere, why they hammered and shat upon the island next to them worse than they ever did the hindoo or arabesque populations is a mystery to me, what is the story with the ancient enmity between the angles and the celts, I hope our dear blessed Jesus can forgive the imperialist slavemaster pagan bastards their foul and lurid crimes against the chosen people because we cannot and I am not alone in praying they burn luridly in the seventh circle of hell where roast the violent who have sinned against the innocent, that slime Cromwell the worst among them, he will be riven by rough arrows and mauled by savage dogs with slavering jaws and upon him will rain flakes of fire from the sky all day every day unto the end of days, and etc. in that vein, the old man would go off raging like a fecking volcano unless he had a pint or eight in him which weirdly cooled him off, the reverse of the usual arithmeticalculus. O God that was funny watching those poor anglers, get the joke, hey, *anglers?* They scuttled off the boat fast as crickets, leaving behind among other things bless me a holystone which the poor Irish innocents in the imperialist fecking slavemaster navy used to have to scrub the decks white as snow with every blessed morning, the decks made from Irish oak stolen from the blessed land leaving it naked as a bird and twice as helpless. Jesus. God knows why they had a holystone. Roll on thou deep dark blue ocean, roll! Not blue though. Gray as slate, gray as the face of the old man as he trudged out to his cows in the morning. The ocean of the mud. The desert of the sea as the prophet says. The sea, the ocean, the billowing deep, everybody has some blessed fecking poetic name for it, but there is no It. It isn't It. It's just a roaring amount of water with untold fantastic beings peeing in it all day. World's biggest pisspot. Beings unknown and unknowable. Like the old man. Seething above and below. Oceanic rages. Depths no light ever reached. And his oldest son then went to sea, riven by dark tides he did not know, and thereupon voyaged interminably, never finding that which he sought with might and main, but sentenced to a watery exile, to be fed by salt alone as he wended weary through the trackless waters; yet he was granted companions in his exile, though none knew their destinations, nor the manner of their roads thereto; and they proceeded on, fearful yet armed with hope as if with arrows of fire in quivers of gold.

★

Night on the boat, Taromauri and Pipa asleep, Declan and Piko smoking cigars in the stern, watching the stars.

See, that's the Southern Cross, see that? says Piko. That's how you know you are in the South Pacific. You basically can't see that if you are north of the line. And right near it, see, there's the star Hadar, I always liked that name, Hadar, sounds like a Viking star.

What's the other bright one there?

Rigel Kentaurus.

Bless you.

Haw.

You know your stars.

Well, the sky always seemed like another ocean to me, you know? Like we live between two incredible oceans, and we'll never get to the bottom of either of them. A wet one and a dry one, both of them unfriendly to air.

Don't we know the wet one pretty well after all these years? People been in and around the ocean for half a million years, don't we know it pretty well?

Nope. That's what I found most interesting in my work, to be honest, that we don't hardly know a thing. There's places six miles deep in the ocean, man, and there are caves and tunnels and halls and valleys no one has ever been in, and whole forests bigger than any forest on land, who knows what's there? No one knows what's down there. There's millions of species of plants and animals in there we don't even know what they are. We might never know.

Millions?

Millions, man. Probably thousands of kinds of fish we can't even *imagine*. Isn't that wild? Maybe there's fish that look like you.

Tall fish. Handsome.

Ugly with a capital u. I mean, there could be some new kind of living things there we don't have words for yet, you know? Not animals or plants but something else. What if there was a kind of living rock down there? Or plants that are smart and swim fast? Or a kind of underwater bird? Or animals made of water and whispers? That could be. No one knows. Basically the thing I learned most in my work is that whatever you are sure of don't be, and as soon as you think you know something for certain, you don't.

Story of my whole life so far, says Declan, and Piko can *hear* him grinning in the dark.

Me too, man.

Ah, at least you were sure of Elly.

I guess.

You guess?

We had some hard times.

Sorry, man.

It was like when things were all good we were all good but after the pip got smashed things got smashed too and they never really got back to where they were. We didn't talk to each other much down deep, you know? We just poured ourselves into the pip. And then Elly got sick and we never got all the way back, Elly and me. Not that going back was the best thing, she used to say we *couldn't* go back and neither of us would want to anyways, but maybe we could find a new forward, you know? But we never found that. It was like she was walking ahead of me and I couldn't quite catch up. And when she got sick she poured herself into the pip even more. There were days when they would stay in bed all day just holding each other and making bird sounds. I would take care of them, sure, but it was just taking care of them, is all. And all this was after we decided not to have more kids because we would be taking care of the pip forever. Sometimes I could feel the kids we didn't have, you know what I mean? Like sometimes I would be sitting at the table and suddenly there would be three kids there instead of the one who wasn't even *there* there anymore. After the pip got smashed, you know, she couldn't eat at the table anymore, and Elly was always the one who fed her in her bed, so I didn't set the table anymore, you know what I mean? *I didn't set the table anymore.* No plates and napkins and fork on this side and spoon on the other and exactly the right glass for the pip, *not* the pretty one from Grandma but the chipped one the wolverine man gave us, the guy I knew who studied wolverine in the mountains, he gave the pip a glass he said a wolverine bit a piece from, and she *loved* that glass, man, she just would not use any other glass, and she would always only drink from the place the wolverine's mouth had been, even though I told her not to. I used to look at that poor old wolverine glass every day, stuck in the cupboard, never making it to the table anymore. It was like it had died and was buried in the cupboard behind all the other more polite glasses. Jesus. I finally threw it in the ocean one night, man. I just couldn't stand seeing it anymore. Jesus.

*

The next day for some reason everyone aboard got totally into making and hanging flags and pennants and banners, so by the end of the day the *Plover* looked like a floating laundry barge, with flags and pennants and banners of every conceivable shape and sort and color flittering and snapping and flappering in the wind from the west: Taromauri's dream of what a national flag from her country might look like if ever her country was officially a country which she had high hopes it would eventually be, said country's flag featuring *tabakea,* the turtle, oldest of all beings, the first of all things in the world, on a background of sea and sun and sky; Piko's flag, a frigate bird, mighty *'iwa,* the happy thief, against a field of the bluest blue; Declan's Oregon flag, done from vague memory of the state flag, featuring a football on a background of mist and sage and salmon guts; Piko's flag for Elly, featuring a kestrel in flight against the greenest green he could find on the boat; Pipa's flag, a fairy tern on what seemed to be a *kukui* tree, thought Piko—Taromauri had cut and painted the tern without even asking Pipa what she wanted, but when Piko had begun to paint a black background with stars, to allow the painted tern to leap off the flag, colorwise, Pipa had mewled steadily. Piko knew what this meant, and he set aside the night sky with stars, and kept painting different backgrounds, but she kept mewling until he arrived at tree branches, at which point her music changed and her hands calmed. They concocted a flag for the *Plover,* a testy-looking burly golden plover against a bilious gray sea, and they invented a flag for the gull hanging effortlessly in their wake, and they rigged banners of every color they could find, and they hung blankets and mats and bags for fun and sun, and spent the rest of the day laughing at the cracking and whappering and flippering of the flags and pennants and banners, and reveling in the wild music of it all; a grand day altogether and no mistake, said Declan to Piko that night, as they tucked the pip in tight as a tick in the bunk, and not one of the five of them ever forgot the sheer headlong pleasure of that day the rest of their lives; and for all five of them the day would sneak back into their memories early in the morning, or in fever dreams, and they would lie there, not even half-awake, and suddenly feel the peppering of wind from the west in their faces, and hear the snap and smile of flags, and see, at the very top of the pole, the turtle, oldest of all beings, first of all things in the world, flying over sea and sun and sky.

*

More and more it was Taromauri holding Pipa in the bow as the *Plover* slid gently through moist green mornings and crisp blue afternoons and calm bronze evenings. East and then east. For a few days Piko held Pipa the same as always curled against his long chest with his rope beard braided in her hair and then one morning he let Taromauri hold her and Pipa sank into Taromauri like a pebble into a sea. Declan fished and repaired and tightened and cleaned and tinkered and puttered and hauled and charted and fumed and snickered. Piko set up a dizzying series of experiments measuring salinity, oxygenation, depth, the attraction levels of various baits for various species of edible piscatory populations, and, his opus, a meticulous map of the music on board by *approximate instrument,* as he said, for example the rigging of the jib, which produces a remarkable song in winds of certain speeds, or the door of the hatch, which emits a piercingly sharp solo when waggled energetically, or the subtle sound produced by our gullish friend when he or she banks to starboard, a wholly distinctive sound from, as you certainly have all noticed, the one produced when she or he banks to port. Piko spent most of an afternoon making a detailed musical map of the *Plover,* poring over it with such attention that he missed the jaeger that slid past the bow so fast that even Taromauri, who had eyes like a prophet, caught only a flitting image and not a confirmed sight; but she knew what it was.

★

Enrique refitted the *Tanets*. He sold cargo and bought cargo. He made arrangements. He had discussions. He listened to what was not said when something was said. He hired two silent crewmen neither of whom was totally sure of the names they were supposed to use in this chapter of their lives. One said he was Rapanuian and the other said he was Rungarungawan. They spoke more than Taromauri had, but not by much. It seemed to Enrique that they were brothers or cousins but they denied this. One of them said he had only read one book in his whole life a page a day and when he got to the last page he went back and read the first page again and so on and so on. He claimed he had read the book so many times that the words had fallen out of it and the pages were all blank so he had to read the book to put the words back in or the book would be all forlorn and naked. Enrique forbore to check the accuracy of this claim or even the title of the book, although he did notice the battered red cover had no words on it. The other crewman owned only possessions made of wood or cloth and was reluctant to touch let alone handle anything made of metal or plastic. He said that things made of metal or plastic were the tools of the eyeless ones and must be avoided at all costs. This posed a problem briefly inasmuch as most of the *Tanets* was made of steel and iron and copper and bronze and plastic but Enrique was able to persuade the crewman to conduct the usual and necessary duties on board wearing gloves and a face that flickered with fear whenever Enrique stared at him. It seemed to Enrique that they were surely brothers or cousins not for obvious reasons of similar physique or deportment but for subtler tells and flags; they both laughed hesitantly and then wholeheartedly, rivulet to river; and they sneezed the same way, quick staccato bursts instantly covered with coughs, as if they were embarrassed to briefly explode; and both flinched when the shadows of large birds flickered over the deck; and while only one crossed himself when the shadows came, the other would stand and close his eyes for an instant; Enrique couldn't tell if he was praying or terrified or both. Not that there was any difference between the two, he thought. Praying was only a way to beg not to be beaten, and you were not even begging the right overlord. People who prayed for health or good weather were begging the cold universe for heat. You might as well beg a rifle not to spit its bullet. Better to pray for what was, and what would always be, which is sickness and bad weather; at least you were sure of those things, and so your prayers were always sure to be answered, and in full measure too.

*

Just thinking the crewmen were brothers made Enrique think of his own brothers. The lost tribe. Scattered to the seven seas. Some to the stars and some to the sea. Some sailed some jailed. We all left. Poor Mama. One after another. Seven brothers with no mothers. She left too. She left early. Her body stayed but the her of her left. Burned on the altar. That little room in the back where she said she could see Papa burning in the prison and then burning in the lake of fire. He never shrove his sins and now he is ash and so shall we all burn. Her eyes burning and her voice burning into the baby. He never did have a mother that brother. Even their names are burned away. Unto ash we shall return. The house burning the sun burning our eyes burning. If everything must be burned I will do the burning and so I will not be burnt but be the fire. Everything I ever loved burned and so I will be the burning. There is nothing but that which must be burnt. Women will burn and children burn and houses burn so I will be nothing that can burn. I will be the fire. The fire has no home. The fire goes where it wants. The fire arrives and departs and none can account the meaning of its travels. Everything I ever touched burned. The prison burned and no man escaped not one. It was an accident. It was unavoidable. No man could be saved. No man can be saved. All men must burn. And Mama burned away, day after day she stayed longer in the back room among the candles, and she would not eat, and she burned away, and the baby cried, and my brothers left one by one, and Mama's eyes burned, and in the end there was nothing left of her but her eyes burning in the dark, even the candles had burned away by then, and they came for us, and the little house burned, the house that used to be us, and they took the baby, and his voice is burning me. Where are you, brother? When are you coming for me? They took me away and I said your name and you did not come and I am lost and burning and when are you coming for me, brother? When are you coming for me? Remember we would talk about the water, the blue water and the green water and we would live in it and nothing could ever burn us again and we would be green and wet and safe, you remember we talked about that, about the water? Remember that, brother?

★

Piko and Taromauri sitting in the stern. Two of their twenty toes are touching; neither one knows this. Pipa asleep in her chair; her left foot is tucked under Piko's ponytail. Declan asleep with his head pillowed on the hatch cover; his right foot is touching Taromauri's right hip; neither one knows this. The gull is asleep on the stern railing with his or her tail brushing Pipa's hair.

Well, says Piko, it started the same way every guy's beard starts, as a third armpit, you know. You grow it because you can. Even if you really can't. Even if it looks silly. Probably *because* it looks silly. Guys are like that. Then suddenly it changed color, to a kind of red. *That* was weird. God knows why *that* happened. Then it changed *again,* to a kind of silver. Elly and Pipa thought this was hilarious so I couldn't cut it off then and so the moment for cutting it passed and it became part of the old facial landscape, you know? Like when you plant a tree and you don't think about it after a while and then suddenly it's thirty feet tall and shoving the shed over so bad that you have to turn sideways to get your tools, and you think, man, I better cut down that tree, but you forget, and about two minutes later it's too late, man, that is a serious tree, you can't cut down a tree *that* big, you have to just build another shed, you know? Trees win when it comes to pushing matches with sheds. And my beard kept changing colors by itself, and Pipa really got into putting feathers and coins and messages and pencils and crayons and mouse bones and little flags and notes and stuff in it, and you would have to be an idiot to cut a beard that your kid is leaving *notes* in, am I right? I still have all her notes somewhere in a box. She used to write tiny notes on walnut shells and hazelnut shells and scraps of bark and spruce fingers and stuff like that. For a long time she totally got into writing on maple leaves. You ever see big-leaf maple leaves? They're like *rugs,* man, and they float forever when they get loose, they are a kick to watch. So Pipa would load up the old rope beard with maple leaves with little messages she'd written, and then we would climb a tree or go up to the top of the hill, someplace where we could get our faces into the wind, and I would shake the old noggin, and her messages would soar out over the yard, or the valley, or sometimes when we did it at the beach we would watch them float out over the surf. *That* was cool. I thought of that a lot when I was throwing fire at Makana, that I was sailing messages again, sort of, like me and the pip used to do at home.

And your hair? said Taromauri.

Same principle. Just fun to let it grow. The pip ties it to my beard when I am napping. Tied it, I should say.

I hear her voice inside her body, you know, said Taro-mauri.

Pardon me?

I can hear her speak. She laughs like bells.

She did, yeh.

Does.

Did. So, listen, what's the story with your tattoos? I never saw totally blue arms before. What are you, the village newspaper?

I think perhaps she is more awake than you know.

Your tattoos are history lessons, or religious things, or what?

Why do you not talk about her?

I was going to get a tattoo once but I figured what's the point, you know? Paying someone to punch holes in your body, that's nuts. Life punches enough holes in your body for free, right? Plus I kept seeing myself age eighty with my tattoo sagging down to the ground. Not a pretty sight, right? What's to talk about? It is what it is.

I hear her voice.

You don't know the kid from a hole in the wall.

I lost a daughter too. I can't hear her voice anymore. But I hear this one.

Piko doesn't say anything to that. He wants to say everything to that. But he says nothing. What's to say? No one says anything. No one says anything for a really long time.

★

Danilo Somethingivić tried on new names. He tried on new voices. He tried not speaking at all again for weeks at a time, because he noticed that if you do not speak then people do not see you very clearly, if at all. He swam as much as he could in the warm water and he sang as often as he could in the church choir and he worked as many hours as he could at the tiny airport saving as much money as he could and learning every scrap of every language that came by whether in mouths or boxes or songs on the radio or squawks on the intercom. He learned Abu and Ama, Foi and Gal, Bima and Basa. He learned to pilot a small plane. He learned some words of a language called Hermit, which was said to be extinct but wasn't. He learned to fish at the edge of the reef with the younger guys from the airport cargo crew. He learned some words of a language called Kewa which was different depending on which side of a mountain you lived on. He learned to sing solos and duets and trios and one time a slate of barbershop songs from an American pilot from Iowa who said his given name was Mister, that his mama figured if she named him Mister that would save enough time over the course of his life where he would get an extra year of life. He learned some of a language called Mamaa which is only spoken by women. He learned to read and speak American and English and Australian, which are three different languages. He learned some Maguindanao and some Masbateño. He fell in love with three girls one after another each one for almost a year but not quite. He tried to forget his brother and their childhood and the snow and the fear and the forest but he couldn't not quite. When he first awoke in the night in his cottage near the beach and found himself deep in the snow deep in the forest he would leap up and run to the ocean and dive in and swim in the warmth, but as the years passed he learned he could just sing away the snow and the forest and the fear, that if he sang as hard as he could the snow would melt and the forest fade away and he could get back to sleep before dawn; and slowly, so slowly that he did not even notice the ebbing of the tide, he stopped dreaming about the snow and the forest. On the day he turned twenty he sat on the beach and learned some words of a language called Tobi from a man who told him in the old days when ships came out of the sea you could tell if they were good or bad from the songs of the birds, and that you would welcome a good ship but with a bad ship you would dress up like a monster, with a huge thatch monster mask, and dance and caper on the beach, and the bad ship would fill with fear like water, and sail away, and then everyone would sing on the beach. That is what happened in the old days.

One time it rained so hard for an hour that really and truly you could not tell if you were underwater or on deck under deluge, and when the rain stopped there were fish squirming all over the boat, enough to eat for three days for everyone including the gull who ate so much she could not fly for a day and made happy groaning noises. One time when the wind was high and all sail set Piko tied himself to a longline and tied his feet to cedar planks and surfed behind the boat until the rope snapped and he described a somersault very nearly landing back on his feet again in the water but not quite. Another time a pod of whales swam right at the boat their massive foreheads like seething walls in the water but at the last possible second they split into two lines and slid past the boat making booming sounds so deep and thorough and amused that Pipa mewled happily for an hour afterward. Another time a shark circled the boat for an hour until a leap of porpoises shot past and hammered the shark mercilessly until it fled. Another time flying fish flew over the boat east to west in such numbers that it seemed the *Plover* was covered with a silver sheen, silver snow, a living shroud, a moist blanket, a shivering roof. Another time the sky was so stuffed with stars and so many of them shooting stars that you would swear the stars were plummeting into the sea faster than the sea could drink them. Another time something enormous in the water rolled not five feet from the boat and an eye the size of a refrigerator opened and then closed and whatever had been there wasn't and no one was quite utterly totally sure that there had been something there except for the memory of that epic eye. Another time it seemed inarguably true that two suns were rising out of the ocean to the east until one of them vanished as if someone had flipped out the light. Another time fairy terns appeared out of a clear blue sky by the hundreds and perched along the rigging and on the mast and along the railings and on the wooden engine box and on the cabin, crowding the discombobulated gull, until suddenly at some silent and mysterious signal they rose again as a body and swirled away east so swiftly and thoroughly that again no one was quite utterly totally sure that they had been there except for the inarguable evidence of what they had most recently eaten, which the captain of the *Plover* suggested *ought* to be cleaned off by the *father* of the child who probably *summoned* the birds with her blessed Jesus fecking *magic* somehow and me personally as the captain I might personally suggest that said *father* use his useless *goat's ass* of a *beard* for a mop whereas you might as well make that third armpit do some *useful* work around here bless my soul.

★

Sure, things went wrong. Sure they did. Declan hurt his back jumping into the hold and it hurt so bad for two days that he lay in his bunk and cried. The rudder pin broke for no reason at all. Pipa got so sick that her lips and fingers turned blue and she threw up until there was nothing left to throw up but air. The gull sheared off suddenly and was gone for two days, leaving the boat curiously naked. The patch on the hole from the storm worked itself off an eighth of an inch and had to be jiggered back into place with a great deal of sweating and cursing. The engine cover cracked in half one afternoon for no reason at all. Piko crushed a finger working on the hull patch and his finger tripled in size and turned purple and when finally in frustration he listened to Taromauri's advice and trailed it in the sea for an hour to reduce swelling, a giant trevally made a run at it and very nearly nipped it off, and when Piko made a grab at the fish's tail on the off chance of free meat he lost his balance and fell in and it took half an hour for Taromauri to turn the boat around and retrieve him. One tank of water unaccountably went bad. One volume of Burke's collected speeches, from 1790, the year he and his dear friend Fox fought bitterly and their friendship died, unaccountably rotted. The two *kiore* rats found and ate all the snails, reducing the passenger list by four. The tiny warbler, *bokikokiko,* the eighth passenger, emerged cautiously from under the water tank and discovered that her right wing did not at all answer the bell when called upon for flight. One afternoon the ocean boiled into a series of sickening swells so irregular and relentless that everyone aboard threw up, including the rats and the warbler. One morning there came an unaccountable dark hour in which all four human creatures lay abed afflicted with despair, and wondering why in heaven's name they were sentenced to this voyage, and when they would ever escape this tiny wooden prison, and under what unimaginable circumstances had they arrived in this bleak and sterile predicament, and when they would ever see or smell or touch or knead or walk upon or kneel upon or embrace or scrabble in or paw or even bless me gobble the sweet thick rich black holy soil of the earth which was the antidote and medicine and angel to the faithless unsturdy demonic sea. Even the two island rats, with memories as thin as smoke, had vague memories of another life that might have been on land; and it was Pipa who plunged deepest, remembering the shiver of alder, the moist of moss, the sting of sorrel on the tongue, the red shout of elderberries, the whir of winter wrens, the nodding of foxglove flowers, the depth of duff at the foot of the biggest firs and cedars and hemlocks and spruces; there were some trees near their house when she was little with duff so deep she could crawl in and cover herself with it like a blanket; and once, she remembered, she dug down into the sea of brown needles and found a rabbit warren, which she followed until she found the nest, with nine tiny creatures no bigger than her thumb; and as she stared at them, so new they had no hair, one opened its eyes for the first time ever; and she wondered after that for a long time what that new creature thought he saw, when he opened his eyes and saw her face like a planet above him; and when she told that story to her mother her mother said why, darling, whatever that little rabbit thought he was seeing, that's another one of your names, whatever word popped into his head when he saw you and you saw him, that's your name in *his* world, sure we have names in other worlds, wouldn't it be cool to know all your names in all the other worlds? Maybe that's your work, my little button, you'll be the greatest translator that ever was, the greatest name catcher ever. That could be. That could most certainly be.

★

But the darkness passed and on they went, the days brilliant and the nights more so. Piko, in an expansive scientific mood, one sunset, as all the *Plover*'s passengers, including the rats and the warbler, gaped at the indescribable colors of the sky:

Of course, the air is an ocean also, he said. Of course it is. It weighs five quadrillion tons, did you know that? And it heats and cools, expands and contracts, it's always in motion. It has currents and layers and secret places where no one has ever been yet although someday. It has currents with names like the ocean does. Currents that have been steady so long we slapped labels on them. Sirocco, chinook, monsoon, knik, matanuska, pruga, stikine, taku, aajej, arifi, beshabar, datoo, ghibli, haboob, harmattan, imbat, khamsin, nafhat, simoom. Typhoons and cyclones, tornados and hurricanes, storms and squalls. The air carries water like the water carries air. Maybe they are lovers, you know what I mean? Air has a little hydrogen and lots of oxygen and water has lots of hydrogen and a little oxygen. Mostly air is nitrogen, though. You know where nitrogen comes from? The *stars*. Isn't that cool? What you breathe used to be *inside stars*. Makes you feel a little taller, hey? And there's air in the ocean, of course. Also in every creature in the ocean. Every being has air in it like transparent blood. Way down below us there are beings with air in them. Dragonfish and anglerfish and flashlight fish and lanternfish and viperfish. *Miles* down there. And there are other beings down there no one ever saw yet or even *imagined*. But they have air in them. We know *that*. If you don't have any air in you, you're dead. We know *that*. One oceanographer friend of mine, her theory was that air was born from water, that billions of years ago sunlight and lightning bolts jazzed water vapor and made gases, which eventually grew up and became air, which then went into business with water and dirt. That could be. No one knows. Although if anyone would know *she* would know. She was one electric being, that one. She used to remind us all the time that we were mostly made of saltwater. Babies are made of more water than older people, she would say, so her theory is that we all came from the ocean, and babies remember this better, and we forget as we get older. We dry up. Another theory she had was that we went from water to air to dirt as we aged, that we started as mostly water and then became mostly hot air and then ended up aiding and abetting dirt, this was the contract water and air and dirt had agreed on, billions of years ago. That could be. No one knows. Although if anyone would know, *she* would know. Just before she died she asked us to make sure she went back to the ocean when she died, she didn't want to help out dirt, so after she died we took her out on the boat and gave her back. Beautiful day. Two men and one woman helped me lower her into the ocean and it seemed to us that she weighed about four ounces, that she was mostly air, and we were a little worried she wouldn't sink, you know, and that we would have to tie weights on her to sink her, but she sank down gently and didn't come back up, and later the woman who was with us said it was like the ocean was inviting in a dear friend, which I guess it was. She was one electric soul, that one. Yes she was.

*

Pipa hears this from her chair and is fascinated by the words dragonfish and anglerfish and flashlight fish and lanternfish and viperfish and she sends her big soul down to find them. Down and down and down. The light changing as she goes. She did this more often in water than air. It was hard to do it on land. She had tried but couldn't get her soul past soil. Stone was impenetrable but air and water were friendlier. Air was almost *too* friendly, though, and you had to be careful to keep your soul together because it could get too big too fast and you could lose yourself. This had happened before and it was terrifying and the first time it happened it took days to get herself back together, three days during which her parents thought she was in a coma but she was retrieving herself. Water was best. You could travel through water but stay coherent. She wondered if other people and animals and insects did this too but no one talked about it. Maybe this is what the Jesus man did in the tomb for three days. Maybe he lost his big soul and had to be silent and dark to get it back again. She arrives on the seafloor and bounces along among coral and caves. In one cave there is a soul ancient beyond reckoning but she does not know what kind of soul it is. The ancient soul is startled to feel her young soul, having never felt a child's soul before. She stays with the ancient soul for a while and they feel each other out. The ancient soul is confused and fascinated. For more years than it can remember the souls that it encountered belonged to beings that were either good to eat or not good to eat. That was the law of the world into which it was born: eat or do not eat, be aggressive or be afraid. Pipa is a different law. Also her soul does not wrap her being. Her being is elsewhere. How could that be? Pipa is a different law. The ancient soul brings its being out of its cave. It has not been this curious and startled for more years than it can remember. The other beings on the reef flee the scene at the speed of terror. The ancient being stretches and blinks and slides along the seafloor like a vast shadow. Pipa's soul goes along for the ride. The ancient being is so large that the waves on the surface of the sea are shivered. No one notices except Declan who notices everything about the sea. He notices a vast swatch of darker water for a while and then the darker water lightens and Pipa opens her eyes and sees her father grinning and she wants to say Papa you wouldn't *believe* what I just did but tonight her mouth has decided to sound like the warbler on board so she burbles and whistles and Piko laughs and rubs her legs and tickles her and cups her face in his hands and kisses her forehead nine times, one kiss for every year you have been the most beautiful amazing girl in the whole history of the world, Pip Pip. I hope you know how much I love you. I know you can hear me in there and I love you more than there are stars and songs in the sky. Yes yes yes Pip Pip Pip. He unbuckles her from her chair in the stern and folds her into his chest and Taromauri reaches over and touches her left cheek and Declan reaches over and tickles her right foot and Piko says *bedtime for bonita* and Pipa whistles and the warbler, delighted to hear her own language, answers at length from under the water tank.

★

Sir, said one of the brothers or cousins on the *Tanets* to Enrique, what is it you are hunting?

What are you talking about? Get back to work.

Sir, clearly you are hunting something and we would like to know what it is.

It's not your business. Nor are we hunting. We are a cargo ship.

Yes, sir.

Enrique couldn't tell if this was the Rapanuian or the

Rungarungawan. After a day or two he had ceased to care who was whom. He cared about their work. He did not care about their names. He cared about their burl and brawn. He did not care about their empty books or their aversion to metal. He cared about finding the *Plover*. He did not care why he was so intent on finding it. He did not care for introspection. He cared about efficient operation. He cared about control. He cared about money only insofar as money offered control. No money, no control. He cared about loss of control as insult offered. He did not care who offered the insult. He avenged insult to regain control. Control bred efficiency. He did not care to think about his hunger for control. He did not care for reflection. Control bred freedom. He did not even care for his ship. He cared for what the ship allowed. It provided control. He went where he wished to go. He hired whom he wished to hire. He fired whom he wished to fire. When insult was offered in any shape or form whatsoever it was repaid with twice the force. Reputation abetted control. Disguise abetted control. Mobility abetted control. He who was neither here nor there could not be controlled. He had often thought of changing his name serially but as yet saw no need to do so. Those whom he hired called him simply sir or captain. He who had no name or label could not be controlled. He who controlled his words and story controlled time. Controlled violence bred control. The threat or specter or suggestion of violence bred control. The ship with several registrations and names and permits and passes and bills of lading could not be controlled. He stared at his charts and for a moment considered that he did not care overmuch about the crewman Taro, and that Taro's departure from the *Tanets* did not actually affect or diminish his control of the ship and its commerce, and that in fact he had replaced Taro with two crewmen who together equaled the proximate labors of Taro and Something Somethingivić for slightly less money than he had paid the last two crewmen, and that in fact his intent pursuit of the green boat with the red sail might in a sense be a distraction and therefore a reduction or diminution of his control of matters; but then some slow rage rose in him that *his* ship had been offended, *his* crewman taken or persuaded to abscond, *his* will flouted, and he bent grimly over his charts. Where would they go, where would they hide, where would they flee?

★

There's a little island that way where I think we should put in for a while, said Declan. Fresh water, villages, even a little airport if we want to turn the boat into a plane. Also fresh fish. Also I bet there are pigs to be had. Me personally I could use a roaring pork dinner. With fresh coffee. And fruit. And cigars. And fresh coffee. And cigars.

And the name of the island is . . . ? said Piko.

Actually I think it has about eighty names. I think it changes names every three years. It's like a law there or something. The guy who first told me about it called it Torino, but he was from Italy. Another guy I knew called it Manhattan, and then a scalloper I know called it Eel Island because he said there was a lake there with eels in it but I don't know if that's true. I heard there was a lady who called it Betsy Island but I don't know if that's true. I do know there's freshwater there though. Guys who fished this far south would stop there for water because it rains like hell on this island and there's plenty of water. Also pigs.

We call it Maraia, said Taromauri.

Maria?

Maraia.

What does that mean?

It means dangerous.

Oh, lovely, said Piko. Just lovely. We are going to land on an island named Dangerous. Lovely. Why don't we slide past Dangerous and land on Undeniably Safe?

Quit pissing and moaning, said Declan. Better be despised for too anxious apprehensions than ruined by too confident security: Burke. Let's pull in there. We need the water, and I wouldn't mind hiding out for a few days in a corner of a lagoon or something. Be good to get the pip some fresh food too, you know? North by west. Bag of almonds for the first person to see land.

★

Are we still all telling stories? asks the gull. Because I have a good story.

God, says Declan, what *is* it with that bird, she doesn't say anything for days and then you can't shut her up.

Well, says the gull, a little offended, *we* don't keep babbling away with small talk, *we* only say something when we have something to say.

Man, listen to her shriek and cackle, says Declan, you would think she's telling a dirty joke or something. There were these three gulls in a bucket . . .

See, that's just rude, says the gull. I *was* going to tell

you a story about this particular island, but if I am just going to be insulted I have other matters to attend to.

I tell you, says Declan, I would give my left nut to know what she's saying. If she's a she. I haven't checked. Not that I want to know. Maybe she's a boy gull.

Do *I* make sniggering remarks about *your* genitalia? answered the gull. I do not. And how easy it would be to observe that *you* do not have a mate. *I* have a mate. Could it be that none of your species wishes to mate with you because you are rude and insulting? Could that be?

It's almost like she's saying something tart and blunt, you know? says Declan. Look at her with her face like a schoolmarm. She looks like an old preacher reading me the riot act.

Fine, says the gull. Fine. You think this is funny. But I have stories to tell that would make your head swim. There's a boat hunting you, did you know that? I have seen it with my own eyes. Where do you think I go when I leave? And this island is indeed dangerous. We do not land here. No gull has set foot on this island for more years than there are fish in the sea. Even the albatross people will not go near it. And why is that? I could tell you but you are not interested in what *I* have to say. I thought we were shipmates. *You* enlisted *me*. You asked if I was in it for the long haul, and I was honored to be invited, and I signed on for the voyage. But here I am being mocked and insulted. After all we have been through! Fine. You are the captain, you make the decisions, I will just zip my lip. You go right ahead. Land where you shouldn't and stop moving when you should be moving twice as fast. Fine.

Minutes later as Taromauri and Pipa were sitting in the
bow they saw . . . something we should investigate, said
Taromauri quietly to Piko. Declan aimed the *Plover* at the
object. Not a boat, not a mat of vegetation or garbage, not
a dead animal. So much of what we see we identify by
what it is not. It was a raft. There was a body on it. Declan
hove to. The raft was raw—a few logs lashed together,
not carefully. The body was a man. He was clothed but
barefoot. His right foot hung over the side of the raft. His
hands and feet and face were so burnt by the sun that
strips of blackened skin had peeled here and there showing
bright pink stripes of newer skin ready to burn in its turn.
The raft knocked politely against the *Plover*. Piko slipped
overboard and felt the man's wrists and neck. Alive but
not by much. Declan slipped overboard and he and Piko
lifted the man up to Taromauri. Pipa felt for a larger soul
but there was no answer. They laid him on the hatch and
crouched alongside.

The raft?

Let it go.

Young guy.

Yeh.

He'll barf whatever we give him, you know.

Yeh.

Too bad we don't have ice.

Yeh.

They dripped water between his cracked lips and after
a while his tongue woke up and tried to explore the water
but it took a while for the engineering of his face to get

back into gear. His face was cracked and burned something awful. They spread salve on all the cracked and burned parts they could find easily and figured his shirt and pants had protected the rest. He had a jacket, it turned out, which he must have been using for a pillow or blanket on the raft, because it was rolled up tight and stuck to his neck, which had cracked and burned so that blood had seeped into the jacket and hardened and now the jacket was glued so tight to his neck that the shock and pain of removing it was what woke the man from his coma. It took a while for him to get his eyes all the way open, the skin on his eyelids also being badly cracked and burned, and it took him an even longer while to get his voice up from his chest and through the raw desert of his throat and across the blackened waste of his lips, but after more water and salve and hard work on everyone's part he got his parts all moving together again and after a brief period of croaking he said *you* and *yes*.

Excellent start, said Declan. Good word choice. If *you* is a question, the answer is that this is a boat called the *Plover,* and yes, we will carry you to a doctor, we are heading that way anyways.

The man looked at Piko.

Just along for the ride myself, said Piko.

The man tried to say something else but his voice had retreated to croaking again and Declan said my sincere advice is for you to stop talking and keep sipping tiny drops of water. Also the more salve you get on the better. The ship's medical officer here will remain in attendance. Dr. Piko?

Dr. O Donnell?

Your patient, sir.

Thank you, sir.

★

The island was small but thorough. It was three miles long by one mile wide and there was indeed a lake with eels in it, some of them mammoth. Most of the island was dense with palm trees that seemed as if they had never been cut in the whole history of the world. There were coconut crabs everywhere and lorikeets and terns and boobies and turtles on the beaches. As the *Plover* slid past the landing wharf Piko pointed out egrets and plovers along the shore. There was one airstrip and six coconut plantations and eight small villages and one village almost big enough to be a small town. The smallest village had thirty people and eleven dogs in it and the biggest village had hundreds of people including a doctor and a reverend mister and a skid row district and more than one hundred dogs. Piko jumped out and roped the boat to the wharf and Taromauri stepped off carrying Pipa on her shoulders like a nut on a tree.

You not coming, Dec?

Nah. Stuff to do on the boat. I'll stay with the guy and you find the doctor.

You coming, gull?

Nope, said the gull. I believe I made it clear that we do not set foot on this island, and indeed even being roped to it like this is unnerving.

I tell you, said Declan, every time you ask that bird a question now she answers right quick. I think she understands us. I would give my—

No no, said Piko, keep your nut, you and your pal keep an eye on the boat and we will see what's up. What's my shopping list, fruit and water?

And fish and coffee. And the doctor. See if there's pork to be had. And cigars. Cigars are important.

Why are you not coming? The burned guy isn't going anywhere.

Stuff to do on the boat.

Why really are you not coming?

I don't want to land.

Pardon?

Not ready to land yet.

You don't even want to set foot on a beach? After all those days on the boat?

Nope.

Okay. Fruit, water, pork, fish, coffee, doctor.

And cigars. Cigars are—

Important, yeh, I got it. All right—see you in a couple hours.

*

In the second-largest village there is a chapel surrounded by ferns. The chapel is made of palm trees and screw pine and catchbird tree and there are little exquisite worked details cut from breadfruit wood. In and around the chapel are strings and pots and bunches of frangipani and hibiscus. To the west of the chapel there is a grove of guava and to the east there is a grove of papaya. At the foot of each tree in both groves there is a nameplate with the name of a deceased person whose used body was turned to ash and the ash planted with a new seedling so that as a person died a tree was launched and the person's energy fed the tree from which came food for the families of that person and for other families if the person's tree was especially generous.

In the chapel this evening the choir is practicing. The choir has eleven members, one of which is the Reverend Mister, who sings bass or baritone, depending. The Reverend Mister was almost ordained a priest but not quite. Matters conspired such that he completed his study and training and took final vows but found himself pastor of the chapel and its small attendant congregation before achieving ordination. It is a long story and not especially interesting, as he says. It is the stuff of low drama. Whereas our choir is the stuff of elevated aspiration. The choir is his baby and his pet. He recruits widely and well. Among the members are two boys with voices as nearly perfect and pristine as you can hear in this world. This perfection cannot last but we will savor it before it flees into croaking maturity. There are three young women who sing like birds like angels like the murmuring sea. There is another man who sings bass if the Reverend Mister sings baritone and vice versa. They call themselves the Alternators when they are in their cups. When they are in their cups they sing Jimmy Rushing songs. There are two older women who love to sing and do not sing at all well but they sing with passion, and awkward passion is so often so very much more admirable than mere achievement, isn't that so? We also have a new member this evening, a visitor from another island, where he was a man of great service to his community; let us welcome him with our usual grace and warmth, and assure him that here he is among friends. You stand back row center, sir—bass far left, baritones center, tenor to the right. With that nose, you are surely a baritone. Tonight I will sing baritone and our broad-shouldered comrade Toba here will sing the bass line. Our tenor . . . but ah, here, as if entering from the wings on cue, is our tenor, prompt and punctual as always. Danilo, welcome. Ladies and gentlemen, "Be Thou My Vision," on three . . .

★

Taromauri carries Pipa along the beach. Terns swirl around them like sentinels. Your legs are longer than they were yesterday, says Taromauri. Are you growing an inch a day? And soon you will be eighteen feet tall? Eventually you will be tall enough to walk in the ocean and pull the boat? Pipa the Giant! With one foot on one island and the other on another far away. Birds will build nests on your shoulders. Or you can be a bridge from one island to another and people will walk along your spine and think it is a range of lovely gentle mountains. It is not so bad to be big. I have been big forever, I think. When I was little I was big. People were angry that I was big and for a long time I wondered why they were angry and then I figured out that they were frightened of me. Yet big people are rarely frightening. It is small people who are frightening because they are frightened. This is the way of the world, I think. I was so big when I was little that people didn't talk to me. People shouted at me like I was a stone or a storm. The first person who spoke gently to me was Kekenu. I think that is why we married each other. He understood that I was a person inside my big body and I saw that he was a person inside the powerful armor of his body. He had tides and storms inside but his face was set like a stone or a sea and people thought he did not feel things painfully but he did, very much so. Did I ever tell you about the last time I saw him? He was on the beach and he took the last letter he had written to our daughter and he made a little fire and he burned it. I watched him do this thing. Then he took her clothes and toys and a book she loved and her sleeping mat and her bracelets and hairtwists and a flute she loved and he burned all those things too. He sat by the fire with a stick making sure that everything burned properly. I watched him do this thing. Poking the fire with his little stick so that every single thing burned away. He crouched there for hours until the fire burned everything through and burned down to ash and blew away. That was the last time I saw him. I miss him very much. I wish that we could see into each other again but I don't know if we will ever see each other again. That is the way of the world, I think.

★

The doctor in the largest village, on hearing about the man found on a raft at sea, sent a truck and two men to carry him from the boat to the clinic. The two men were small and silent and efficient and they shouldered the burned man gently into their truck. One of the men had lightning bolts tattooed on his cheeks and the other wore intricate blue-and-green feathered earrings that hung to his shoulders. After they drove off Piko and Declan stashed the fruit and water Piko had bought, and made coffee with the o my gawd fresh coffee he had bought, and commiserated that sadly there was no pork to be had whatsoever absolutely, and Piko with a flourish produced a bright golden box of cigars, and said me personally I suggest that we wait to enjoy these until we have circumnavigated the island, and walked it stem to stern, and explored the teeming jungle, and quartered the compass, and spent a whole blessed day on terra firma, a boat that doesn't rock even a little.

Nah, said Declan. I am staying with the boat.

The boat's not going anywhere, man. Let's wander and wonder.

Nah, *misneach,* stay with the boat, rule number one.

We're not *at* sea, for a change, Dec. Come on, man, Taromauri will keep an eye on the boat and the pip, let's have an adventure. Why else did we land on land?

Nah.

You serious?

Yup.

We just spent *weeks* at sea, and you are not going to even set foot on this island.

Correct.

What's the matter with you?

Nothing's the matter with me, man. Just not leaving the boat. Calm down.

What is your problem? says Piko, and for once he is angry; he is *never* angry and in the way of guys who never get angry, when he gets angry he is slightly too angry. What are you running away from? Why don't you want to land?

Are you going to live on a little stinking boat the rest of your life? *What* is your problem?

Little boat? says Declan, trying to cut the moment. Stinking? Don't call my boat little. This is a fecking cabin cruiser. This boat is almost thirty feet long. This boat is an island, man.

This is chickenshit, Dec, says Piko.

Long pause.

Who are you to talk? says Declan, real quiet; dangerous quiet. Who are you to bark at me? Who ran away from home to throw fecking firesticks? What are you, ten years old? Everything is going to be better in the fecking swaying fecking palms of the tropics?

I left because Elly died and everything was finished, you dumb fuck.

So did I, you stupid ass.

They stare at each other, furious.

What's to go home for? says Declan. What home? And what's to land for? Where the hell would I live? What would I do? This is what I *do*, you stupid ass. I run a boat. At least you *had* a home where someone loved you and you loved them. I *know* you loved Elly. I know it hurt when she died. I am not a fecking idiot. I know it hurts, what happened to Pipa. But get a fecking grip, man. You *can* go home. You *have* a home. You can go back and get a job and have fecking neighbors and a fecking mortgage. At least you *have* a daughter. What would *I* go home for? What home? What fecking job would I do? I fish. I have a boat. This *is* home. I live here. You don't want to be here, don't be. Fecking run away like you did from your life. Jerk.

Piko comes real close and sticks his nose about half an inch from Declan's nose and says real quiet, fuck you, Declan O Donnell. You don't know what you are talking about. You never got married. You never had a kid. I am playing in the big leagues. My wife wasted away and died and I live in that hole every day. My baby girl got smashed and she'll never come back and I live in that hole every day. Fuck you. Don't talk to me about what you don't know a fucking thing about. Stick to talking about fish. You know fish all right. Don't talk to *me* about running away. *Your* wife dies, *your* kid's crippled, *then* you talk to me.

Declan shifts his right shoulder and Piko tenses his whole body like the string on a bow.

Listen, man, says Declan even quieter than before. You wanted a ride. I gave you a ride. You are my brother and I love the pip. But don't give me shit, Piko. Don't do it. You want a ride, you need a place to stay, there's bunks for you anytime. But do not, do *not,* give me shit. I got enough shit already to last me a lifetime. I got twenty years of shit at home. I am not taking shit from anyone again, ever. This is where I live and how I live and it's not up for debate. Get it?

Pause. Boat creaking. Taromauri and Pipa just visible at the far end of the beach, a big dot carrying a little dot with terns whirling all around like snowflakes in summer.

Fuck you, Dec, says Piko just as quiet as Declan. We'll find somewhere else to go. Fuck you. You don't want to talk about real things, fine. You want to be alone on your boat, fine. Thanks for the ride. That was real generous and we are very grateful. We'll get our gear off before sunset. Thanks for the ride. If Pipa could talk she would say thank you too.

★

That night Declan pays a kid strolling by the boat to go get him a bottle of whiskey and he gets so drunk he slips in the stern and sprawls in the slosh. The starry heaven. That's old Ed Burke. Éamon de Búrca. Never used his Irish name. Poor old Ed. Two sons died. Never a penny. The story of the race. The sea of sons. The silent She. I should have been a pair of ragged claws scuttling something something the shilent sea. The thtarry thee. Scuttled o yes scuttled. Piko not coming back. Pipa not coming back. Taro not coming back. *Declan* came back. Good old Declan! God gold Declan! Declan O Lonely. Captain of nothing. I have to pee like a horse. One hand for me and one for the boat. Oldest adage on the She. Up we go, captain! One for the boat and one for the dolt. Oldest adage on the She. Ahoy, mate! Present yourself, Mr. Johnson! Avast your waving and man the pumps! Sure yes sir! Bless my soul that is the single greatest feeling o my God in the history of feelings. No fecking novels about *that,* are there? Back to quarters, Mr. Johnson! Sir yes sure! One hand for the skipper and one for the zipper! Sir yes sir! Permission to stand on the cabin roof and imitate the gull who used to be there, captain! Permission granted, sir! Gull not coming back either. Must be a dull gull, sir! Pooped on the poop deck, sir! This makes Declan laugh so hard he loses his balance and he lurches and shoots out a hand for the mast but misses it and falls to port and smashes his arm on the railing as he falls and then he crashes into the water, the stabbing pain in his arm so immediate and huge he opens his mouth to scream and the Pacific Ocean, which has been waiting patiently for many years for exactly this chance, rushes into his mouth as fast as it can go.

VI

THE TWO YOUNG ISLAND RATS, *kiore,* and the tiny warbler, *bokikokiko,* had long ago come to an understanding, a tenuous peace, something like a truce on the boat; one of the rats had made a gesture toward attacking and eating the crippled warbler, but the warbler had bristled and cocked its one good wing like a grim fist, and the other rat had intervened to calm things down, and an arrangement had been negotiated whereby the rats were masters of the lower reaches and the warbler master of the deck, ruling from her headquarters under the water tank; all three were respectful but wary of the gull, and generally leery of the human beings, especially the smallest one, who knew everything about them although she did not move on her own but was carried about by the other three. It was the warbler who saw the *kai,* or trees, as she called the human beings, in their most active modes, working the boat, fishing, talking, laughing; the rats, on the other hand, saw the human beings active only when they were cooking in the tiny galley kitchen; inasmuch as the human beings came below only to sleep or shelter in their bunks from wild weather, the rats had concluded that they were a generally somnolent and nocturnal species, and, for all their epic size, probably harmless. But they too felt the thorough attention and curiosity of the smallest of the human beings, the one who was carried around by the others; no matter where you hid on the boat, no matter how far *that* one's body was from your body, as one of the rats noted to the warbler, *that* one sees you.

★

Declan falling down and down and dark and down.

Well, you useless rat bastard, I see you've come to your sorry end at last, says his father.

Declan is so shocked to hear his dead father's voice in his ear that he opens his mouth wider and more of the ocean roars in snarling.

Poor boy, says his dead mother. Close your mouth and stand up straight. You look like a trout. God alone knows what to do with that hair. You'll never be handsome but you are a clever boy and if you work hard you'll get by somehow.

Drowning while drunk, says his father. What a surprise. What a shock. Fecking sorry bastard. His sister is a better man than he is.

You're too hard on that boy, says his mother. You drench that boy in your own bile.

He's a useless flop of a child and he'll end up a rudderless drunk, says his father.

Because you are a failure he has to be one also? says his mother, grim and cold.

You're an icy bitch, says his father, and he steps toward her suddenly but Declan jumps up faster and closes his mouth and swings as hard as he can at his father's bony white face and his hand slams against the rudder and he hauls himself desperately up and his head breaks the surface and he retches and coughs and hauls in air and retches and sobs and coughs for longer than he can later remember. After a while he tries to grab the rudder with both hands but his left arm screams and refuses to answer the bell. Some parts of him are screaming and raging but the seagoing parts are calm and patient. As long as he is touching the boat all will be well. *Misneach.* Find the anchor cable, first of all. How deep is the moorage? Not so deep. It's a sandy bottom. Stay with the boat. *Misneach.* No passion so effectually robs the mind as fear: Burke. The water is warm. There are no sharks in the lagoon. With two arms he could haul himself up on the stern step and so reach the railing from which hung Taromauri's tent; but with one arm dead he could only wait, or swim to shore. Probably the arm is broken, which means shock and loss of blood. Which means try for shore now while you have the gas. Jesus. Drowning while drunk. Misdemeanor. Misneachdemeanor. It's not like there's a choice. Swim. Jesus blessed Christmas. But just as he lets go of the anchor cable a hand grabs his collar and he sees Piko's rope beard swaying silvery in the dark and hears a voice say *my turn, man.*

The feck are you doing here, says Declan, after Piko hauls him in over the stern and examines his arm and splints it and wraps it tight in duct tape. Thought you were gone, man.

Felt bad about abandoning ship. *Misneach*. Can you walk, you think?

Yeh. Not drunk anymore.

You got drunk? Tonight?

Yeh.

Jesus.

Yeh.

Piss-poor idea, that.

Yeh.

You swore you wouldn't touch a drop the rest of your life.

Yeh.

So why did you get drunk?

Because I did.

What the hell does that mean?

I'm a drunk, man. Why do drunks get drunk? Because they can.

We have to get that bone set right or you're screwed.

Yeh.

On the beach Declan staggers a little but he's not drunk anymore, he's stone sober. The trees are like bones all pale and jagged. He can hear a dog whining in the woods. The shadows have weight and teeth. He can hear dreams and whispers. He staggers again; the land has a different tilt and tide than the sea. He can hear the seethe and hunger of what

lives on the land; it snaps and quivers in the wind; everything clamors in the razored air; nothing is muted by
the merciful and murderous waters, nothing damped,
shrouded, muzzled; on the land there is a blizzard of noise,
pulsings and moanings, barking and groaning, coughing
and gulping, growling and praying, thickets of sound, a
wilderness of music so dense and loud that Declan staggers
again; he felt like his feet were plowing through snow he
couldn't see, an avalanche of noise he never heard afloat; at
sea, he thought distractedly, all I hear is the sea. Then they
were in a small tin building where a balding man with
spectacles missing one lens silently unwrapped his arm, examined the break, wrenched and snapped the bone ends
into place again, and rewrapped the arm. Take this pill
now and tomorrow take that pill, he said. Come back in
three days and let me see your arm. Pay me whatever you
can. Sleep on your right side. Avoid saltwater. Do not drink
alcohol. Alcohol is the demon child of the east wind. Try to
face west whenever possible in the next three days. Drink
as much freshwater as you can hold. Note the first bird you
hear or see every morning for the next three days and report them to me when you return. Remember to face west
and drink as much water as you can hold. Questions? No?
Good. Pay me whatever you can whenever you can. That is
the way of things here. Questions? No? Good.

★

The burned man is sitting up in his bed in the clinic. He
is more bright pink than black now, most of his former
skin having peeled away and fallen to the floor like shreds
of bark.

I feel like I am in a tighter suit, he says to the tall thin nurse. I feel like I have been poured into a new and smaller vessel. This is refreshatory but also uncomfortable. I think I am slightly too fat for this skin.

How did you come to be on the raft?

I believe I was placed there by unfriendly forces.

Pardon me?

Various contingents on the island where I used to live were uncomfortable with the direction in which I wished to suggest we as a society should proceed, and I was ejected.

Assaulted? Beaten?

Not that I remember.

Pardon?

I remember walking down the street and the next thing I knew I was on the raft.

You were kidnapped?

Kidnapped is a very interesting word, said the minister for fisheries and marine resources and foreign affairs. Meaning not at all what you would think it would mean. It sounds innocuous and even pleasant, a kid taking a nap, but no. I would say in my case that it's more that I was bundled off stage, in a manner of speeching. Perhaps exile is a more accurate term, considering that my return is unwelcome. I would imagine that physical violence awaits, and following that, my demise, although my demisery would be a criminal act, of course, with possible repercussions.

Do you always talk like this?

Only since my mouth works again.

Are you going to press charges?

I have an idea for a different approach to the matter, said the minister. I have a bigger idea than revenge or restoration. I have an idea, which, if it takes root, and spreads widely, and flowers in myriad ways that even I cannot see, will change matters, on such a scale that the men who stole my life from me, and nearly caused my death, and exiled me from my home, and tried to thieve and quash a vision that I can articulate but that many people already share, a vision possessed and owned by no one, a vision that cannot be kidnapped or killed or set adrift on a raft, well, those men will be defeated in their reliance on theft and violence, and their crime against me will be redressed, but I will take pleasure not so much in justice delivered in one small incident, in the long view, but in the ever so much larger, or oceanic, arena.

The nurse, one of those remarkable women with a stern implacable face but a joyous musical spirit behind the mask, laughed aloud, changed the bandages on his neck, told him he might very carefully sponge himself with a wet cloth if he wished to approximate a bath, checked his vitals, brought him a bowl of poi, and told the doctor that the patient was essentially recovered and could be released in the care of the boat. He's bubbling away a mile a minute in there, she said. It's like he has to catch up on all the words he didn't say when he was on the raft. No, he has no money. File him under indigent.

Not under emergency care?

Yes but no, she said. It was an emergency for *him* but we'll never get reimbursed for that. I'd file him indigent or impecunious and call it a day. The man with the broken arm will pay his fee, but the burned man has nothing but the remains of the suit he was wearing.

Impecunious it is, says the doctor. I note that the impecunious file is fatter than the indigent file, why is that?

Longer word, says the nurse, and they both grin.

★

Enrique called cheerfully to passing fishermen to ask after the green boat with the red sails. It is my cousin, and I must tell him of a new baby in the family! He asked radio operators on islands about the green boat. I owe the captain money, and I want to pay my debts! He asked harbormasters and shipping agents. That captain is my business partner, and we are being sent to Tahiti! He seemed to be splitting himself in half. One part of him was the old Enrique with a cold eye for money and a brain like a machine for profit and odds and percentages and corners to cut. The new part was a sort of ravening, a hunger that got worse every day that it was not fed. He lost weight. He spoke less. He had visions. He could feel himself splintering. He was afraid of *nothing,* nothing could ever faze or terrify him ever again, he was a silent verb in a world of clownish nouns, he would rain fire upon that which must be burned; but some shred of him *was* afraid, some deep sliver of the boy he had once been; and with mounting anger he squelched this boy, the small boy in a dark corner watching the candles, he cornered the fear and burned it in rage, but he could not erase it completely, and sometimes he sat for an hour over his charts terrified that the price for finding the green boat would be losing the last seeds of himself—his truest and deepest self, not the man he had created but the man he might have been, might still be; the man with a mother and a father and brothers; the man who might one day marry and have children; the man who might not be a grim verb, a fuse, a simmering machine, a human orca, but something else altogether; something he could not imagine, or not let himself imagine; but he knew it was still barely possible, and that it could only grow from the seeds of the boy in the dark corner, and that those seeds grew more brittle by the day. One time when he was a small boy an uncle gave him a handful of seeds to start his own garden. It was his seventh birthday and he took the seven seeds and hid them from his brothers and took them out only late at night to gaze upon and touch gently in amazement that they were his and they meant food. The season for planting came and he did not plant, and the season for harvest came and he did not harvest, and a second season for planting passed, and still he did not plant them, but only took them out of their secret box late at night to roll them in his fingers and gape in amazement; until one night when they had grown so fragile and brittle that they shattered when he touched them, and there was nothing left in them but dust.

★

The Rapanuian and the Rungarungawan are in the engine room of the *Tanets*. They are sitting face to face. Both have their hands on the book with no words. One has his eyes closed and the other is speaking very quietly. This is about death, says the one with his eyes open. You can see this coming and so can I. But *we* are not about death. We are about living. That is why we are together. That is what happened to us. Neither of us sought what came to us but it did and it is the very opposite of death. We are about living. We are about joy. We are not the children of the eyeless ones. We are the very opposite of the eyeless ones. That is why we are sworn together. That is what we are about. You know this and so do I. We can stop that man's imminent action or we can leave the ship before it happens. But we can only stop him with the tools that he uses. We can only stop him if we are violent. But we are sworn against violence. We can only be who we are. He must be who he is. Today he is a child of the eyeless ones. He might awaken to his next self but we cannot force that to happen. That is what we swore not to do. We vowed not to force things to be what we thought they should be but rather be open to them and allow them to be what they inarguably are. That is who we swore to be. So we must leave the ship. We must step away and let things happen as they will happen. We are sworn to be examples and not agents. So we must leave. We can swim. We can hold each other. We are together. The two of us are one.

Let us pray, said the other man, and they both sat silent holding the book for a few minutes, their eyes closed.

I feel that an island is coming soon, perhaps an hour, said the Rapanuian, and he folded the book into a blue cloth and slipped it into a waterproof bag. The Runga-rungawan waited until the book was safe and then he kissed each of the Rapanuian's eyes and the Rapanuian kissed each of the Rungarungawan's eyes and they went up on deck, the Rapanuian carrying the book as carefully as you would carry a baby.

*

Declan wakes up slowly in his bunk. His left arm says *about time you awoke so I can get some things off my chest. I am snapped in half.* What were you thinking, drinking? Did we not, as coherent body parts, all make a decision months ago to cease and desist with the drinking? Has anything good *ever* come from drinking? Have we ever not been battered bruised and broken as a result of drinking? Have we not seen through the ostensibly social veneer of drinking and perceived the inherent and incipient darkness of the habit? I speak for the fingers and toes and nose and ears and wrists and collarbone and even one *eye* socket when I say that drinking has never been *remotely* a productive enterprise in the least whatsoever for us and you *know* this which is why we all agreed to desist months ago. It's no good saying you forgot. We all know this is not true. Nor can you plead a broken heart or the urge to suppress great bodily or emotional pain and trauma. The fact is that you lost your temper and you lost your compass and this is *not* acceptable to the parts of the body that in concert compose you. You yourself appealed to us to help you in this matter and we have worked hard for months now to make that happen. Again I speak for the other parts of the body when I say we are *very* disappointed by what happened and we certainly hope it will not happen again. You can well imagine how particularly disappointed I am, having been *snapped in half* by an ostensibly accidental fall after drinking.

I do not think we have unreasonably high expectations for you. We have been with you from the beginning. We have always served with a will. We were all in it together. But you still do stupid things deliberately. We have no idea why. And the stupidest of all is to do the very thing that you know and we know will only bring turmoil and trouble. Not to mention significant and nearly fatal injury. That was very nearly the *end* of us last night. In a sense we are very lucky indeed to come away from last night with only me *snapped in half.* Do I sound a little bitter? Well, I am not thrilled about being halved but I will accept the blow if you promise us to stop drinking. You know and we know that cannot end well, and there is *so* much ahead of us. We cannot get there without you and you cannot get there without us. We are your crew, Declan. And you wouldn't casually place your crew in danger, would you? You wouldn't carelessly put your crew in harm's way. In fact you would do everything in your power to *protect* your crew. Not just from a sense of responsibility, but because of your character. Look, we have no illusions about the mistakes you have made but we also have no illusions about the quality of your character. We have known you all your life. We have seen the growth and defiant courage. The fact is that you are a good man with every hope and expectation of being a great man, if you marshal your undeniable tools and talents. Now, *I* have no idea what it is you will be at your apex, I am just your left arm, but you know I am right, and you owe it to yourself to be the best man you can be. Well, that's all

I have to say, and it's probably time to be up and about. It's after dawn, and there's a *lot* to be done.

★

Think of the Impacific Ocean not as a place but as a language, said the minister to the tall thin nurse, who had asked him about his work, and then been so startled by the cheerful river of his talk that she had to sit down to catch it as it poured forth.

Everyone who lives here speaks this language, he continued, and the language influenced who we are, and how we act, and how we think, and how we see and smell and hear and savor the world. So if we all speak the same language, and we all have a certain mindset and heartset about our lives that came from this ancient language influencing how we developed, and we all live *in* this language, on the tops of hills in the huge sprawl of the language, then we are a nation, isn't that so? Isn't that what a nation *is,* a coherent region where people gather under a certain set of ideas by which to live their lives? Now, some of those ideas are easy to see, like the color of your skin or what name you call God, but some of those ideas are *not* so easy to see, like how long your tribe was in that one place, or what war deep in the past gave you a story under which to claim that place, or what new ideas led to a new story under which to live there. And some ideas are very hard to see because of the miles involved. This is the case with our Impacific Ocean nation, I believe. But once some of us see that we actually *are* a nation, the nation of Pacifica, then we can start to *talk* about it, and believe it, and the more people who handle an idea, the more the idea becomes a place to live your lives. Do you see what I mean? So even this conversation, in which you entertain the idea of the nation of Pacifica, means that the nation just grew in population by one person. It doesn't even matter right now if you *believe* in the idea of the nation of Pacifica; it just matters that the idea is *in* you now, taking up residentialness. Ideas are like seeds and they grow some places and not others, but you have to scatter the seeds everywhere so they have a chance. So that is what I do. I am the seed scatterer. I do not own this idea. I am not the boss of the idea. I am just an agent of the idea. I am the first ambassador for Pacifica. I think it is a true idea and that the more people who receive the seed the more people will think about how we could be a very interesting nation, the nation of Pacifica, and the more people who think about it, the more likely it is to be born. And how often are new nations born? Not so often. It seems like a good idea to me that a new nation would be born, especially here where there never was a nation before, and other nations came and took what they wanted and left nothing for the people who stayed here after the other nations left. We could be a new nation unlike any other nation that ever was, too. That would be excellent. We could be a new kind of nation that never has a war, for example. Maybe we could be a kind of nation that invents new ways to solve problems. We are already a nation with the most remarkable volume and sun and range and amount of salt water and countless numbers of beings many of which we do not even know what species they are, but maybe we could also be the most inventacious nation there ever was. Maybe inventingness would be our National Product. That could certainly be. So everyone would want to get some of our inventingness. We could export *that*. We could import problems and export solutions that we invented. That could be. That could most *certainly* be.

★

Pipa had dark days. Sure she did. How could she not? She had dark *weeks*. How could she not? But something always flittered up and she could not stay down there in the dark. She had no words for how this was. It just was. It was some irrepressible bone at the bottom of her bones. Sometimes she tried to put a name or a shape on it but the name or shape would never stick and even when she was little she knew trying to name the bone was only a mask. It just was. There were no rules for its rising. Sometimes she would fall silent for hours, swimming in a darkness she could never imagine ever lifting ever again and could never have explained even if she had a voice with which to try to scream it, and then the irrepressible bone would rise up and the darkness would recede like a tide. It was like the darkness was afraid of the bone. Sometimes music drew the bone up to her surface. Sometimes birds. Sometimes angles and corners of light. Sometimes the way someone held her. Sometimes the gleam of a coin in her father's beard. She learned to trust the bone. It could not be called or summoned or controlled or bent to her will but when it came it came thoroughly and effortlessly without sign or signal and when it came the darkness shrank away and fell away thoroughly as if cowed and defeated. The darkness always came back. Sure it did. How could it not? But after a while she knew in her bones that it would not stay forever, and that up would rise something with raw defiant snarling joy in it, and that that would be a door opening to an ocean of light, and when this happened she was overcome with silent wriggling laughter, and shot through with some kind of electric wriggle that made her fingers flutter and flicker and her voice leap out thrilled even in its motley tatters and shreds, its halt and stammer of music; and there were times when what she heard herself saying was not the sputtered mewing and mewling that other people heard when she opened her mouth, but songs in languages of their own, music that used her as its instrument, not so much broken as newly shaped, shaped in a way the music had never traveled before; so that in the rare times even now when she tried to explain the bone in the bottom of her bones to herself, she would think of it as music that had to be sung somehow, and had chosen her, battered shattered Pipa, for its delivery. Why this would be so she could not understand, but that it *was* so was inarguable, and that it *was* so, she often thought, was the strangest and most amazing of gifts she had ever received.

★

Declan is in the cabin on deck staring at his charts. He is eager to be at sea. Enrique is in the cabin on deck staring at his charts. He is eager to reach the island. Taromauri is on the beach with Pipa. They would not at all mind staying on the island for another month or nine. Piko is walking through a forest negotiating the purchase of pork with a woman who says she is one hundred years old but looks older. The nurse at the clinic is still listening to the minister for fisheries and marine resources and foreign affairs who has now moved smoothly into his ideas for education in the nation of Pacifica, specifically ways and means to accomplish universal literacy despite problems of geographical enormity which seem insurmountainable but which actually are utterly surmountainable largely through the invention of media which seem unimaginable at present but which will soon be invented primarily by brilliant children who are not aware of the impossibility of the project. The gull is aloft, quite high, so that she can see the *Tanets* with one eye and the *Plover* with the other; she is singing something to herself. The doctor at the clinic, a naturalist by avocation, is studying slides of eel scales in an effort to determine if the eel species on the island is indeed as he suspects not only native but unique, occurring nowhere else, and occurring here not from seeding from foreign shipping but from a peculiar set of natural circumstances such that the freshwater of the lakes is occasionally infused by brackish water from inlets opened and closed by storms. Danilo is walking along the beach and will meet and greet Taromauri and Pipa in seven minutes. The Rapanuian and the Rungarungawan are together at the stern of the *Tanets,* silently watching for the island, the sighting of which is their sign to slip overboard, the Rapanuian carrying the book. Some of the molecules of what had once been Something Somethingivić wash up against the western beach of the island, a few of them touching the sand for an instant, until they are drawn gently back into the sea. By now Something Somethingivić in his new form has traveled much farther than he ever did while a coherent whole; he now stretches from Russia to Australia to Japan to this beach, where sanderlings and whimbrels and turnstones and curlews and plovers sprint and skitter, chasing savory flashes in the surf.

★

Piko follows the woman who says she is one hundred years old to her village, which looks to be about twenty tiny houses on a tiny lagoon. Twice she says the name of the village but Piko cannot catch the word; the word sounds like otter. Behind the village is the tallest hill on the island, which looks to be about twenty feet high. She says the name of the hill, but Piko cannot catch the word; again it sounds like otter. Here I am in Otterville, at the foot of Otter Mountain, he thinks. She leads him to a tiny enclosure in which three large pigs look annoyed at the interruption. She gestures that he should choose one and cut its throat but pay for the privilege first. He offers her dollars and she picks through the dollars looking at the engravings of men's faces until she finds a face she likes: Hiram Ulysses Grant. Piko, grinning, asks if she is absolutely sure she does not want to choose the brave and admirable Abraham Lincoln but she insists on Grant and he grins and hands her the fifty. By now several neighbors have gathered to watch the proceedings and stare at Piko's silvery beard and ponytail. A small girl tiptoes closest and reaches for the gleaming coin in his beard. Piko squats on his haunches and says ah I cannot give you that coin, little fish, that is a gift from my own daughter, but if you want to braid something in there yourself, be my guest, and she runs away quick as a cat, and Piko stands up again thinking maybe he has scared her and thinking of Pipa running just that way just that speed quick as a thought, but just that quick the girl is back again with a tiny wriggling green lizard, which she carefully imprisons in Piko's beard. The neighbors laugh at the way Piko's beard is now alive and squirming at the tip. Piko offers the girl dollars but she backs away. The woman who says she is one hundred years old is growing impatient to have one less pig and she gestures again that the time for murder has come. Piko contemplates the long walk back to the boat with a serious amount of deceased pig on his shoulders. He asks the neighbors if they would mind sharing the road and the load but they laugh and say no thanks in their language. The woman hands him a knife. Piko chooses the smallest of the pigs and snags her by her right rear leg and as she shrieks he deftly slits her throat and lifts her rear legs so that her head dangles and her blood drains into the sand in a wild gush and the small girl laughs and claps her hands.

*

It takes Piko a while to get back into the hang of dismantling a being that was a moment ago alive and coherent, but his hands remember the thousand times he has edited fish, and soon what had been a pig is several piles of steaming interior, some of which will become energy inside people and fish and birds and a little of which will become energy inside a brilliant dog who at the moment is watching from the hillside and considering his options. This dog is one of the most amazing dogs in the history of dogs, a

dog with unbelievable intellectual and physical gifts, but
with none of the arrogance that so often is the price for
even a small genius. You would say that this dog is blessed
beyond belief, if you were the sort of person who used the
word blessed. There's no reason you can see why this dog
would be gifted far beyond the usual gifts of dogs, but the
fact is that he *is* so gifted; he learned to swim by watching
the little children in the village learn to swim, he watched
and remembered as schools of fish chose certain refuges in
the tiny lagoon, he has explored the island's lake and knows
how to catch eels, he noticed that catchbirdtrees actually
do catch birds and lizards and insects on their sticky fruit,
he understands almost all of the languages he hears from
people and other animals, he knows who among the villagers tends toward kindness and who toward greed, he
knows the arrival and departure times of the cargo planes,
he knows which of Danilo's fellow workers at the airport
is smuggling drugs in secret compartments in copra shipments, he knows which ships illegally dump sewage at
night in the harbor, he knows when a subtle change in
the wind means cyclone and when it means a stretch of
rare blue weather on this most humid and rainy of islands.
He knows that there are other islands beyond the horizon,
some of them vast, for he has heard and pondered what
people say of the world beyond the island of eels; and while
he feels a small curiosity about other islands, he is brilliant
enough to know that horizontal travel is not as nutritious
and revelatory as vertical travel; so he has concluded already, at what would be age twenty for a man, to explore
and plumb and plunge into his own island so thoroughly

that he would know something of everything; the work of a lifetime, perhaps several; but perhaps we are issued several lifetimes, and are not apprised of those before and after the present one, for reasons of decorum or bookkeeping. This could be.

*

Even with one arm Declan works the boat. Examines the hull patch with a cold and ruthless eye; is that going to last through a cyclone, a ferocious storm, a scorching dry lull when wet wood shrinks? Finds one last bag of almonds, each one so dry and brittle it snaps like a twig in his teeth. Examines all hoists and junctures. A boat is not unlike a body in which the joints are crucial and surrender first to gravity and entropy. Indeed a boat has knees, and can be said to shoulder through the sea, and how often the *Plover* has elbowed its way through a crowd of other fishing boats the other crews jeering the horse of a different color, the orphan of the species? He examines the sails, looking for the inevitable flaw, a poorly stitched seam, a thin place; *caol ait* in the old tongue, thin places, the windows between this world and the others, the worlds everywhere extant but never seen, everywhere sensed but rarely explored. He examines the engine and the engine house and the hatch and the hatch cover and the running lights and the rigging and the wheel and his chart box and the life preservers and life jackets and sight reduction tables and collected speeches of Éamon de Búrca. He sighs over the paint and stares at the creosote daubed thicker than paint at the bottom of the mast. His father had given him that creosote, or rather sold it to him, at cost plus ten percent;

and while he had done the daubing himself, cursing the old man's penury and thrift, the fecking cheap old goat, he had known full well that the ten percent would be soaked back into the land where he was born, into the cows and timber of that slice of Oregon where he and his sister and brothers were raised by the snarling old man, bitterer than ever before after his wife their mother left one day wordlessly dragging her suitcase thumping down the driveway, so that the small profit he made over to the old man would come back to him snarling probably as food; and now that he sat and remembered the transaction he recalled that for once the old man had ill-temperedly said hell, he would help tar the mast to make sure it was done right and not done piss-poor as you have so many times done ill, boy, and Declan had as usual paid the old man in the same coin, and snarled back that he would do it himself and do it right and not have a crank as consultant, and now Declan, sitting in Pipa's chair in the stern, saw that maybe the old man was opening a tiny window in his castle that day, and that his oldest son had slammed it shut, slammed it in his face, slammed it without the slightest thought that it was anything but bile. So it is that I have become my dad, thinks Declan, quick to think ill and quicker to speak it.

*

Danilo, walking home through the palms and pines, realizes he has come to a crossroad in his life; a man can only savor not being dead and frozen for so long before he wonders what he *should* do. What *was* his work? Why had he been spared in the winter woods? Should he find his brother, who must certainly by now be a man of substance in their country? Should he return to their country and do what he could to make it whole? Should he join a new country, and add his salt and song to a new national music? Go to sea? Sink roots in this island? Seek a wife, build a small country of their children? Try to earn his living with his singing? Enter holy orders, and be like the Reverend Mister, whom he much admired for his cheerful grace and lack of ego? Danilo was young and muscled, healthy and hale, unencumbered by debt or despair, draped and adorned by no responsibility at all; but he was wise enough even at twenty to see that what many would call an utter and admirable freedom was also a sort of thicket or wilderness, in which, by virtue of being able to take any path he chose, he was lost in a dense jungle of the possible, the sheer welter of which sometimes overwhelmed him. The irony was, he thought, that as soon as you chose a path, you mourned and regretted the ones you did not choose; but to choose none was to moon uselessly over them all, and thus be imprisoned by impasse. How very many people, he thought, as he walked through the catchbirdtrees by the lake, were frozen by the weight of their potential, the imposing alps of their dreams? There must be so many people who, because they could do anything, did nothing. Was this the secret cost of civilization, perhaps, that once people were free from want, free to act as they liked, they did not act at all, but only stared at themselves, sentenced to solipsism?

Thus his line of thought in the dark as he made his way along the west rim of the water, listening with all the eleven ears his years in the forest had given him. He heard a dark thrash in the lake and thought of the fabled eels, and wondered if the sound was courting or fighting; and then with a start he saw a brilliant white bird caught fast by feet and wingtips to a cluster of catchbird fruit. It was a tiny tern, which he freed with one hand while guarding his eyes with the other. The tern, loosed from its sticky trap, vanished so suddenly that he spun around looking for evidence of its flight; to no avail.

★

Piko divvies up the pig, handing pieces hither and yon, and everyone is smiling and laughing, and soon there are cooking fires, and he sits with two men on the beach grilling a little of the meat before he sets off back to the boat, and he teaches them how to throw firesticks, they take a few sticks from the fire and he shows them how to throw *into* the wind, with a snap of the wrist to impart spin, sort of like throwing a curveball, he says, so the stick actually *floats* out over the water for a moment; and he explains with a smile that you can throw fire a lot better when you have some elevation and an updraft, and they are fascinated, and they keep practicing until there are no more sticks in the fire, and then, consequently, no fire. In his capacity as veteran fire-throwing consultant Piko advises them to try it after dark from the hill behind the village; while the wind will have reversed, and be blowing out rather than in, still, they might have enough lift to get some serious throws in. It was all a matter of practice and experience, he said gravely, and then smiled to remember the time he had been so confident of his skill, finally, after much practice, and had thrown a *papala* stick at exactly the wrong angle, at exactly the wrong instant, and nearly roasted his hair and that of his close companions on the mountain in Makana. In the old days, one of his friends had said, the people out in the sea in canoes would try to catch the firesticks, and mark themselves with the ember of the stick they caught, to make a sign on their skins of the occasion, and these scars were honorable and revered, but in his case their marks would have been earned by the worst throw in the history of fire throwing, which would certainly be memorable, if not exactly revered.

Piko gazes out at the ocean, watching fishing boats and children in the surf, and there's a whisper of breeze cooling everything, and gulls and terns float past like incarnated bits of the wind itself, and the men are smiling as they teach him lewd and vulgar words in their language, and Piko thinks, you know, all in all, this is better than a stick in the eye here, this is a kind of life we could live, this wouldn't be a bad place for the pip, I bet we could get a cottage for ten bucks here, and I could fish, and maybe recruit some grant money for scientific study of this particular finger of the ocean, and the weather's decent, and there's plenty of freshwater, and the neighbors seem generally decent; but then his relentlessly honest scientist's eye begins to see beneath the bucolic. The children are thin; more than a few are scrawny. There is a mound of broken liquor bottles behind the village; a modern midden. One woman has a black eye; another has a bruise on her shoulder exactly the size of a large man's fist. Several half-hearted fences are missing slats and look like broken teeth. Several men and women are missing teeth. Several houses have broken windows or no windows and shreds and shards of useless things scattered about them like old accidents. Several dogs are mangy. The house nearest to where he sits on the beach, he notices, is listing slightly to starboard; as he watches, a man emerges from the back door, squats in the yard to defecate, and then walks back into the house; over the back door, Piko notices, is a faded painting of Queen Victoria. A line from his grandfather pops back into his head: *Her Majesty Victoria, by the grace of God, Queen of Britain and Ireland, Defender of the Faith, Empress of All India, the scabrous old battleship, enslaving the poor for her baubles and beads, all queens should be put to work scrubbing floors, and all washerwomen elevated to thrones. . . .*

★

Pipa in her chair in the stern of the *Plover* has her eyes closed in the bright sunlight and is cruising her soul around the lagoon, amazed at the wealth of colors and beings and shapes and sculptures and angles of light and astonishments of graceful and terrified propulsion. Taromauri had been repainting the cabin as per instructions from the captain, but something about the gull perched on the cabin roof has caught her eye, and she has been staring intently at the gull for several minutes. The gull had been dozing but felt her attention and now is awake and has cocked one eye at Taromauri. They regard each other with interest.

There's more to you than meets the eye, says Taromauri quietly.

The gull cocks her head to port.

What is it, though? Who *are* you?

Gulls do not grin, not having lips, nor do they hoist their eyebrows, not having eyebrows, but if ever there was a gull who *seemed* to be hoisting a brow and grinning, it's this one.

Declan says you understand every word said on the boat.

No reply.

I think maybe you understand everything that isn't said as well.

No reply.

Declan could be wrong but he's right, isn't he?

No reply, but a flurry of feathers; do the gull's eyes grow more intent?

We are verbs in noun packages, as Piko says.

Again what would be a grin if gulls could grin.

Piko could be wrong but I think he's right.

No reply.

I think you are far more than who you appear to be.

Now the gull is undeniably intent; and she steps daintily to the edge of the roof, closer to Taromauri, and stares down at her. They are perhaps a foot apart, and oblivious of everything else in the universe: Pipa's gentle burble as her mind explores a cave with an eel the size of her leg and the eel startles at her touch; the sway and creak of the boat in the cradle of the lagoon; the startle of terns along the stern railing, three on each side of the murmuring child; the rhythmic *thwap* of the rigging against the bones of the boat; the throaty humming of the captain down below tinkering with the hull patch for the hundredth time; the faint faraway drone of a cargo plane; the steady smash of surf on the reef; the rustle and rub of trees and bushes and thickets and copses; the infinitesimal whir of wind through the wings of an albatross just past the surfline; somewhere fainter than faint, the sound of voices in song.

I know who you are, says Taromauri, so quietly that if you were standing next to her you could not be sure if she had spoken aloud or if she had thought those words, and somehow you had heard them in your head.

I know who you are. You are one of the thirteen. You have taken this form and come among us. You are one of the shining ones.

The gull chortled; did her eye again double in intensity?

I see you, said Taromauri in an awed whisper. I *see* you.

It is so, said the gull, and again, if you were standing there on the deck, inches away from this bird and this woman, as close to them as you could decently stand, you could not absolutely tell for sure if the gull had actually formed those words with her beak and her tongue, or if you had heard them as if they were cut into your mind as sharp and bright as lines of fire.

Yes, said, or thought, the gull, it is so. You see clearly. And we see you. We cannot give gifts, we cannot change what is, but we can open things that are closed. We are allowed to remove obstacles. We are the thirteen servants.

Taromauri began to weep so silently and copiously that the tears slid down her face like a sheen on a rock and the top of her immense red cloth darkened with the wet. She bent to kneel but the gull said, do not kneel; remember we are your servants. We see you. What is it that we can open for you? Remember we cannot change what is, but we are allowed to open that which is closed. You must say it with your mouth. *Manewe,* as you say in your tongue, the thing must be sung. So many tongues in which to sing.

But Taromauri was overwhelmed, and could not stop weeping, and all her love and pain for her vanished daughter and hollowed husband, all the grim nights when she sat awake swaying and praying in the hold of the *Tanets,* all the pain and loss she had witnessed and tried to ameliorate, all the kindness and courage she had witnessed and tried to celebrate, all washed over and through her like a tremendous tide, and she did kneel, she couldn't help it, and weep from the cellar of her soul, and place her forehead upon the wooden deck, and heave sobs not of sadness but of release, and then relief; the latter not because her people had been right to believe that there are always thirteen shining ones in the world at any one time, taking any and all forms according to their incomprehensible designs and predilections, but relief in some inarticulate way that she had been *seen,* she was *known;* without ever admitting it to herself, she was lonely beyond articulation, so lonely and bereft that she had plastered over the pain with a grim mien and constant work, even fending off what few friendships were offered; but that *this* bright being, one of the blessed ones, of whatever nature it truly was, had *seen* her, seen the holes the size of her slim daughter and burly husband; this knocked her to her knees, and she wept.

The gull waited patiently, peering over the edge of the cabin roof; then again she felt a piercing attention on her skin, and looked up to see Pipa staring at her with eyes like wild oceans. The terns leapt into the air and swirled protectively around the child, darting like swallows. Down below, Declan felt some electric jolt in the air and stopped humming, puzzled; what, Jesus fecking *lightning,* on a clear day, in the blessed fecking tropics? Is this how a cyclone starts? Taromauri also felt the shock and stood up, instinctively reaching for Pipa. At the other end of the island Piko felt it also, and turned instinctively toward Pipa, although the top half of his mind thought is that an earthquake? Taromauri saw Pipa's stare and turned and looked at the gull and suddenly knew what to ask.

Can you heal the child?

We cannot change what is, said the gull.

Can you . . . open her? asked Taromauri.

The gull bowed ever so slightly from the roof of the cabin. We *are* allowed to remove obstacles, she said, or thought, and then the words *be opened* were in the air, shimmering, and again the gull bowed slightly and without the slightest effort sailed away into the gracious air. Taromauri watched her soar along the beach until she was a thin white line against the tangled green trees; and just as the gull banked seaward and vanished against the surging surf, Pipa said *Papa?*

*

Piko, startled by the electric shiver in the air, concluded that he better get moving, and he rose from the sand, and turned back toward the village to pick up his pieces of pig, but his eye is caught by what surely must be porpoises! just behind the surf line; his mind automatically processes speed (fast), color (black and white), furl of propulsion (considerable), and dorsal evidence (minimal), and he thinks *Phocoenoides dalli,* this far south? *Phocoena dioptrica,* this far north? Intrigued, he follows the porpoises—almost certainly *dalli,* amazing!—along the beach, until they vanished, all at once, in an instant, their speed and grace in the water just as awesome to him now as the first time he ever saw them as a boy, from a boat on the Oregon coast, nine porpoises flashing alongside the boat suddenly so fast and powerful that he gasped, breathless at such beings he had never imagined in what had seemed a bleak and ponderous sea.

He turns inland, smiling at the verve and power of the creatures, and sees a faint trail toward the village through what looks like a muddy swamplet; once inside the scrim of trees the trail becomes a worn wooden walkway, winding through an increasingly deep and fervent swamp. Piko is a student first and foremost of the ocean and its creatures, but he is alert to all of nature's profligacy, especially moist gifts, and he examines the welter of plants, some of which he can identify: arum, fern, bulrush, palms of various sorts and hues, and what seems to be an orchid; also there are flitterings of tiny birds, warblers and brilliant little parrots of green and red and blue.

He kneels down on the walkway to get a closer look at a nest tucked deftly into an old coconut husk, when he sees a second nest built into a soldier's helmet. Then he sees a circle of ferns bursting from an old tire. Then he sees shards of metal and cloth and men, little by little, as if his eyes were clearing and the swamp was revealing itself as the moist graveyard it had been for twenty years, untouched by the villagers, left to haunt and molder; the villagers had carried out their own dead, two boys blown to bits in the shivering clearing, but left the rest of the soldiers for the bog to bury, and buried they were now, by ferns and bulrushes and flowers; here and there still a flash of metal could be seen if you looked close for it, but the men— boys themselves for the most part, tall beardless boys, except for their sergeant, who had a beard like a bush—sank and dissolved, their atoms and molecules feeding the vibrant green things, the green things feeding the birds, the birds feeding the crabs, the crabs and birds and plants all eventually feeding the swamp again; the swamp always hungry, always patient, always inviting, always gentle in its acceptance of what falls into the shimmer of its surface, and then slowly plummets, the thick warm water closing over the memory with a sigh.

*

The warbler, smelling land and trees and ferns and bushes and flowers and mud and bogs and lakes, emerges slow and shy from under the water tank; and for the first time in many days she comes all the way out into the overwhelming light, which feels so warm and luxurious and nutritious that she stretches and flaps and whirs and chirrs; and her wing works! her wing works! Not very well, and it's *very* sore, but it works! the parts are back in play! A thump and curse from belowdecks sends her skittering back under the tank for a moment, but she cannot resist the light and out she comes again, this time more sure of herself, thrilled by her wingfulness; still cautious enough to see where the Huge Ones are—the largest One and the smallest One are sitting on the stern rail, One is down below, One is missing, that One with the long feather hanging from his chin—but jazzed by the light and by the irresistible smells of soil and sand, which together mean food. For the first time she hops all the way out onto the deck; and then with half a hop and half a flutter she makes it to the top of the water tank; and then, all systems go! and all caution thrown to the wind! she flutters up to the bow railing, and then bounces to the prow, and back to the railing, and if you can imagine a bird essentially the size of your thumb laughing with pleasure and leaping around with a sort of antic joy, go ahead and imagine that. Back to the water tank, quick as a sneeze; back to the prow, then all the way up to the cabin roof—where's the big white bird, the gull, who lives here?—back to the railing, liquid as water; a tiny feathered pinball, quicker in flight than you can easily follow; she moves so fast that she's more like a gentle brown blur than a bird giggling at being back in her first form. Then she remembers the *kiore,* and calls to them in that rippled voice warblers have trilled since before there were people in the world; and one by one the two young wood rats emerge, blinking, from a crack in the hatch cover; the first time they too have seen full sunlight in many days. The warbler launches an incredible tumultuous song covering many subjects, especially the unimaginable foods available and waiting on shore; and there is a moment to savor, as the boat rocks gently, and the warbler sings of vast mountains of fruit and hillocks of seeds, and the *kiore,* overwhelmed by the song, and the extraordinary light, and the green dense wet redolence of the island in their noses, shiver with pleasure; and fear.

VII

22° NORTH, 165° WEST

PIPA WAS STILL CRIPPLED. Sure she was. Her hands and feet were no different than before, flittering and flapping and wriggling when she was excited; she still could not sit up, or kneel, or walk, or run, or jump, or spin, or skip, or shuffle, or amble, or shamble, or shake hands with another being of any sort or species, or cup miracles in the bowls of her hands, or rub her eyes in weariness or amazement, or dance in a fling of limbs, or thumb-wrestle, or punch someone in the nose, or lean back grinning and weary with her hands behind her head, or wipe away tears, although tears did rise in her eyes and fall down her face, free and untrammeled; as they are right now, when she is so happy and overwhelmed and startled and croaky and out of practice with her voice that every time a word comes out of her mouth she regards it for an instant with absolute astonishment, as if it was a new and brilliant creature emerged from the holy cave of her mouth.

Declan came flying up the ladder from below when Taromauri shouted, and he too stood there agape as Pipa spouted and sang and bubbled and burbled in her chair. For a few minutes she poured out every word she had wanted to speak for the last four years but could not force past the prison of her teeth; she poured them out in no particular order, and there was no sense or syntax or structure to them at all, just a wild laughing jumbled spill of one headlong word after another, an ocean of phrases, and shards of stories, and threads of tales, and comments and observations, and remarks and ejaculations, and imprecations and recriminations, and jokes and puns, and explanations and fulminations, and musings and murmurs, and jollities and raileries, and snidery and speeches, and drollery and drivel, and mutterings and mumblery, and sarcasm and witticism, and falsification and rationalization, and songs in imitation and reverence for birds; and then, as the minutes passed, more and more songs of her own design and device, for in the four years during which she could not sing or speak, Pipa had somehow become a startling musician, crammed to the ears with notes and chords and snippets of song and rills and trills and runs of melody; and out they flew between the open gates of her teeth, her hands fluttering like wings, as Declan and Taromauri stood there entranced; and just as Declan turned to Taromauri to ask what in the fecking name of Jesus blessed Christmas had happened to the pip, there was a thump as Piko vaulted over the railing and landed by his baby girl and knelt and cupped her face in his hands and she shouted Papa, I can talk! I can talk! I love you! I can *talk*! Papa, I can *sing*! Listen! My mouth works and my voice works and I can *sing*! I *love* you! Listen, *listen*!

The two men who had kidnapped the minister for fisheries and marine resources and foreign affairs and marooned him at sea on a raft of rough planks were soon enough in their turn marooned by other men for offenses against the ruling cabal; and they drifted east for days, increasingly thirsty and desperate, until one morning they saw a tiny atoll, so tiny it had no name or map coordinates, and treeless and arid and caked with guano it was also; but nonetheless it was fixed and substantial, a refuge, however inhospitable, and they paddled madly toward it, with their blistered hands and blackened feet; but their raft was destroyed by the crushing surf, and one man was flung upon rock and coral, to be cruelly battered and torn, and drowned, and rendered into pieces by two sharks lurking for exactly this happy providential chance; and this man's bones did drift to the bottom of the sea, and there were covered by silt and the detritus of time, until such a day as bones be revived, if such a day shall come.

His companion survived the crashing surf, and achieved the atoll, but once there was again marooned, this time in a tiny sea of salt and sand, scoured by the wind and at all times drummed by the roaring of the sea; and there he did bake, and slowly wither, and drown in the heat, and grow so parched that he did drink of his own bodily fluids, even unto his own blood, which is exactly as salty as the sea was when life was born in it, many years ago. After he died his body dried, and dissolved, and was blown back into the sea and into the crevices of the rocks beneath the sea; and so ended the two men who had kidnapped the minister, and set him to drift in the vastness of the ocean. What were their names? Lost and barren, sea and shark, silt and ashes, whispers and insinuations, sounds spoken less by the year until finally they are only words on pages of old ledgers on their island; and even those words will dissolve, in time.

*

There was a tense intense hour during which Pipa sang and burbled in her chair and then she fell silent for a moment and began to weep and her father still kneeling his face inches from hers said what? what? and she said Papa if I stop talking now will I ever be able to talk again? and then she laughed, realizing that she just *had* stopped talking and resumed talking, and he laughed also, and all was well and all manner of things were well, for a moment. Taromauri tried and mostly failed to explain what had happened, or what she *thought* had happened, and Declan finally gave up, grinning, and said okay, fine, hey, bird, thanks, good job, well done, I'm recommending you for promotion, and the gull flittered and Declan laughed and said all right, are we all done here with fecking miraculous stuff, let's get on the road. So then the ship was prepared for the next stage of its journey, north by west, and stores and provisions laid by, and water tanks refilled, and farewells offered, and debts paid, and gratitude expressed, and so they prepared to sail, taking advantage of a prevailing wind at dusk, the captain still secretly leery of pursuit and confrontation, a feeling he expressed only to Piko belowdecks, as they triple-checked the hull patch.

We could buy guns here, said Piko quietly.

What, my bow and arrows are not enough?

I'm serious.

I know.

You think that guy is still after us?

Yeh. I don't know why I'm sure, but somehow I'm sure. I don't know why.

Pause.

Maybe we should be better . . . prepared, said Piko.

I don't know, man. If we have guns we'll end up using them, you know?

Better us than him.

Can you shoot?

No.

Me neither.

Pause.

Can Taromauri? asked Piko.

I don't know.

Pause.

Is he coming for us or Taromauri?

Does it matter?

I guess not.

She's one of us now, sort of.

Yeh.

Jesus, what a weird crew.

Hey, you hired us. And your gull.

Boy, this turned out to be not at all what it was supposed to be. I was just going to take off solo and whatever happened happened.

We happened.

Yeh.

Regrets?

Nope. I figure carting you all around is payment for my sins or something.

We're your fate, man. You're the ancient mariner.

I am not so ancient. *You* are the guy with the old goat beard. We better get moving. I want to be away before full dark. No moon tonight.

But they look at each other for a second, each man chewing his lip a little; and Declan brings the bow up to the cabin with him.

★

At dusk several people gather on the dock to which the *Plover* is roped. There is the balding doctor with one lens missing in his spectacles. There is the tall thin nurse who listened carefully to the minister for fisheries and marine resources and foreign affairs. There is the minister himself, barefoot, wearing an old suit of the softest tapa. I do not think I will ever wear shoes again, he says to the nurse, it being a shame to constrain or disguise these shining new feet. There is the Reverend Mister from the chapel choir, standing with his hand on Danilo Somethingivić's shoulder. There are two men from the village where Piko bought the pig, bearing a gift for him: a large bundle of dried *hau* and *papala* sticks, cut to the proper length for throwing fire. Piko bows and accepts the gift with a smile. The Reverend Mister asks to speak to the captain of the vessel. He testifies as to the excellent character and inarguable work ethic of the young man who has been a stalwart of the choir and a trusted and respected worker at the airport since his arrival on the island, and then speaks about the natural and understandable ambition of the young to travel and conduct themselves adventurously, within reason; an urge each of us of a certain age remembers fondly and indeed often returns to in happy memory, sometimes to the rue of young listeners. This has been *my* experience, says the Reverend Mister with a smile, but be that as it may I conclude by requesting that you find space aboard your capacious ship for my young friend here, whom the choir and chapel community are sending on his way with a small token of our respect and love; just enough money, perhaps, to defray the cost of his passage. With that the Reverend Mister bows and withdraws, but before Declan can open his mouth to say Absolutely Not, the tall thin nurse asks to speak to the captain of the vessel, and formally presents the minister, whose feet indeed are glowing pink like new babies at the end of his legs, and she testifies to his recovered health, and requests that in lieu of payment rendered to the clinic for the repair of Declan's arm, the minister be afforded passage, as his further residence on the island might put him in the way of unforeseen dangers arising from his past civic responsibilities, and inasmuch as the island community was not equipped to protect guests in such straits and circumstances, perhaps the distinguished

captain would be so kind as to be of assistance in this matter, with something of the same spirit in which he himself
was afforded assistance when he found himself in similar
straits and circumstances; and the clinic would see fit to
wipe all accrued and incurred debt from its books, considering the money to be the cost of the minister's passage. And
again Declan didn't even get his mouth all the way open to
say Jesus blessed Absolutely fecking Not before Piko was
helping the minister over the railing and Taromauri was
showing Danilo where to stash his gear. And so it was that
the *Plover* slid away from the dock at dusk, in a flurry of
terns, with four men, one woman, one girl, one gull, and
one warbler aboard, the warbler having unaccountably returned from the lush island; but the *kiore* had not returned,
and the warbler crouched in her accustomed spot under the
water tank, mourning her companions.

★

Why are there no love stories on this boat? What kind of
voyage is this, with male and female in it, over the course
of many pages and miles, with no adamant and steamy
love stories? But—there *are* love stories here. Have we not
sung them sufficiently? Have we been too subtle? Did not
the Rapanuian and the Rungarungawan kiss each other
tenderly and treasure each other in the bones of their hearts?
Does not Taromauri think and yearn for the man her husband was, and perhaps still is, in his bones? Is Declan not
learning to love a child, and so tiptoeing out of the castle
of the man he has been, and who knows how he might
love, once released from his keep? Is Piko not slowly learn-

ing to love his daughter for who she is rather than who she was? But certainly, yes, there are so many pressing and puzzling questions about love here. Will Piko learn to love another woman other than the one he loved and lost? Will Declan fall in love with *anyone* older than a child in the space of this story? Will the minister come down from his vast perspective of national affairs, and concentrate on an affair with one single individual citizen of Pacifica? And what of Danilo—how is it that a handsome young man with a voice so lovely it stops people in the street and shivers their hearts is not besieged by romance, or himself besieging the alps of ardor? And Enrique—is Enrique a mere thin curtain of villainy, or is he a real man, a complex character of emotional swirl and surge, who finds a way through the prison of his rage, and opens himself to love? And most of all, most tender of all, most sweetly and sadly and gently of all, what of Pipa? Who will Pipa love? Who will Pipa be? Who will love her not as his daughter, not as her new daughter, not as his first lesson in love, not as a small citizen of his new nation, not as a magnet and light for terns, but for *herself,* her webbed and intricate being, her pipatude and pipaness, which has *never been in the world before,* in ten billion years, and will *never occur again,* not in this form, not with this music, not with this singular hammered grace? Any ideas? Or must we simply proceed, trimming the sails as need be, wary of reefs and rocks, secretly a little worried about the death of the old engine, attentive and curious as to the nature of the way ahead, our destination imagined but unfixed?

The morning rain, thorough and insistent, hung like gray sheets above the boat. *Is baisteach ar fhuinneoig ina clagarnaigh, gan sanas air o thitim oiche,* mutters Declan, half-awake in his bunk. The rain is a tattoo on the window, unslackening since the fall of night. Jesus, where did that come from? The fecking old man. *He* knew rain. In the dim he sees the huddled crowded sleepers. He slides the panel in Pipa's bunk open and finds her staring at him.

What are you doing awake, little peach?

Listening to the terns. Hear them?

Nope.

They are telling stories.

You're a nutcake.

Declan?

Pippish?

Can Tuesdays talk? When trees rub their branches together are they kissing or fighting? If you tell enough lies do you go blind? Did Papa *ever* not have a beard? I can't imagine Papa not having a beard. Did *you* ever have a beard? Do fish have beards? What about birds? Can hawks grow beards? Can you not hear the terns ever? Can you hear fish when they talk? All those fish you caught with this boat, didn't you ever talk to them? Are there people who can talk but don't? Are there people who can talk with their mouths but not hear what they say? Are there people who can talk but don't know any languages? Are languages alive as long as people talk them? If no one talks a language and it dies where does it go? Are you ever going to marry someone like Papa married Mama? If you have a daughter will you name her Pipa? Did you really think that Taromauri was a man? Can someone be a man *and* a woman? What if you are in the wrong body, can you switch sides? Do you have to speak a different language then? If you are a woman and you are married and you switch to being a man does your husband have to switch to being a woman so you can still be married? Do you just trade clothes then? If there are certain kinds of birds who know who you are and talk to you and something changes in you will they still know who you are or do you get a different kind of bird to watch after you or do you get no bird at all? If someone dies, what happens to their birds? After Mama died what happened to her ospreys? Did they have to find someone else to watch over? Did they forget their first person?

I need coffee, says Declan. You want some coffee? I need coffee. *You* don't need any coffee. You *are* coffee. You want to help me make coffee? Yes? All right, pipe down so we don't wake everyone up. Hang on, let me get around the corner here . . . all right, here we go . . . sweet Jesus, did you get taller overnight? Your legs are eight inches longer than yesterday. Here, fold up here for a moment. Are we going to have to tow you behind the boat on a long skinny raft? Jesus Christmas. Ever since you got your voice back you are growing an inch an hour. Maybe I can use *you* for a mast. You want juice or juice? Juice? Good. No, you can't have coffee. Coffee is for *captains*. New rule. Hang on one second before you start chatting again and let me get my coffee and then we can go on deck and you can grow some more. A *moist* day, as my sister would say. The rain is raining all around, it falls on field and tree, it rains on something something, and on the ships at sea. All right, ready, up we go, keep your arms around my neck, sweet blessed Jesus! You grew another inch *as I watched!* Don't laugh! We'll have to hire a boat just for your *feet*!

★

Business and Emergency Planning Meeting on the *Plover,* by command of the captain. Here's the deal, says Declan. Piko and Taromauri know the score but you two don't and God knows what the pip knows about anything. A while ago we had a confrontation with a bigger boat. This boat is called the *Tanets.* I don't know what that means either. The confrontation was complicated and I can explain the details later but the short version is that I am sure it's looking for us, with bad intent. This isn't legal but we are not in a position at the moment to complain to the cops or wave cease and desist orders as the fecking thing tries to run us down. So we are going to be prepared as well as we can for whatever happens. I hope nothing happens. It would be great if nothing happens. But we will prepare for something happening. If push comes to shove we have a kid on board and we will protect the kid as necessary. Everybody understands what I mean here? Questions?

A plethora of questions, says the minister, but later.

General agreement.

In other business, says Declan, this is a small boat and we all work. Piko and Taromauri know the drill and can show you what to do. We could use a better cook than the one we have now, so if either of you can cook, speak now.

Who is the cook now? asked Danilo.

I am.

I can cook, says Danilo.

I appoint you cook, says Declan. Congratulations. See me after class.

I can catch fish, says the minister. Also I am a student of sacred theology, if that helps.

Yes to fish, no to religion, says Declan. No religion on the boat. Prayers yes, religion no. Practice whatever religion you want but do so silently. I appoint Taromauri pope of the boat in all religious matters. I appoint Piko boatswain and carpenter. Also oceanographer. Finally I appoint the pip assistant coffeemaker and musician-at-arms.

What does that mean, at-arms? says Pipa.

I haven't the faintest idea, says Declan. Sounds cool, though, doesn't it? Better start singing. Recruit anyone you like for your singing crew.

★

Which she did, the instant Danilo opened his mouth; and instantly they were friends and soul mates; and they sang for hours in the stern of the boat; and she was thrilled by the way he sang, without affectation or noticeable effort, as if his job as a person was only to open the gate of his mouth to free his impatient and extraordinary voice; and he taught her all the songs he could remember from his cold gray childhood, and the songs he invented for himself in the forest, and the songs he had heard when he dove in the sea, and the songs he had learned from the guys at the airport, and the songs he had learned in the choir on the island; and she taught him all the songs she could remember from her wet green childhood, and the songs she had invented for herself in the years when she was silent, and the songs she had heard when she set her spirit loose in the sea, and the songs she had learned from her mother in those last weeks when she and her mother lay huddled in the bed as her mother shrank and vanished, and the songs she had learned from the troops of the terns; for of course the terns had a vast and ancient array of songs and chants, lays and sonnets, litanies and dirges, sure they did. All birds and animals and fish have their own peculiar and particular symphonies and adagios and jingles; just as the stories in and of a species outlive its individuals, so do its songs. In some species some individuals are charged with remembering and teaching the songs and poems; in other species the songs and poems are on their own, and find their chosen vessels among individuals, some willing and some reluctant; there are more manners and means for this sort of thing than can be accounted here, even if we had a thousand pages for just the stories of music among the millions of forms of things granted life; suffice it to say that we know this is true, and so we can well imagine the sweet tumult and tumble of songs in the stern of the *Plover* this morning, as the tall young man and the spindly child perched in her chair singing like birds; the gull on the roof of the cabin, listening intently.

Enrique is in the cabin of the *Tanets* poring over his charts. He has a terrible headache. He has a pistol on the chart table about ten inches from his right hand. His left hand has curled into something like a gnarled paw and no matter what he does he cannot get it to loosen. The pain in his head is worse on the left side than the right. Since the Rungarungawan and the Rapanuian abandoned ship he has tried to run the *Tanets* on his own and he is exhausted. Not even rage and fury can keep a man going day and night infinitely. He is too weary to hijack fishermen as crew. The pain in his head is worse at night than during the day. His left eye does not appear to be working as well as it did in the past. He can hear his mother say *we should get the boy to a doctor* and his father says *doctor? doctor?* Enrique can feel the end of something. An ending is on the horizon. For years he has steered according to the horizon and the horizon never ends but now somehow it is. He has no idea how he knows this but he does. He has tried soaking his hand in hot water to get it to loosen but it won't let go. His mother told him a story once about a man who turned into a bear starting with the left foot. He admitted to himself last night that there is no reason for him to care about the boat with the red sail, the loss of a taciturn crewman is easily replaced, he's done worse to other boats than steal a man, why should he care, why is he so furious, every hour of rage is money lost, money is control, money is power, money is defense, money is an island impregnable to assault, but as soon as the sun stumbles over the horizon every morning he is back in the cabin poring over his charts, guessing, estimating, measuring miles, calculating fuel expenditure and wind speed, gauging the weather. This doesn't make sense. I have always made sense. Reason is control. Nonsense is chaos. There is no such thing as imagination; imagination is another word for nonsense. Imagination is a polite way to say dreaming and dreamers are weak. Yet he could not detach himself from his charts, and he saw the sail redder in his mind by the day; and he loaded rifles and set them in their waterproof jackets everywhere on deck: two each to port and starboard, one each in bow and stern, two in the cabin; and he kept the pistol on his person at all times, clutching it unconsciously with his left hand while he slept.

*

Taromauri and Danilo are in the sea with Pipa. Declan is in the cabin poring over his charts. Piko and the minister are sitting on the hatchway chatting. The gull is on the roof, listening. The warbler is eating dried berries that Taromauri left under the water tank for her. Several terns, unused to Pipa being in the water, are whirling nervously above the stern in gentle circles. It turns out that Danilo is a terrific swimmer and Taromauri has been more comfortable in the water than out of it since she was a child so much bigger than the other girls that people would laugh just seeing her standing with other girls for example in line at school or on the beach for various ceremonies. Danilo can hold his breath for three minutes at a time and several times he dives down below Pipa's dangling useless feet and puts them on his shoulders and kicks up until his head is almost at the surface and she is almost but not standing in the ocean and she is laughing so hard the terns relax. No, no, says the minister to Piko, my vision of Pacifica does not include me as president or prime minister or king or leader of any sort. I do not think there is a word invented yet for what I would be in Pacifica. A sort of uncle-at-large, perhaps. There are all sorts of jobs and tasks to be done and each child can choose. Perhaps when you are thirteen you choose three jobs to pursue, and then whichever job wants you the most chooses you. Something like that. Also each child would have more families than only one. You might have, say, seven families. There would be ambassadors from the nations of children also—perhaps nine from each island. Nine is a shapely number. Perhaps there would be ambassadors from the other species also. Some people would be asked to contemplate numbers and see what we could do about that. Also I would like to see if we could find a way to make weapons forget what they are made of. There should be an unweapon for weapons, I believe. Anti-matter for the matter. Perhaps there is a way to persuade weapons to talk to each other so that one weapon could say to the other, listen, what are we doing here, this is not our fight, let us wander off, or let us dissolve ourselves, or let us go fishing instead, or something like that. Also I believe there should be more religions; the more there are the less any one can insist it is the boss of the others. Religions should be as common as sandals, so that you could wake up in the morning and shuffle out to the porch and grab any two in which to walk for the day. That would be good, I believe. Also I think we should have long weeks and short weeks. In the wet season we could have long weeks, say nine days, so we get a lot more repair work done around the house and boat, and in the dry season we should have short weeks, say five days, so that we have more weeks to enjoy the dry season. Something like that. These are just a few of the things I think. What do you think? Most of all I think we need more thinking. This is why the very first thing we should do when Pacifica is born is to start the National Dreamers. How could you have a new country without excellent dreamers?

★

The afternoon being lazy and his arm aching, Declan retires to his bunk to read Edmund Burke; or rather read *about* Burke, today's reading being selections from the comments of people who knew that most interesting Irishman: "petulance, impatience, intractability, anger, irritability . . . he was often intemperate and reprehensibly personal . . . a vein of dark and saturnine temper . . . sonorous but harsh tones . . . his utterance was often hurried and eager . . . his banter is nearly always ungainly, his wit blunt . . . his gestures clumsy . . ." Hmmph. No wonder I like the guy. He's me, or I am him. The poor Irish. Brilliant idiots. Charming fools. Engaging boneheads. Enthralling nutcases. Entrancing charlatans. Alluring disasters. We are the rocks and reefs of the human sea, tumultuous outcrops, magnets for wrecks. The peaks of mountains you cannot see: that's us, all right. Dark even on the brightest day. Stony and defiant of the prevailing currents until we are eventually worn down and dissolved. Sometimes soaked and sometimes dry as a bone. Hammered by tides and grimly standing our ground against the pounding. Probably even secretly enjoying the pounding. The poor Irish. An island people, as the old man reminded me many a time. A muddy rock soaked by rain and tide and blood. From which we fled for the farther shore. We leave, we left, we have been left. Into the waters of the world. Each of us an island. No man is an island, my butt. Trust an Englishman to make an eloquently stupid remark. I am an island, and the boat is an island. Although bless me how so many other people got on the boat is a mystery absolutely. Jesus Christmas. A bird, a child, four men and a woman. It's the opening line of a joke. A man sets out to sea to see what he can see . . . and ends up driving a fecking bus. Jesus. And where this will end no one knows. Probably we'll just keep picking people up until we sink. That would be about right. A boat that doesn't float. An island at the bottom of the sea.

*

Taromauri tried the dried berries first, thinking that warblers probably eat mostly insects and fruit; and the berries vanished as soon as she turned her back. Then she tried almonds, which did not work; they sat untouched until the minister ate them. She went back to the berries, this time laying out a trail leading out from under the water tank into the sunlight. This worked, and she saw the warbler for an instant, leaping out and back so fast you would not believe there had been a bird there except for the inarguable absence of berries. Taromauri experimented with the distance the warbler would emerge for berries; after a couple of days and many experiments, the answer seemed to be about four feet—approximately the height of a Pipa, as Danilo remarked. Then one afternoon a swarm of insects swirled over the boat and Danilo caught a few in his cap and tossed them under the water tank; the warbler, considering this an act of remarkable generosity, emerged shyly and stood at the very edge of the tank's shadow, looking up at the mountainous beings. Taromauri, with that odd gesture of her hands, folded down onto the deck, and the warbler vanished instantly; but emerged again a moment later, standing in the shadow, only her beak poking into the light. Taromauri slowly reached out and placed a berry between them. For a moment, no one moved a muscle, not on deck, not below, not on the roof of the cabin, where the gull watched, absorbed; and then the warbler bounced out, and stood over the berry, staring at Taromauri, who slowly opened her hands and lay them against her skirt like islands against a sea of red. Another long moment of utter stillness, as the boat rocked gently and the rigging clinked against the mast; and then the warbler, quicker than the eye could see, leapt up into Taromauri's hand, and then to her shoulder, and then into the black lawn of her hair. Pipa burst out laughing, a lovely trilling sound that draws the terns into the air; they regard the warbler with amazement, wondering where this tiny cousin came from; and Taromauri stood up grinning, taller by two brown inches.

*

Pipa and Declan are sitting in the stern.

Where are we going? says Pipa. Are we going to Australia?

Nope. Actually we are going away from Australia.

Isn't Australia an island?

Yep.

So why don't we go there if we have been to other islands in the ocean?

It's too big. It's a continent. An island that huge becomes something else.

Are you afraid of land like that?

Yep.

Why?

I don't know. Your dad has asked me that politely and not so politely and I am not sure what exactly is the problem. It's not like I don't get tired of being on the boat sometimes. It's just that I get very uncomfortable if I am not on the boat. I can be on land for a little while but then I want to get back on the boat even if I hate the boat sometimes and use bad language for which *someone* I know says I owe her money for breaking the rules about using bad language on the boat even though *I* am the captain and I don't remember making that rule. I think someone *else* made that rule and I think she made that rule so *someone* would owe *someone* money.

Are you in love with the ocean?

No. Sometimes I even hate it.

Are you in love with anything?

You. And the boat. I sure love the boat. And cigars. And your dad, in a way. I really admire your dad. Don't tell him. Also I used to love whiskey.

Don't you have a mother and father and brothers and sisters?

I have two brothers and one sister. My mom went away and my dad died. My mom might be dead by now for all I know.

I'm sorry.

Thanks.

Don't you love your brothers and sister?

I guess.

You *guess*? If *I* had a sister I would sure love her. I wish I had brothers and sisters. I wish I had *ten* brothers and sisters.

Did you love my mom?

I didn't know her very well, Pippish, but I could see why people loved her so much.

Will she ever come back for me?

Yes, said Declan, and then he stopped talking, because there was not a hint of another word in his mouth, and he could not lie, not to this child, the child who died in one form and came back in another form, the child he suddenly realized that he did love with a ferocious love, for reasons he did not understand, reasons he couldn't articulate, reasons that swirled with brokenness and courage and amazement and endurance and other arrangements of letters that claim to be words that mean anything other than a shadow of what is.

She will?

Yes.

But will I know her? Will I see her?

No.

No?

No.

And Pipa burst into tears, as if she had broken some-place inside and all the water inside her lean body like a whip of kelp, like a fast fish, like a bird in flight, was flee-ing from her through a sudden hole; and Declan held her shivering against his chest like a secret.

★

We have not spent sufficient ink on the sounds of the sea; so let us do so now as the *Plover* makes its way north by northwest along the Christmas Ridge, a vast drowned mountain range that runs for five hundred miles beneath the sea, invisible from above but epic from below, and how very many things are like that, yes? Massive beneath the surface and absent above, roaring inside, but on the surface not a trace, not a hint, not the slightest indication of sub-terranea; many things, many things.

But here we are on the starboard railing, as everyone dozes in the sun, and there is the riffle of the ship slid-ing through the sea, and the rattle of rigging, and the shiver of sails, and the thrum of the engine, and the croaking complaint of wood, and the arias of attendant gulls, and the flash of fish, and the battering moan of the wind; but these are sounds you would expect. Listen deeper; listen with your throat, with your shins; the ocean is alive with sound discernible with everything *except* your ears; some things you can only hear with the ears you *don't* have, isn't that so?

So then let us spend a few minutes with our orthodox ears closed and our other ears open; and now we hear the uncountable residents of the sea beneath the hull and keel; we hear increase and diminution, swell and fade, wax and wane, ebb and flow, charge and retreat, seethe and mutter; the snick of eyes opening, the sigh of hearts ceasing to beat; at any one instant any billion coral polyps emit their astounding tentacles and wave them alluringly in order to eat, just as another billion retract and reboot; a billion other mouths open, a billion fins flicker; and now we are *overwhelmed* with sounds, more than we could ever imagine, for there are lives below the hull and keel numerous beyond calculation, each one a small symphony of parts and desires, a pulsing narrative of its kind, and no two the same, for all our eager categorization and brave naming; even in this one moment, as the *Plover,* traveling at three knots, proceeds one hundred yards north by northwest along the hidden ridge, it passes over geniuses and singers, captains of industry, sinners and saints, voyagers and teachers, visionaries and thieves; it passes over beings who see further and deeper than any of their kind who have ever been born; it passes sudden murders and awesome births; it passes over more stories than could be told if there were more years to tell them than there are molecules in the waters of the world; and here we are on the waters of just this one blue world. There are more worlds out there, it is said, than there are molecules of all sorts and stripes here; and if this is so, imagine the sounds in those incalculable other seas among the stars; just the dreaming of that music is an extraordinary voyage, isn't that so?

★

Okay, says Declan, silliest stupidest dopiest funniest nutti-est boneheadedest thing you ever did in your whole life, one story each, Piko goes first, ready, go.

Ah, why me, you always make me go first, *you* go first, says Piko.

I am the fecking captain. Go.

Ehhhhh . . . one time I was showing Pipa how to catch crabs in the bay and I told her young crabs react to any-thing that wriggles right near their myriad stalky eyes so I wriggled my toes next to one to prove this and you can guess the rest. The pip laughed so hard I thought she would turn inside out.

I remember that! shouts Pipa, I remember that day! That crab was huge! I was scared and laughing! You told me we would have to go to the toe store to buy new toes!

Your Honor? says Declan.

Only one foolery, when I could choose among so many fooleries? says the minister, with a smile. O dear. The tide of my sillitude is high. I suggest that I simply offer brief short-hand versions of several errors and the assemblery can vote. To wit. I fell head over heels with my teacher and asked her to marry me, in fourth grade, on bended knee, with a ring that I had carved from the vertebraic material of a shark. You can imagine the derision of my classmates. Also I once dove from a cliff a hundred feet high wearing nothing but a smile, to impress a young woman on whom I had roman-tic designs, and in my descent I spun awkwardly akimbo, and landed directly on my rear parts, which hurt for months thereafter. Is that enough for the moment?

Far, *far* too much information, said Declan, grinning. Danilo?

Danilo smiled, and this is a good place to point out that he had the most interesting sidelong subtle smile, a hint of a smile, really, an idea *toward* a smile, you might say; you could tell he was amused, but it wasn't anywhere close to beaming; it was more like a lift of his lips, a flex of his face; not altogether unlike the gull's not-quite-a-smile, come to think of it; but once you got to know Danilo you savored the sly allegation of amusement in the man; like, for example, now.

Hmm, he says. I don't remember much of my early dopery, as the minister would say, but I do remember one time when I was in the forest and I was so hungry and I found a little scatter of what I thought were black eggs or truffles or mushrooms or something, and I ate one, and it wasn't.

Wasn't what? asks Piko.

Any of the things I thought it was.

I get it! shouts Pipa. You ate *poop*!

General moaning.

Probably deer or elk, said Piko, interested in the zoological details.

Rabbit, I think, said Danilo.

More snickering and moaning.

*Any*way, says Declan, Taromauri?

I think I stand with His Honor here in that there are so many choices that . . . well, here's one, she says. When I was a girl there was a brief time when my friends and I were fascinated by the production of interior gas, probably prompted by an uncle of mine who was something of a natural genius in that way, and one of my friends who was obsessed with fire convinced us all to try exactly what you think we tried, and by chance the resulting flame caught my grandmother's *riri,* her cloth skirt, and what you think happened did happen, and you can imagine the rest.

Pipa is laughing so hard she loses her voice for a second and looks up terrified at her father but he is on task and smiling and he claps her on the back and she coughs and her laughter returns, startled and a little abashed.

Pip?

Yes, Captain?

This gets a general laugh; one of the subtle pleasures of the pipster getting her voice back is that she has a sly wit all the more entertaining for its dry emergence from a gangly child.

Your silliest stupidest dopiest funniest nuttiest boneheadedest moment? Choose only one.

But she, of all the beings on the boat, has to think about this for a moment; for one thing she has not lived as long, and had as many misadventures, as her shipmates have; and for another she spent the last four years silent, sending her large spirit out exploring in ways and realms she has not yet tried to explain to her father, let alone anyone else, although she finds that she wants to explain this to Taromauri almost as much as to Piko; so there is a shard of silence for a moment, as the boat rocks and thwaps; Taromauri notices suddenly that the gull is back in her accustomed position on the roof of the cabin.

The stupidest thing I ever did, says Pipa suddenly in a voice as sharp and gleaming as a knife, was dancing in the road before the bus came. Papa told me not to go in the road *ever,* no matter what, until the bus *stopped* and put its *sign* out and blinkers *on,* the *blinkers* were the sign for me to move, and *not before the blinkers,* he told me that One Million Times, and I *knew* that was the Rule, but I *did* go into the road that morning, because I started to dance in the bus stop, and the bus stop was too small for my dance, so I danced out of the bus stop, and I should have stopped when I got to the road, but I *didn't* stop, and I danced right out into the road, and I *knew* it was wrong, I *knew* it, but I couldn't stop dancing, I could have stopped but I *didn't,* and it was *my* fault what happened, it was *my* fault, and that's what killed Mama, and that's why I am crippled, because it's *my* fault what happened, if you break the rules you have to pay for it, so I am paying for it, and I'll never see Mama again *ever,* and it's my fault.

There are some silences that are so huge, and fraught, and haunted, and weighted, and shocked, that they just *are;* there's nothing you can say about them that makes any sense. All you can do is witness them, and feel some deep ache that such things arrive, and must be endured, with wordless aching all around. Eventually someone will clear his throat and break the silence awkwardly; but that moment will not come for a while yet.

★

Late that night Declan could not sleep and he went on deck. Taromauri was asleep in her tent in the stern and Danilo was asleep on the hatch, the evening being warm. Everyone else was below and asleep, the minister snoring like a walrus with a cold. Declan climbed up on the roof of the cabin to sprawl; the gull rustled but did not wake.

Scoot over, bird.

Stars by the millions and billions. Fireballs as far as the eye can see. The sea of the stars.

When I was a kid, whispered Declan to the gull, I dreamed about spaceships, and voyages in the stars, and what it would be like to steer by the stars *among* the stars, you know what I mean?

No reply.

Which you probably do, am I right? Steer by the stars? That's how you get around, right? With like a magnet in your head? Because I have not seen you haul out a map or chart.

No reply.

Not to say you don't have maps and charts somewhere, like a secret pocket.

No reply.

Because everyone has secret pockets, am I right?

Absolutely so, says a quiet amused voice.

Jesus, says Declan, the bird speaks!

No no, says the voice. The bird's asleep, bless her.

Declan sits up and looks around but there's only Danilo, asleep, and Taromauri, asleep, and he leans over the cabin roof and there's no one on the ladder or in the cabin, and he thinks, not for the first time, Jesus, hearing voices again, it's the nuthouse for me soon enough.

No no, says the voice, and now it's right by his left ear, not in his head, but clearly *outside* his head, but there is, really and truly, nobody attached to the voice, which is again wry and quiet.

And you are?

Don't get all rattled, says the voice, but I am actually your death, come to visit.

My *death*.

Yes.

You came to take me?

No no. Just a casual visit. I happened to be in the area.

You are *my* death. My death is a guy.

Yes.

Just paying a social call?

You could say that.

Why?

Why not?

I could die of fright, for one thing. Or go mad.

Well, you are not going to die of fright, I can tell you that. Nor is madness in the cards.

What *do* I die of?

No no. I can't tell you that.

Do I live a long time?

Can't tell you that either. Listen, I just dropped by to chat, not to be examined.

This is a dream, right? I am dreaming?

If you want to later consider this a dream, sure.

What was it you wanted to chat about?

Oh, I don't know. I suppose I just wanted to get to know you a bit. A rare impulse for me. Usually it's just the one final meeting. In your case I thought we could just converse a bit beforehand.

You did.

I did, yes. Don't mean to scare you. Really.

Are you the only . . . agent?

No no. There are many . . . agents.

You know them all?

No no. Far too many. I know some, that's all. And we come in all shapes and sizes, of course. No two alike. Some better at the job than others, also.

I beg your pardon?

I know one . . . agent, for example, who couldn't find the fellow he was supposed to escort. Try as he might he just could *not* pin down the man's whereabouts. Very embarrassing.

What happened?

Long story. Another agent, not once but twice she escorted the wrong person. The first time it was a nomenclatural problem, the second time cosmetic, I heard. Plastic surgery or something. I am not totally sure of the details there.

Am I really having this conversation?

It's more like question and answer, I think, but yes.

What happened to my dad?

You know the answer to that.

Do you?

No. We are not issued biographical material, nor do we keep an eye on you in any way. We just escort you when the time comes. Agent is a good word, actually. Now, can I ask you some questions? Because I am only here for a few moments. I have an engagement elsewhere.

What if you miss it? Does the person live forever then?

I wouldn't know. We don't miss engagements.

You've never made a mistake?

Not yet.

But you could.

Theoretically. But again, let me ask *you* questions for a moment.

Shoot.

When someone you love vanishes, do you always have a hole in you afterward?

I am not the one to ask. Ask Piko. I don't love anyone, so no one I love can die. See? Good system, eh? Everyone *I* love will live forever.

Is food as good as it looks?

Yes.

What's the best food of all?

Fresh water. And berries.

Don't you love the little girl?

Pause.

What little girl? says Declan, very quietly indeed.

The girl on the boat. The girl who can't walk.

She's not here anymore. We left her on the last island. At a hospital.

Really? I thought she was still with you.

Nope.

My mistake.

Don't you have an engagement elsewhere?

Indeed I do. I must go. Do consider this a dream tomorrow when you awake.

Will do.

See you again someday.

I hope not to see you again for sixty years. All due respect.

I understand. I'd best be off.

Thanks for the visit, I guess.

Anytime.

No thanks.

And there was a silence, during which the stars glittered more than before; and then the gull rustled and fluttered in her sleep, and Declan went below, rattled and thoughtful.

★

Danilo was up first, before dawn, an old habit; so he was the first to see the *Tanets* on the horizon. He woke Taromauri so that she could keep an eye on it, and then he woke Declan. Who stared at the horizon for a moment and said fecking fecking feck and woke Piko.

Is that him?

Yup, said Declan. I know that hull. I climbed that hull.

What do we do?

You and Taromauri get the sail up and I will run the engine.

Can I help? asks Danilo.

Do whatever Piko says.

Are we running?

Yup.

Can we outrun him?

Nope. But we can make him work all day to catch us.

Then what?

I don't know. I'll figure it out. Wake up the minister if you guys need help.

They ran. They ran all morning at full speed, Declan

nursing and wooing the engine, everyone else taking turns nursing and tinkering the sail. No one ate. The *Tanets* drew closer by the hour. The minister and Taromauri took turns sitting with Pipa and answering her questions. She had many questions. Her terns swirled confusedly for the first hour and then settled into a steady flight in a small phalanx something like a diamond. The gull also lifted off and hung in her usual spot nine feet above the stern. Taromauri said something to the gull but the gull just hung in the sky and didn't say anything or look at anyone. Just as the terns settled into their diamond formation an albatross appeared and surfed along behind the gull over the stern. Early in the afternoon the engine coughed and died but Declan got it humming again within four minutes a new fecking world and Olympic record the fecking old thing made of spit and rust. Late in the afternoon the wind began to wither. Piko tacked in every direction to catch every last breath; to no avail.

Dec . . .

Yeh, I see. Haul it in and hope for dark.

★

On the *Tanets* all Enrique could see was the red sail and the blue water and the dwindling daylight. Everything else was outside the narrow cone of his vision. I see you, he said aloud. I see you. You cannot hide. The night will do nothing for you. I know where you are. I know where you are going. You stole from me. You took what was mine. This cannot abide. One theft leads to ten. And then where are we? Adrift. Disorder disrupts order. I give the orders. I command both our boats. I command you to flee. I command fear. Having committed disorder you have brought disorder upon you. It is the law. I command that you will be caught one hour after full darkness and your boat destroyed and my property returned and no evidence of your existence or destruction will be found evermore. What you were will sink to the bottom of the sea and be lost and none will remember or testify.

But with a real start of surprise he heard himself talking aloud in a loud cold voice, and some deep part of him was frightened; he sat down and put his face in his hands, and was startled at the shocking heat of his skin and a slather of sweat so heavy his hands glistened. Am I sick? Is this a bad illness? His left side ached from his eye to his toe. Nausea rose in him like a tide. He sat hunched and haunted for a few moments, and then stood to splash water on his head and face and was there steam? Steam rising from his face? Or was that smoke? Smoke! He jumped to the railing just in time to see another burning stick whirling right at his head; he leapt aside, furious, and the stick crashed against the cabin wall and shattered into smoking wreckage. Bastards! Bastards! He reached for the first rifle he could find under the railing and fired on the red sail just as the *Plover* swerved and slid past his stern. Enrique sprinted around the corner and along the port railing, cursing and firing, but the smaller boat was either deftly swerving or he was losing his vision altogether, because the red sail seemed to be shimmering—there for a moment and then not there at all, and then suddenly there again, but not where it had been before; and then somehow it vanished altogether, just as Enrique realized he was perilously close to the reefs of what looked like atolls so low that they were probably underwater most of the time. He sprinted back to the cabin and hauled the *Tanets* to port, but not before the boat scraped against the reef with an agonizing shriek; then he was in deep water again, and so angry that white flecks of froth appeared on his lips. He bent over the railing and heaved his bile into the darkening sea. When he stood up again, staggering, the sun was gone, the *Plover* was gone, and his left hand was locked so tightly on the rail it took him fully ten minutes to pry it loose.

★

Jesus, said Piko. That was close. His chest heaved and his hands were black with char. He and Declan bent over the charts, their faces an inch from the maps; no lights on the boat, by command of the captain. We can slide through this passage, said Declan, and then run all night, but he's got a bigger boat, and more fuel, and he'll catch us eventually. But I think it's just him. I didn't see anyone else on his boat. Did you?

No. But I didn't get a great look.

Jesus Christmas, said Declan. My hands are shaking.

Let's go get him, said Piko.

They stared at each other.

There's no moon, said Piko, and if we don't get him now he'll get us tomorrow. He won't let us get close enough to board him. We have to get him.

Again they stared at each other, each man thinking many thoughts at once: how did it ever come to this, the pipster, the infinitesimal chance of all five able bodies on the *Plover* boarding the *Tanets* at once, a vision of a bullet hole between Taromauri's eyes, a vision of Pipa weeping at the loss of her mother and her father; also both men thought of the word murder but neither said it aloud. Each was startled at the grim willingness to violence in the other; but neither spoke of it.

There's a smokestack above the engine in that boat, said Piko in the dark. It's a mess down there. Oily rags everywhere. Plus who knows what his cargo is. Maybe it's oil or gunpowder. I drop a stick in there and he's got a fire that will keep him busy for a week.

Can you do that?

Silence.

I don't know. Yes.

You'll have about three tries max, you know. He'll shoot as soon as he sees where the sticks are coming from. He can't miss us forever.

Silence.

Can you do it? asks Declan, very quietly indeed.

Silence; the lapping of waves against the boat in the shallow passage between atolls; the faint crush of surf on the reef; the sharpest ears might catch the breathing of the four rattled beings belowdecks, and of the warbler beneath the water tank.

Yes, said Piko.

★

On the *Tanets* Enrique was sick again and again, as if his body wanted to empty itself completely. He hung exhausted over the stern. He knew he should be alert; he had been boarded once by the man on that boat, in a manner Enrique still couldn't figure out, his hull being sheer and slippery; but his fury had ebbed to embers. His mind rattled and leapt with images: his mother's eyes in the firelit dark; dust swirling around his brother's feet; broken adobe walls; dry mountains lined along their ridges with lovely swaths of pines and firs and mountain cedar. That is what heaven had seemed like to him when he was a boy, those dense thatches of cool forest in the sky; he had climbed there a few times later, when he was a teenager, and never forgot the clarity of the air, the cool shade under the trees, the sharp scent of the conifer trees. For a moment he stared into the darkness and saw another life he might have led, in the mountains, the bushes filled with butterflies every winter, the occasional lynx or mountain lion glimpsed like a russet shadow on a ridge, his axe and saw the tools of his trade, coming down from the mountains occasionally to the big rivers, or the coast, or the city, for weddings and wakes; but then the burning part of him rose again and he went around the ship checking that the rifles were all loaded. In the cabin he stared at the charts showing a thin passageway between the two low atolls. Half his mind calculated odds and percentages, wind and current, angles of approach, the relative weights of the two boats, ramming speed, the maximum number of rifle shots he had at his command; the other half, first silently and then mumbling and then speaking quietly, said we could just turn around and go. We could just go. We could sell this last cargo for a good profit and sell the boat for a serious profit and burn everything else behind us and go to the mountains. We could go. We can make decisions. Circumstances do not dictate decisions. Decisions dictate the process of circumstances. We can decide to go. That is not surrender. That is magnanimity. With a wave of the hand we spare their lives.

But the burning half of his mind was grim and silent. He was finally two men, one weary of rage and the other starving for it, one desperate for the drug and the other finished and done and sure at last it would lead to death, one immersed in the past and the other dreaming of the future, one stoking his fury with the past and the other wishing nothing more than to be done with it forever, one lawless and the other lawful, one at war and the other at peace, one heat and the other cool; and they strove in him mightily, this last moment in the cabin. His head throbbed and he reached up his left hand to rub his eye and he saw that his hand had become an unusable claw. He stood up and made a sound like a sob or a scream and he spun the wheel and the *Tanets* slid toward the two low atolls.

*

Again Danilo and Taromauri built a small fire on the hatch cover, and roasted firesticks, the minister holding a canvas tarpaulin over his head to hide the light; again Pipa shivered in her bunk, and sent her spirit into the deep waters, to see what she could see. Declan maneuvered the *Plover* out of the inlet and into the ocean, peering desperately into the gloom for the lurk and loom of the *Tanets*. Piko shimmied up the mast, and balanced himself for a moment like a dancer on the tip of it, feeling for the wind, for he knew that he would need every hint of wind for these throws; *oahi* depended not on strength but on skill, the ability to read the wind, the deft snap of the wrist, the perfectly burning stick; the wood could not be too burnt, or it would fall apart in the teeth of the wind; it could not be insufficiently burnt, or its weight would cause it to plummet; and the glowing stick had to have just enough of a handle for the thrower to launch it into the wind without hurrying the throw to save his hand from scorching.

He shimmied back down, the coins in his beard clinking against the mast.

Can you throw from up there?

No. Can't keep my footing.

He jumped up on the cabin roof, nearly crushing the gull, who leapt away silently into the darkness, and then he bent down to whisper to Declan in the cabin.

Dec?

Soon. I hear his engine.

For a moment there are only the gentlest of sounds: the pitter of waves against the boat, the faint thrum of the *Tanets*, the faint thump of surf, the faint crackle of the tiny fire under the tarp, the faint shuffle of the minister's feet as he tried to evade the smoke, the quiet groan of the *Plover*'s engine, a faint snap as Danilo fed the fire.

Declan tapped on the roof and Piko bent down again.

I'm going to slide by once slow enough for you to get two throws. Then I'll come around and go back along the same side real fast. That will give you one more throw.

Got it.

Ready?

Yeh.

The *Tanets* loomed out of the dark suddenly, moving slowly—loomed just as it had that night long ago, thought Declan distractedly for an instant, before he cut the engine and turned the *Plover* to parallel the larger ship, perhaps twenty yards away. Taromauri reached into the fire, caught a stick, and handed it up to Piko, who set his feet and whipped it end over end into the darkness. It seemed to hang in the air for an instant, and then shattered against some hard surface; they could see the deck of the *Tanets* illuminated for an instant by the sparks, and a flash of Enrique's body running along the railing. Taromauri handed Piko another firebrand, and he set his feet, aiming four feet above the last one; but this one, perhaps traveling too fast, also smashed against something unyielding and shattered, although somehow it seemed half the impact of the first. By now the *Plover* was nearly past the *Tanets* altogether, but Taromauri snatched a third stick from the fire and tossed it to Piko, who caught it, whirled to his right, and threw; and this stick, like the first one, seemed to hang in the air for a remarkably long time, before it winked out as suddenly as if it had been extinguished. At exactly that instant a bullet from the *Tanets* shattered a starboard window of the *Plover*'s cabin, passing directly over the steering wheel. Taromauri screamed; and then the *Tanets* exploded with an incredible roar and sheet of flames.

★

We read and talk about explosions as if we know much about explosions, said Piko much later, but very few of us know anything at all about explosions. Explosions are *terrifying.* They are so huge and sudden and immediate that there aren't any decent words for the horrific assault on the senses. You can say *shattered* and *obliterated* and *destroyed* but none of those words give the right sense of absolute naked terror and fear, and displacement; as Piko put it, it's like the world you were sure you knew doesn't behave, for a moment, and then when it rights itself there's a terrible mess, and after that you never think quite the same about what you thought before. Also explosions are *indecent.* They're obscene. They offend nature; they're unnatural. Even when they are ostensibly natural, like volcanoes. Twice I have seen volcanoes explode, once on land and once at sea, and both times that was the end of the nature that was there before the volcano blew, and everything and everyone was unsettled essentially ever after. Talk about offending nature, you know? But explosions caused by human beings; I don't know, there's something really and truly obscene about that, I think. Believe me, I know what I am talking about. I caused an explosion that I will never forget, and I have *tried* to forget it sometimes. You could argue all day long that it was the right thing, we had the right to self-defense, the theory of just war, violence can be fairly met with reciprocal and commensurate violence, violence is the default mammalian function when offspring is threatened, blah blah blah. I've heard it all. I've *thought* it all, I've taken refuge behind it all. Believe me, on dark days I have blamed evolution for my mammalian default function when offspring is threatened. But there are still a lot of nights when I see that ship explode into a million pieces, man. I see it in front of me as real as can be. I am standing on the roof of the cabin and the universe shatters and I hear screaming and I can't see for a while. Sometimes I think I will see that particular explosion until the day I die. Maybe afterwards. Maybe.

★

Declan felt the bullet slice past his face, by a hair; he had leaned back from the wheel to look up at Piko. He spun away from the wheel toward the stern and was coming up fast from a crouch when the world exploded. Piko, on the roof, dropped to his knees instinctively, covering his head, and then leapt off the roof for Pipa. The minister, still covered with the tarp, was knocked down by a shard of flying wreckage and was crumpled against the railing to port. Danilo, who had been crouched by the fire on the hatch when the *Tanets* exploded, had the wit to scatter the fire with his feet just as wreckage fell and waves from the explosion nearly overturned the *Plover* and he went sliding into the huddle of the minister. Declan counted people instantly without thinking and shouted for Taromauri and Pipa but Piko, already down the ladder, shouted from below that they're all right! we're all right! you all right? Declan leapt back to the cabin for the wheel and gunned the engine and shot the *Plover* ahead a thousand yards, listening with an unconscious ear for the rumble of surf to be sure he was not gunning the boat right into the reef, and then he suddenly had to pee so ferociously he thought his groin would burst. Holy shit. Holy holy shit. Holy shit. Holy holy holy shit. Calm. Calm. Regroup. Boat. Pip. The minister! He turned from the wheel again but Piko was kneeling by the minister, with a groggy

Danilo, who had cracked his head against the hatch cover in his slide; and the minister sat up, also groggy, but saying something animatedly to Declan, it seemed; his mouth was moving but no words were coming out. The minister stopped talking, and looked like he was waiting for an answer; and when Piko and Danilo also turned to look at Declan, Declan realized that he couldn't hear a thing.

★

Are there survivors? is what the minister had said. We should look for survivors. The *Plover* was still reeling from the waves caused by the explosion, but Declan realized what the minister meant and he went back to the cabin, started the engine, turned around, and then stopped for a moment; do I *want* to pick up that guy, if he lived? Wasn't the whole point to get rid of that guy? But something in him clicked the questions off like a light switch, and he nudged the boat back to where the *Tanets* had vanished, shaking his head to try to get his hearing back. Must have been the explosion. Hate to be deaf. Fecking fecking feck. Never hear the pip squeak again. Shards of wreckage seething in the sea began to bump and jostle the boat, and Declan slowed to a crawl.

Piko, he said quietly, and heard himself say the word; wheeeew.

Dec.

They okay below?

Yeh. Taromauri was down there in a flash and had the pip wrapped up bug in a rug.

Man. Nice shot. I can't believe you actually pulled that off.

Me neither.

Look for the guy. Look for anybody. God knows who or what was on that ship. He must have had explosives or oil drums or weapons or something. Get everyone to keep their eyes peeled. Use flashlights or whatever.

Okay.

You okay?

Yeh. Rattled.

Me too, man. Me too.

They stared at each other by the faint light on the chart table.

Now what? said Piko.

Look for survivors and get the hell out of here, I guess, said Declan. It's not like we can file an accident report with the cops. Listen, take the wheel for a minute, okay? I have to pee like a racehorse.

*

At the instant the *Tanets* exploded Pipa's large spirit was some three hundred feet below Enrique's boat, which was just over the slope of the reef where it descended precipitously to a trench half a mile deep; her spirit flinched at the powerful shock in the water, and she instinctively hugged the slope of the undersea mountain as fish fled past her at incredible speed; in another context, at another time, she would have been thrilled by the rocketing colors and flashings sheets of animals zooming past, headed for the safety of the deep. Angelfish, butterflyfish, parrotfish, wrasses, triggerfish, sharks, eels, turtles, dolphins, what looked like a small whale, and at least two seals shot past her quick as a blink. A series of shivers in the water rocked and shook everything that clung to the slope, and then odd objects began to fall slowly from above: large shards of metal, immense steel drums painted bright red with WARNING! stenciled along their flanks, a series of large metallic tubes, various sizes and pieces of piping, several dark wooden boxes that were so heavy they did not turn end over end like the other detritus but fell smoothly, with a stolid lumbery dignity; and last, a large safe, which struck a ledge above Pipa's spirit, somersaulted over her as slowly as if it was in a slow-motion film, and continued bouncing slowly down the slope until it vanished into the darkness below. As it careened ever so slowly over Pipa she noticed the bright silver combination mechanism gleaming like a brilliant silver eye; and twice, as the safe tumbled slowly into the depths, she saw it flash again, before it vanished for good and all. She waited another few seconds, to be sure the shocks were past, and then fled back to the *Plover;* when she opened her eyes she found herself wrapped in a life jacket and wrapped in Taromauri's arms, just as her father leapt into the room, covered with what looked like ashes.

*

It was Danilo who found Enrique, or what was left of Enrique; as Danilo said later his eyes had spent so much time in the darkness of the forest that he and the darkness had come to a sort of understanding, and he spotted the slightly darker jumble of sopping limbs that turned out to be Enrique, unconscious and badly burned, but not fully dead yet, said Taromauri, after examining him carefully, Danilo and Piko standing over them in case of tumult—as if anyone on this earth could overpower Taromauri, said Declan later, the very idea is laughable, she's the strongest being I have ever seen, male, female, or vegetable.

They stripped off the wet tatters of his clothes, cleaned and anointed his burns as best they could, and put him in Taromauri's tent, posting a watch of two at a time until morning. Taromauri and Danilo, the strongest of the six, took the first watch. Piko, now shivering uncontrollably for some reason, went below to sleep with Pipa; the minister, nursing a burn on his right foot, curled up below; and Declan set a course northeast by east for an hour, after which he shut off the engine, threw out the sea anchor, and fell asleep so fast in his bunk that when he woke in the morning he thought for an instant he was in his childhood bed, his sister snoring on the other side of the thin wall between them; but then he realized with a smile that it was the minister snoring like a seal, not a foot away. The events of the night before flooded in on him then, and he leapt up the ladder to discover a brilliant sky, an empty blue sea, the gull floating effortlessly nine feet above the stern, and Danilo grinning over a sleeping Taromauri. She just fell asleep an hour ago, just as the sun came up, he whispered to Declan. Let her sleep. I'll keep an eye on the guy. You got any coffee? I could really use some coffee.

VIII

WHERE ARE WE?

I think we are sitting on the blessed Jesus Tropic of Cancer, believe it or not, if I have read my charts and sight reduction tables correctly, which of course I have, being the blessed Jesus captain.

Longitude?

What the hell do you care for?

Eeeeasy there, Captain. Just curious.

Longitude was invented by an English bastard anyways, so who can trust it?

Somebody's all viss and pinegar this morning.

Well, hell, I am running a fecking ferry service, as far as I can tell. Look around. There's people as far as you can see on the boat and God knows how many are below. I lost count a few days ago. This trip started with one people, me, and now there are more than I can count.

Seven. Counting you.

Jesus.

He's not here. Although He did go on a boat, didn't He? Fishing boat, too.

Jesus blessed Christmas. Take the wheel. *I* am going for a swim. *I* am abandoning ship. *I* am leaving the ship in your hands, despite you having a college degree. Don't screw up.

Take the pip with you. She loves the water.

Okay.

Which is why one moment later a long-legged girl, age nine, screaming happily, is flying head over teakettle through the air, nine feet above the water behind the stern, to the astonishment of the gull who usually camps out there, and the woman who threw the child effortlessly high into the air as casually as you would toss a walnut is laughing, and two men in the water flanking the spot where the child will land in a second or two are grinning, and another man with bright pink feet is poised teetering on the stern railing also, ready to launch his considerable bulk into the air as soon as the child lands safely, and a man with a long silvery ponytail and a long rope of a beard stitched with coins and feathers is sitting grinning in the cabin, with one eye on his daughter and the other on a man sleeping under a tarpaulin rigged between the hatch cover and the starboard railing; and the gull quiet on the roof of the cabin, and the warbler huddled companionably next to her; and ten is the number of beings on the boat, not counting the barnacles and algae and microfauna attached to the hull below, who have accreted to such a degree that now unbeknownst to the captain his boat has a long green scraggly bedraggled beard very much like Piko's, but without, as yet, coins and feathers.

*

Later that afternoon the captain of the *Plover* issues a command that all hands will set to fishing, as he has a hankering for fresh fish, and the boat could use an infusion of fresh fish, and there are more people on the boat today than there were yesterday, cutting into the extant food supplies, so everyone sets to fishing, even Pipa, who sits in Danilo's lap in the stern and his hands hold her hands on the fishing rod and she feels the strikes and sprints of creatures she cannot see, trembling through the rod; but when Danilo securely hooks a bonefish and begins to haul him in she wriggles her hands off the rod; and he understands, and sets her down in her chair, and walks with the rod toward the bow, where he kills and cleans the fish, offering a tidbit to the warbler.

The minister and Declan are sitting in the bow, fishing, their legs dangling.

Where is it you are headed, if I may ask? asks the minister.

East.

A certain destination?

Maybe. Why do you ask?

I feel that I have imposed upon you, and should probably be destinatory myself now.

Plans?

I would like to return to the work I began, which was truncated by . . . events.

What work?

I believe that what is popularly called the Pacific Ocean, and is improperly, in my view, broken up into endless entities and territories, many of them set to compete with the others by former and current imperial powers, is in fact not only one consistent and coherent territory, enormous in scope, populated primarily by undersea residents, and rich with not only the resources that have fed the greedy maw of commerce for millennia, but with other products having to do with creativity, as yet untapped, and in most cases, perhaps nearly all, undiscovered and unimagined. Thus I believe, and I am refreshingly not alone in this conviction, that a remarkable new nation called Pacifica may, and indeed should, arise, from the smatterings of islands and archipelagos, conjoined with the vast wilderness of the ocean, and that this new nation may, and indeed should, be a whole new sort of nation, in which the human residents do not view themselves as kings and conquerors, and indeed cease to war and compete with each other, but instead apply creative thought and energetic imagination to providing food, shelter, safety, cultural stimulus, laughter, spiritual depth, interspecious respect, a general compassion, and freshwater to all residents, whatever number of legs, wings, fins, or antennae they have, or do not have, as the case may be. Certainly this will take some imagination, but it is my conviction, and refreshingly I am not alone in this belief, that the ocean of creative ideas among the countless residents of Pacifica is unimaginably deeper and more extensive than the extant ocean of water, and that if the residents are apprised of their own extraordinary potentialities, and awakened to the re-markable proximity of a nation unlike any other that has yet been invented or imposed, then matters will take a most interesting turn, which I will be most interested to observe, and, if at all possible, enjoy as a citizen of same.

Pause.

That's . . . ambitious, says Declan.

Certainly so, certainly so, says the minister. But if we do not dream, then I think perhaps we are misusing our heads. They are not on our shoulders only to be farms for hair.

Good point, said Declan. I think you have a fellow citizen on your fishing line, by the way. If I am not mistaken that is *kawakawa,* the small tuna.

★

Later Danilo and Pipa are swimming off the stern; or rather Danilo is treading water, and Pipa is sitting on his shoulders, her hands flittering in the water.

I think you *can* sing underwater, she says. *I* don't see any reason why not. I just don't think we have figured out the right *song,* is all. I think there are right songs and wrong songs and we just are stuck on wrong. That's what I think. We are on Wrong Island. Sure we can sing underwater. Why not? Didn't we all have gills when we were living inside our mothers? That's what my mama told me and my mama never told any lies that I know about. So we must have sung underwater then, right? So why couldn't we figure out how to do that again? We figure out *lots* of things. You figured out how to get out of that forest, didn't you? And you were singing all the way. So really you sang yourself out of that forest, right? So maybe we can sing our way out of problems, couldn't that be? And everyone sings even if they say they can't sing. That's what Taromauri says, that she can't sing, but she *does* sing, she sings at night when she thinks no one is listening but *I* am listening. She sings in her tent. You can only hear her if you try *not* to hear her, though, isn't that interesting? You have to try to not try. If you try hard enough to *not* try then you can hear what she is singing but if you *try* to hear it you can't hear *anything*. Isn't that amazing? *I* think that's amazing. And the gull sings sometimes, sure it does, I have heard her. She doesn't sing any words, though. And Declan sings those songs with the bad words when he is fixing something and then when he sees that I heard what he sang he gets grumpy and barks at my dad and my dad barks back at Declan and then they laugh. They are always saying things to each other that mean something other than what the words mean. Isn't that interesting? One of them will say something to the other and they both will laugh but what they said didn't have any jokes in it. I think they speak some kind of code or something. I think they are maybe secret agents and we are on the boat to conduct secret missions. That's why we picked up the minister, because he's a secret agent too. Don't you think he could be a secret agent? He knows all the kinds of fish and birds and weather and everything, even more than Taromauri, and *she* knows when the wind is going to change, she knows what kind of fish we are going to catch before the *fish* knows it's going to be caught. That's what my dad says and he never told me any lies that I know about. Are *you* a secret agent? Is that why you escaped through the forest? Was everything arranged so that you could meet the boat so we can finish the secret mission? Am *I* a secret agent too? Do I get to save everybody? I *like* secret missions. Are you hungry? Want to go eat now? Because *I* am hungry and if I am hungry I bet *you* are hungry. Want to eat? Then can we swim again for a while? Want to swim underwater and see if we can sing? Want to?

A greater person, says Taromauri to Piko, would seek the thirteen blessed beings with all her heart and soul, and strive to obtain their blessings, and honor them, and celebrate their works and miracles, and make the world aware of their blessedness, so that the world might be elevated by this, but I am not that person.

She has just explained to Piko, in detail, minute by minute, exactly what happened, or what she *thought* had happened, with Pipa and the gull and Pipa recovering her tongue that morning, as far as she, Taromauri, had seen, or heard, or thought she saw and heard, and then she and Piko sit quietly looking at Pipa as Pipa stares happily at the tern feathers in her father's beard.

A greater person, continued Taromauri, would change her life completely, having witnessed such a thing, and start anew. But I am not that person.

What did it feel like when it happened to you? Piko says to Pipa.

Like somebody opened a door in the back of my head, says Pipa. My head itched for *hours* after that. Taromauri finally did something with oil and it stopped. Danilo says all the brokenest parts had to march to the back of my head and squeeze their way out through the door but there were a *lot* of them and they were in a hurry so they crowded and shoved as they went through and *that's* why my head itched, because the door was sore. Is there a door back there really?

What kind of a person *are* you, now, after that? Piko asks Taromauri.

A new one, says Taromauri. But I am not sure what this new person is supposed to do. I think I should find my husband. Did I ever tell you what happened after my daughter vanished? You think what will haunt you is what they left behind, their shoes and combs, the glass she always left in the freezer so it would be icy when she wanted it for a cold drink, her toothbrush with the rubber band on it to serve as a warning that it was *hers* and *no one else* better use it; those are the things you are afraid of because they are tombstones, they are lonely things without their person. But worse was seeing places where her things *weren't*. She rode her bicycle everywhere and she would just leave it sleeping in the grass and never bring it in out of the rain, she said it loved the rain, which we told her many times was silly talk and would end with a little heap of rust in the grass, and then there was grass that should have her bicycle in it but didn't. I didn't know where her bicycle was.

Piko perches Pipa in her chair behind Taromauri and folds Pipa's hands into Taromauri's hair and Pipa's hands flutter in the brief black thicket like birds in a bush.

I should know, said Taromauri. I should know where it is. I suppose it's in the shed behind the house but I do not know. I *should* know. For the longest time I couldn't say the words *death* or *die* or *drowned*. I would say *vanished* or *visiting*. It wasn't that I didn't know. It was just that I couldn't get my mouth to be where everyone else's mouth was. I knew she wasn't coming back. I knew for certain when Kekenu stopped writing his letters and staking them in the sand. He knew before I did. Did I ever tell you what happened last? He wrote one last letter, a really long letter too, it was probably nine or ten pages, and he went down to the beach and made a fire and burned the letter and the ashes blew into the ocean. You know how there are some things that even when you are about to die you will remember them as if they happened that morning? I will remember that, the way he crouched there and the ashes blew away.

★

Enrique is awake in the tent, moving gingerly. Taromauri alerts Declan, who comes over and sits down companionably with his Dick Groat baseball bat. Piko leans in with a cup of water.

This is the ship's surgeon, says Declan. You may remember him. His name is Piko. You ready to chat?

Easy, Dec, says Piko. Easy. He's bad off.

Yeh.

Enrique tries to speak but his lips are burned and his tongue is swollen and no words get past the gate.

Here's the deal, says Declan. You're not dead but you're bad off. You need a real doctor and a hospital for a while. I'll drop you off somewhere where there are doctors and hospitals. A sensible guy would have let you drown but I am not too sensible. I'll assume we are quits now. You created a problem, we solved the problem, the end. I don't care what your name is or what your problem was but in my view we are done here. Can you hear me? Nod if you can hear me. Good. Want some more water?

Piko leans in with more water.

I don't like problems, says Declan. Problems are not my thing. I don't like drama and mysteries. I like things real straight. I like being left alone. I don't like guys sticking guns in my face and kidnapping my buddies. I especially don't like guys shooting at my boat and endangering little kids. So I would be sorry about *your* boat but I am not sorry at all. In my view we are now all square. Is that your view? If that's your view, nod.

Easy, Dec, says Piko.

That looks like a nod to me, says Declan. Good. The surgeon here will keep an eye on you until we get you to a hospital. If you need water or you're in bad pain, tell the surgeon.

★

That guy was burned pretty much everywhere you have skin, said Piko later, except, weirdly, his feet. He was like the reverse of the minister, whose feet were burnt the worst of all his burns. Although the minister, characteristically, looked on the bright side of even *that,* saying that he was one of those lucky guys who get issued new wheels halfway through life. Very rarely does a man get a new set of personal pedestrials, he said. He was like that about everything, that guy. He never had a bad word about the guys on his island who dumped him in the ocean, never moaned about the loss of his life there. He must have had a house and a girlfriend and status and stuff there but he never spent a minute complaining about what he used to have. He was all for looking ahead, that guy. It's not like he was one of those go go go guys you want to hit with a rock because they don't have a reflective bone in their bodies. Guys like that are afraid of themselves so they keep running ahead, you know? They have to be busy or they are afraid the dark will eat them or something. Not the minister, though. I mean, he had a vision and everything, but it wasn't pie in the sky for him, he really *meant* what he said and he knew how it could actually happen, against all the odds and percentages. You would listen to him and the first time he explained the Republic of Pacifica you thought, okay, this guy's nuts, and the second time you heard him explain it you thought, okay, this guy's totally working a con somehow, but the third time you heard it you realized that he was serious, that he wasn't into it for power and money, he really had *thought* about all this, he really *did* see way ahead, and suddenly it didn't seem quite so crazy. It seemed like a hell of a good idea and why don't I help this guy? That kind of guy. He was a really remarkable guy. I hope that he and Danilo are actually making it happen. I open the newspaper every morning expecting to find a huge headline that they did it somehow, and all the heads of state are harrumphing and issuing terse statements and conducting hurried press conferences, but it's too late, a huge new blue country was born overnight without all the pompous people noticing, and it's too late to send in armies, and it's not like you can beat up the ocean, anyways. A really remarkable guy. As is Danilo. That guy, for all that he was so young, he had that kind of warm electric thing that just cuts through all the walls people build up, you know? You liked him right off because you got the immediate sense he was the real deal and he was a gentle honest guy. Plus, my God, could he sing! That guy would be the most popular singer on earth if he wanted to be, I bet, but he's another guy without a con bone. I liked that guy from the first two minutes he was on the boat. For one thing he and Pipa immediately *got* each other, which is a good sign, and for another the first thing he did on the boat was offer to help. I wish them the best. It was hard to see them go, yes. More than anyone anticipated.

*

Business meeting on the *Plover,* by command of the captain. Dusk. Pipa in her chair in the stern with the terns along the railing. Everyone else crowded around the hatch cover. Enrique in the tent. You can listen but you don't get a vote, says Declan. I'll go first. Decision time. We have to leave this guy in a serious hospital. There are serious hospitals about four days east, in the islands. It's also time to haul the boat in for serious repairs and refitting. It's also time for us to admit we actually don't have much money. It's also time for us to realize we are running low on food. If anyone feeds that warbler one more of the dried berries that *we* could be eating, I will throw that person overboard, even if she is bigger than me. Also there's no more toilet paper. So. Thoughts?

Is this a vote or are you making the decision? asks Piko.

Old Ed Burke says that all government is founded on compromise and barter.

Surprise and butter? says Pipa, which gets a laugh.

Danilo and I, says the minister, have been discussing possibilities, and we have concluded that we could pool our energies to be stimulatory to our shared idea of a new and far more expansive republic on and among these waters. We conceive that we could recruit support among a fairly large population of people and so begin, so to speak, a movement.

Danilo?

If we can get enough people interested and excited about it, says Danilo, then it's started. We are not sure about details but I think the minister is right and it's time to start. I am very grateful for your generosity in taking me aboard.

Taromauri?

But she shook her head silently and pointed to Piko.

Doctor?

The pip and I have been talking to Taromauri, says Piko quietly, and we think maybe we three will throw in together for a while. Pipa and I would like to go back to

Makana, where you picked us up, rather than the mainland, and Taromauri wants to make her way back to her island. We were thinking that we could all three throw in together for a while, get some work, and save enough money for Taromauri to go back. She wants to find her husband, and we would like to help, but we need to stash some cash.

Where would you live?

I have a good friend who lives near Makana who has a house. He'll put us up as long as need be. He's a good guy. Kono. He's the guy who delivered my letter to you in his canoe.

Taromauri?

But again she shook her head and then put her huge hands over her face.

And, hey, Dec, says Piko, we thought we would take the guy with us. Take him off your hands. We can get him to the hospital and fill out forms and all. Least we can do to thank you for all this. You took us all on board and that was generous.

You sure?

Yeh.

Thanks.

We owe you.

Captain? says Pipa, and everyone smiles.

Pippish?

What will *you* do? Will you come with us?

Pause; the gull steps to the edge of the cabin roof to listen.

Well, I'll be working the boat for a while.

Then what?

Then probably working the boat some more.

Then what?

Pause.

I don't really know, Pip. I am not much for land lately.

Will you come with us? Please?

Ah, I don't know, Pip.

Why?

Because I am not much for land, *Pipa,* says Declan, with just a hint of cold and formal in his voice, as if that's the end of the discussion, and it's just the slightest infinitesimal touch of cold and formal, but the chill of it stabs Pipa like a dart.

All right then, says Declan. Forward ho. Meeting adjourned. Dinner at eight bells. Danilo is cook and the minister is kitchen crew. Piko and Taromauri on medical watch. I am on chart duty. I suggest that the musician-at-arms coordinate an hour of music before dinner, if the musician-at-arms remembers her assignment as musician-at-arms, and hops to it.

But the musician-at-arms is huddled in her chair, her hands still, and not even Taromauri can entice her from her crumpled castle.

★

Enrique in Taromauri's tent, the flap open and secured in such a way as to provide shade while allowing a breeze. Danilo to starboard, fishing for trevallies, keeping half an eye on Enrique. Everyone else dozing in various states of sprawl, except Declan. He is poring over his charts and weighing subtle matters like if there is what you might call an accident at sea, and there is a sole survivor of the accident, and another boat picks up the survivor, and generously transports the survivor to shore for medical attention, does this second boat, or more specifically its captain, bear a legal responsibility to report the circumstances of the accident to civil authorities? Does this captain bear any financial responsibility for medical attention provided the survivor, and what are the chances of testimony being required on the parts of the captain, some or all of his passengers, or the survivor? If one boat destroys another, no matter what the context or sensible reasons for said destruction, does the surviving boat, or more specifically the captain, bear a *moral* responsibility for the care of the survivors, if any, even if the first boat, the one that was destroyed, sought the destruction of the second boat, the one that was not destroyed, but that picked up the sole survivor, who was in fact the casus belli, the agent and cause of all the trouble in the first place? If a boat lands several passengers on an island, and the passengers have no official visa or passport or forms of identification, is the captain of the boat responsible for legal ramifications of possible customs or immigration violations, even if the captain can fairly claim that he rescued all of the passengers being landed from various forms of threat and danger, and indeed in two cases was *importuned* to do so by medical authorities on the island from which they departed? If a boat lands several passengers on an island, say under the cover of darkness, and the boat then departs, and is a number of miles away the next day, when the civil authorities become aware of the arrival of the undocumented passengers, can the civil authorities prove any link between captain and passengers, except that of unsubstantiated claims or testimony from the passengers? Can a captain who has never been a father, and has had no particular desire or interest in being a father, actually feel *paternal* toward a child, if the captain has no experience whatsoever in paternity, that he knows about? Could a man who has often and pointedly claimed independence from all constraint and relationship, and insisted with asperity on his solitude against any and all calls on his time and resources from family, friends, or civic entity, suddenly reverse course and throw in with friends as a sort of amateur and untrained uncle, without inviting loss of independence, not to mention ridicule? Can a man who has often and pointedly claimed independence from all constraint and relationship continue on such a course for his entire lifetime, whether in marine or terrestrial context, without finally arriving not at a welcome solitude but at a fearsome loneliness and desiccation of the soul? Does a man who insists on his own compass and geography and direction, without acknowledgment and correction for the courses of others, risk becoming cruel and lonely and hard as a seed that never gave itself a chance to open?

★

Taromauri gently spreads ointment on Enrique's burns. His eyes are closed. Danilo and the minister are making flags and pennants of their own to hang in the rigging: green for Danilo, blue for the minister. Piko is gently bathing his daughter. Her eyes are closed. Declan is watching Piko and Pipa from the ladder. In *our* family, says Piko, we begin with the feet. The feet are where we touch the earth and so we start there. Begin with the foundation. Then to the legs, which are what separates us from fish and moss and lichen. Not to say that things that don't have legs are losers but yes to say that legs are *excellent* ideas and they should be treated with respect. You should be the *best* of friends with your legs. *Your* legs have been sleeping for a long time but they might wake up. That could happen, you know. They might wake up one morning and say *where the heck have we been, we have some sprinting to do!* That could happen. That might happen. So we will keep them loose and limber, yes we will. Then the private parts, and then the seat of the soul, which has a button right *here* in case you need to open it. This is called the belly button, and I know you are ticklish, you don't fool me with your eyes closed, my little *manuoku*. Then the arms and shoulders and chest and neck and finally we finish with the book of your soul, the space of the face, and then those epic eyes, aha! I knew you were not dozing! says Taromauri to Enrique also, at the exact same instant Piko says it to Pipa. Enrique opens his eyes but doesn't try to speak. She works down toward his feet. You are as burned as burned can be, she says. Why did you want to live in the fire? The fire is no place to be. Whatever it was you were looking for isn't there. It was never there. You cannot command the fire. The fire is not ours. You can visit the fire but if you try to live there, this is what happens. This is the time for you to think about the next person you want to be. You cannot stay the same person all your life. If you are still a child inside this body you need to come

out now and become a man. You need to have this ointment every day now, twice a day if possible. I will put it
on you for four more days but then you will have to do it
yourself. You forget that I worked for you for a year and a
day and I saw you with the fire. I saw how you talked to
it. You didn't think I saw but I saw. I think there is a young
man inside you who should come out now. Whatever it was
you used to be is burned and gone. This is a good time to
think about a new skin. You still have your old feet but
everything else will be new and who will live inside your
new parts? That's what you need to think about. Close your
eyes now and get some sleep and I will wake you for dinner,
says Piko to Pipa, at exactly the same instant as Taromauri
says it to Enrique.

★

At dusk the minister called their attention to an albatross
once again hanging effortlessly over the stern, and they
gathered to stare at the bird's enormous wingspan and
startlingly white plumage. How that bird stays so clean
in a world this dirty is a mystery to me altogether, says
Declan. Then it is dinnertime. Somehow sometime over
the past few days they have adopted the habit of eating in
a rough circle, using the hatch cover as a table. Pipa perches
in her chair, Enrique is supine in the tent, and everyone
else sits around the hatch. Tonight we will be dining on,
surprise! fish! says Declan. Our chef this evening is the
young man to my left; a round of applause for the young
man. Danilo smiles and bows his head. They eat, murmuring about this and that. Taromauri stands at one point
to share a scrap with the gull, and she makes a point of

also leaving a trail of berries for the warbler, which makes Declan growl, which makes Pipa laugh. The minister and Piko get into a discussion of bioluminescence, which is fascinating absolutely, says the minister, and in Pacifica we will have to find a corps of bright children who can figure out how to channel all that light for secondary use after primary use by progenitory creatures. Perhaps for example there is a way for alphabets to be written on the surface of the sea at night, so children can study at night as well as during the day. This could happen. Near the end of the meal Taromauri scrinches over to the tent and feeds scraps of fish to Enrique, and Danilo inches over to be closer just in case although as Declan has often said why in heaven's name *we* worry about protecting *her* is a mystery to me, she could throw us all off the boat two by two without breaking a sweat, and if we really wanted to be efficient with energy we would turn the engine off and have her get in the water and push us toward the Jesus blessed islands. Danilo stares at Enrique and Enrique feels the stare and returns it. There's no way either man will ever know that they have, had, Something Somethingivić in common. It just will not happen. Enrique never knew the name of the pilot's brother, and Danilo never knew that his brother ended up a pilot on the *Tanets,* but still they stare at each other, each sensing some odd ripple between them. They'll never talk about Danilo's brother, they'll never even suspect that the pilot who washed overboard that night was the man who sold himself to save his brother, but still they sit there in the stern, staring, as night sifts into the boat. And soon enough both of them think of

Something Somethingivić, just for a moment, the thin man with a leer and a cigarette, young in Danilo's mind and older in Enrique's; but Enrique does not go so far as to stare at Danilo and discern the structure of the brother's face, and it never occurs to Danilo that the burned man huddled in the tent is the last person on earth to see his brother whole and hale, before his brother stepped into the storm and never returned; and then dinner is over, and all hands turn in; the minister takes the first watch.

*

A fishing boat like the *Plover,* originally designed for a crew of two (four in a fishing frenzy), is sparse with space even with an orthodox complement of crew, so you can imagine the press and bumble of a crew of *six,* one of whom is enormous, four of whom are men of substantial sinew, and the one who must be carried everywhere being long limbed and extensive in splay; plus a passenger, immobile as yet, but full-grown and occupying a good deal of the decking under the stern railing; and this is not even to count the gull and the warbler, who do not take up much space and are able to vacate the premises temporarily if need be; nor do we count the albatross, who, floating effortlessly nine feet over the stern, is not technically aboard the boat; nor are we counting the many small passengers on the hull and anchor and rudder, among which we find barnacles, algae (red, green, and brown), flatworms, chitons, sea spiders, sponges, sea squirts, and a flourishing village of mussels (tiny for the moment, but ambitious); a rough count of the passenger manifest, if we were being thorough, would be a thousand, ranging in size from

Taromauri to an infinitesimal acorn barnacle, just born as this sentence began, and no bigger than the period which is about to arrive, here.

So that at night, when everyone is asleep, they are as close to being bundled and piled as possible without actually being entwined and entwangled; Pipa alone gets a bunk to herself, the horizontal closet, as Piko says, but Piko and Declan are ranged immediately alongside her, their shoulders pressed against either side of her box; the minister, despite his bulk, somehow sleeps jackknifed into a space half his height, from which he unfolds himself in the morning very much like you unfold and open a slipknife (and this is a good place to point out that somewhere along the line the minister became a serious student of knives that open and close, and once had, in his previous life, as he says, a collection of wooden-handled knives among which he counted a canoe knife, a sunfish knife, and a butterfly knife, any of which, as he says, had he had it on his person at the time of his vanishment, might have prevented or adjusted the manner of his emigratory adventure); and Danilo, on rainy nights, has slept in a space at the foot of the ladder that no kidding looks to be about twenty inches long, how *that* guy sleeps in *that* space is a Jesus blessed mystery to me, as the captain has said; and Taromauri, until she gave her tent to the burned man, slept in her tent in the stern; where exactly she would sleep in a storm now is another mystery to me, says Declan. Probably on the roof with the bird, who probably can say something that turns rain into carrots, for all I know. Jesus Christmas, the things that have happened on this boat.

And in the morning, when they wake, there is a comical jostling and muttering as they unfold, like a giant bleary bedraggled fist, and pull the pip out like a sardine from a can, extracting her, giggling (her feet are ticklish, and they tickle her feet every morning, Piko holding them up like chins to be chucked), from her redolent bunk, and make their way up the ladder, Pipa riding someone's shoulders, into the brilliant day (for each day is lovelier than the last, these days), to find Taromauri sitting calmly on the hatch cover, waiting for them; at which point Declan orders her below to sleep, which command she gently declines, just as Danilo comes up with a pot of coffee, and they get their cups from where they hang in the cabin, and lounge sleepily in the sun for a moment, sipping the coffee, and Danilo gives Pipa coffee in a tiny cup that he and Taromauri made for her from palm wood. Soon enough they will get to work, and there will be cooking and fishing and course correction and safety inspection and medical rounds, but those first few moments, sipping coffee, ranged around the boat, blinking and stretching and yawning, not yet talking, their mouths and noses and ears washed with crisp salted air—those were the best moments of all. Those were the moments, years later, that all six of them remembered most; early in the morning, waking slowly, untangling and making jokes, hoisting the pip up the ladder, sipping coffee, listening to gulls and terns and the lap and slap of the sea, not yet doing anything except delicious nothing, yet. Those were the moments.

★

Later that morning it was Piko who noticed a slight change in the wind, a slight change in the species of birds lazing by, the advent of vegetative detritus in the water; the latter probably from a storm or series of storms washing over a sizeable landmass, he says. The Leewards, says Declan. We should be among them this morning. Nihoa and Nalukakala, Kauo and Kanemiloha'i, Punahonu and Papaapoho and Pihemanu, Mokumanamana and Mokupapapa, recite Piko and Pipa, happily recounting the *Plover*'s first venture among the Seamounts, forever ago, back when I was talkless, says Pipa, grinning.

A pod of whales, and then a second, followed a little later by porpoises, in arrowed phalanxes and formations; a second albatross, crossing the path of the first as precisely as a stitch; more terns by the hour; and then, far to the southwest, what certainly looked like an osprey but could not possibly have been an osprey, said Piko, unless it was.

It was Taromauri who noticed that the gull on the cabin roof had dozed all morning, which was unusual; and by noon the bird had slumped over and lay on her side, gasping fitfully. Piko climbed up and examined her, but found no evidence of disease or damage, not that I am an expert on gull anatomy and physiology anyways, he said. But I think she's dying, yes. I have no idea why but I am pretty sure that's what's happening.

Taromauri lifted Pipa to the roof and clambered up herself and they sat with the gull. Taromauri put the bird's head in Pipa's hands. The gull's eyes were closed and her breastbone heaved and staggered. The men climbed up one by one to touch the bird and make some last quiet remark to her; Declan muttered *misneach* and said quietly, bird, you were a hell of a good crew when it was just you and me, and you were even better later, and I owe you, and then he climbed down and went below to work on the hull patch for a while. Early in the afternoon they all heard, or thought they heard, the gull murmur something gentle, in the tone that people use when they say blessings or thanks, but no one could quite make out the words. Late in the afternoon the gull died, her head still cupped in Pipa's hands. Taromauri lifted Pipa down and Piko sat with her in the stern. Enrique, sitting up, watched silently. Danilo made a small fire on the hatch cover. When it was hot enough Taromauri placed the body of the gull in the flames and they all watched as the fire ate the gull. When the first ashes fluttered up the minister reached for them but Taromauri shook her head and after that the ashes swirled and flew wherever they wanted. Some ashes got caught in various hair and some spun into mouths and noses but no one sneezed or gagged or said anything. The fire burned all the way down to tiny embers. Most of the ashes swirled up and over the railings and out to sea but some went into the cabin and peppered the chair and wheel and windows. One little group of four or five ash grains went into the cabin and swirled around like they were looking for something and then jumped all together right through the hole in the window from Enrique's bullet and whirled away to starboard. Danilo used a long thin stick to push the embers closer together as they ebbed until there was nothing left to burn and the fire went out. Still no one said anything. After a while Danilo used his stick to separate what was left of the fire and when the ashes were cool Taromauri and Piko scooped them up carefully and carried them to the stern and let them sift into the sea. Piko saved a last little pinch of them and put them in Pipa's hands and Pipa didn't say anything but her father knew what she meant and he helped her open her hands and let the last of the ash drift into the sea. By then it was time for dinner but no one felt like cooking so they had fruit and tea and two bags of almonds that miraculously appeared between Volume the Sixth of Edmund Burke's Writings & Speeches *(India: The Launching of the Hastings Impeachment)* and Volume the Seventh *(India: The Hastings Trial)*. Then everyone went to bed early, Declan taking the first watch.

*

He watched the stars be born; ever since he was a boy he loved to sit outside as dusk slid into dark and one by five by fifty the stars emerged, insisted, flared awake; in the worst years with his father raging or icy or drunk he would climb out of his attic room and sit on the roof, watching nighthawks and owls whir against the stars; the first few times he crawled out on the roof he was frightened, but soon enough it felt like the deck of a boat up there, tight and safe, above all seethe and turmoil; many nights in late summer he had slept on the roof, tied to the chimney with the first jackline of his maritime career, made from shreds of rope, shards of horse harness, plaited blackberry and plantain and spruce fibers, and the braided inner bark of cedar trees; he had worked for weeks on that jackline, and well remembered his father's sneering laugh when he found it. Yet that line had lasted all the years of his childhood, and indeed never broke; it was lost overboard in one of the first storms he experienced when he first bought the *Plover,* and was learning how to maneuver it through thrashing water. Probably that jackline is alive and well somewhere under the sea to this day, he thought. Probably being used by a young seal or something, jacklining himself to his rock perch at night, a thought that made him grin in the dark.

Sir? came a voice in the dark; Enrique.

What?

Can we talk?

About what? says Declan, realizing that his baseball bat is tucked under the stern railing, right behind the tent.

What happens now?

What happens now is that we drop you off on an island.

Then what?

What do I care?

Pause.

Why did you rescue me?

I didn't, says Declan. Another guy did. I would have left you in the water, probably.

Really?

Probably.

Pause.

I'm sorry.

For what?

All of it.

Yeh. Whatever.

I caused fear and I am sorry.

Yeh. We're still dropping you off at a hospital. Make your own way.

Pause.

May I have some water?

Declan considers for a moment. He could wake Taromauri, who is sleeping in the bow; he could tell the guy to wait until morning; or he could lean in and get the bat with his left hand as his right delivers water. He gets water and leans in and gets the bat with his left hand as his right delivers the water.

Thank you.

Yeh.

My name is Enrique.

Yeh.

That is my real name. My mother blessed me with it.

Sure.

What is your name?

Captain.

Pause.

I understand your anger, said Enrique quietly, and there is nothing I can do now but apologize. I am sorry. I am especially sorry to have frightened the child.

Pause.

I see how you love your boat, said Enrique. I liked mine, but I didn't love it.

Pause.

I liked what it could do, said Enrique, but not the way you like yours for what it is.

Yeh, whatever, says Declan. You want more water?

No, thank you.

Pause.

Thank you for rescuing me, said Enrique, so quietly that Declan unconsciously leaned in another inch in the dark to hear him. I thought I died. It never occurred to me that I would live. I thought I died in the fire. What a surprise to wake up here.

Declan felt a silent presence behind him; Taromauri, who had heard the voices. She took the water cup and filled it and gave it to Enrique and sat down. How a person that large can fold down without a sound is a total blessed mystery to me, thought Declan. No one said anything for a long time and during that time about a thousand stars appeared without the slightest fanfare. We take stars totally for granted, as Declan said later to Piko. Jesus blessed miracles, they are, and we casually look up and say stupid things like *hey, stars,* when we should by rights be moaning and gibbering in wonder and fear that fecking nuclear furnaces are burning in the sky in numbers and at distances we cannot even imagine let alone bless me calculate. After a while Taromauri put her hand on Declan's shoulder and he got the message and left her on watch and went below to sleep.

*

In the morning Declan and the minister are in the cabin sipping coffee and Declan says are you actually serious about this whole Pacifica thing or is this some kind of political con or shell game or circus or what?

Quite serious, said the minister. I am aware it sounds unworkable but I believe it can happen, with the right stimulatory activity and shepherding of creative energies. Nor is this a subtle entrepreneurial venture in which I stand to make a great deal of money. I believe that I have a role to play in helping a remarkable idea come to fruition. I do not wish to command the idea, I do not wish to profit from it, but I do very much wish to see it accomplished, and I believe it is eminently accomplishable. Consider the relevant facts. There are some thirty thousand islands in what we call the Pacific Ocean, although that immense basin has been called many other names over many millennia. The basin itself measures something like sixty million square miles. It is the biggest thing on Earth. But because it is mostly water with mountaintops peeking up here and there, we do not think of it as we think of other sorts of space, which are mostly contiguous mountains with water glimmering here and there. These latter constructs we consider countries, but not the former; this seems odd to me and I would like to amend the way we think about this. It seems to me that an enormous blue place in which hundreds of thousands of people live riveting and creative lives, in manners and cultures established over many centuries by their ancestors and forebears, surrounded by natural resources of intricacy and wealth for the most part still beyond our understanding or abuse, is indeed a country, a remarkable nation unlike any that ever was, and I cannot see any reason why it should not be called so, and organized as such for the protection and celebration of its character and inhabitants, and seen and saluted as such by the other nations of the world, not one of which can boast the natural resources and fascinating creative possibilities of Pacifica. Also I do not see any reason why any former imperial power in Pacifica should be given any sort of control, possession, or preference here, considering that imperial powers by nature arrive and steal and commit destruction as a matter of course, nor do I see any reason why current or rising imperial powers, of any sort or stripe, be they economic, cultural, or political, should be acknowledged as having the slightest right whatsoever to commit ruin and theft upon the people, lands, waters, and atmosphere of Pacifica. It seems to me that Pacifica is a proud and remarkable country, and should be defined and acknowledged and protected as such, and not be treated as a playground or gift basket for countries that think they can pluck islands here and there like ripe fruit, and thrash as they like through the ocean for all manner of treasures and riches, and treat people like slaves and serfs, and cut islands in half and pit the halves against each other, or persist in thinking that a theft that occurred centuries ago has any modern legitimacy by virtue of its hoary age. It seems to me that the residents of Pacifica ought to be able to decide for themselves how to organize themselves as a coherent economic, cultural, and political force, and that any former, current, or rising power that has the gall to insist that it can or should decide for the residents of Pacifica how they ought to organize themselves and conduct their lives is foolish, ridiculous, selfish, and criminal.

Thought this through a bit, I see, said Declan.

A bit.

What about violence?

What about it?

People shoot people who take away the money trough.

I think there are ways around that, said the minister.

Around violence?

Yes.

Are you an idiot?

I don't think so.

You know your history, said Declan. You know how it works. Violence is who we are. Our daily bread. Hey, you got kidnapped and dumped at sea, you know what it is. Not to mention you were just in a gun battle, basically.

I think there are ways around it, said the minister. I don't think this is the way it always has to be. I think if people imagine new ways to be then there will be ways to work in different ways than the ways people have worked in the past. I think violence will eventually be useless. It will wither away because no one uses it, like a muscle that never flexes. Too many people will laugh at it for anyone to use it anymore.

Nah, said Declan. It's our oldest skill. We're great at it now and we'll get better. Eventually we'll get so good at it that we'll wipe ourselves out and the world will reboot and probably gulls or jellyfish will run the next version.

Well, said the minister.

Yeh, weird line of talk, let's get some breakfast going for *our* country, what say? Whyn't you catch some fish, you got the touch, and I'll get a little fire going. Can't believe the captain allows fires on the hatch. What are we, fecking Sea Scouts?

★

Two hours later they came upon a lovely little atoll and anchored for a while to stretch and swim and fish and clean the boat and air out bedding and collect firewood and doze and gab and yawp and laugh and repaint the hatch because *someone* has been making fires on the cover and the paint job is *not* what it should be on a blessed shipshape ship as if this was a shipshape ship for chrissake look at all the gull poop on the roof and there's a bullet hole in the cabin window my God *who's* in charge of maintenance here? Taromauri and Danilo carried Enrique to the beach and walked him up and down for a while to get his new skin used to movement; that must have hurt like hell but he never said a word, observed Danilo, after they established Enrique in a little shady grove and Taromauri had again thoroughly rubbed him down with ointment.

That was maybe the greatest day in the history of days, said Pipa much later, to a gaggle of children who stared at their teacher like you would stare at a person who was telling you about her cool voyage to Mars when she was a child. That was an even greater day than the first day we spent in the Leeward Islands, when my father and I were first on the boat, because this time we had three new friends, maybe four. There were birds everywhere, all sorts of brilliant birds. There was *manuoko* the tern, and *'a,* the booby, and *'i'iwi* and *'o'u'* and *nukupu,* the honeycreepers, and *pueo,* the little owl, and *'io,* the hawk, and *huna kai,* the sanderling, and *uau,* the petrel, and the plover—what is the word for the plover, who can tell me? *Kolea,* that's right, very good, Mahealani. Who can name another bird that I would have seen in the Leewards? Anyone? *Ukeke,* the turnstone, very good, Puanani, yes, there were turnstones on the beach. One more? Anyone? *Amaui,* the thrush, good, Marcos—we did not see a thrush that day but yes, *amaui* could well have been there. One more? *'Iwa,* the thief, the frigate bird, good, Mehana, yes, we saw *'iwa. Piha'ekelo,* the mynah, no. No parking lots with food scraps for old *piha'ekelo*—he is not much of a wild bird anymore, I think. *Very* good guesses, though. *Five* extra minutes' recess today! But let me finish telling you the story. We had some absolutely great days, the greatest great days, on that journey. There was the first day we were in the Leewards, when I got sunburnt and my father caught a fish with his hand swimming underwater and Captain O Donnell tried to catch fish with his bow and arrows and we laughed so hard I thought our eyeballs were going to fall out and roll across the deck, but they didn't. There was a day when we saw a blue whale right next to the boat and the whale was so much bigger than a boat we thought it was a blue island until it rolled and smiled at us and slid away into the deep like a dream bigger and bluer than any dream you ever had before. There was the day I got my voice back after not being able to speak for four whole years, imagine all the words that were piled up inside me waiting to come out! There was the day I was washed over the railing of the boat into the sea and almost went to the bottom to be turned into a fish but my father caught my foot and Captain O Donnell caught my father's beard and we were all okay! There was the day I met my dear friend Taromauri whom you met when she came into class to tell stories last week, as you remember. And there was the second day we were in the Leewards, which was the most perfect day of all, the greatest great day we had on that journey, partly because we all knew it was one of our last days together but not *the* last day, which is a delicious and bittersweet feeling, which you will feel near the end of this school year, trust me. Now I will tell you what we did that day, and you take your paints and pencils, and either draw what stimulates your imagination as I tell you the story, or start your own story from my story, or invent a song for a fish or bird or plant or wind or person, okay? Everyone understand the assignment? You decide for yourself what to do, but you have to start something, and have fun. What you start today is your homework for the weekend, and I will look at them on Monday when we are back together. Okay? Ready?

★

While Declan fiddled with the hull patch for the four hundredth fecking time, cursing and humming and trying to recite from memory Edmund Burke's entire speech on reconciliation with the American colonies, and Enrique dozed in the little shady grove, the other five members of the crew wandered the atoll for a while, collecting driftwood and stretching their legs; Taromauri carried Pipa like an oak carries an acorn. Then they made a tiny fire and sat on the beach lazing and talking and vaguely pondering a concerted fishing expedition in the shallows, although as Danilo said after a steady diet of fish it's interesting how the prospect of fish for dinner is not what it used to be. After a while they got to talking about Declan and after more while they essentially quizzed Piko about

Declan because he had known him longest and in other contexts other than captainesque.

Why is he so stubborn about not landing anywhere?

I'm not sure. I don't think he had the happiest childhood, for one thing.

Why is he so gruff?

He wasn't always.

Why does he want to be alone?

Does he?

Seems like it.

I am not sure he does, really. I think some of him is a mask.

Was he ever married? kids?

No.

Girlfriends?

Yes, but never for very long. I think he was leery about letting anyone on his boat.

His real boat? This boat?

Metaphor.

Was he wilder then?

He was . . . looser, I'd say. He'd do anything and go anywhere. He was the one who always wanted to go on crazy trips in the boat. He used to work on his family's dairy on the Oregon coast and fish on the side, so adventures in the boat were a real kick for him. He was always after me to go with him to lost beaches and remote islands and stuff. That's why he put in the mast and the strange rigging system, so he could go farther without paying for gas.

Did you go on adventures?

Not much. I had my work and Elly and the pip and then Elly got sick, so.

What happened to Declan's family's dairy?

He didn't say.

Why did he take off on his own in the boat?

Not sure. I think he wanted to cut all cords with his family and town and land and stuff. That's why he's weird about landing places, I guess.

Doesn't he have any other friends than you?

I thought he did.

How did you guys get to be friends?

Met in a bar on the coast. There was an incident and he jumped in to help me and we got to be friends.

What incident?

Hey, look, a frigate bird, said Piko. Lovely bird, although the Hawaiian word for it is 'iwa, the thief.

Doesn't he like us? said Pipa. If he likes us why won't he come with us to Makana?

I think he likes people more than he wants to admit even to himself, said Piko gently. And I think he likes you the most of anyone in the world, Pip, which really confuses him. I think he decided to be one kind of guy but liking us is rattling that kind of guy and that's why he's gruff and grumpy. I think maybe we just leave him alone and be gentle and maybe things will work out. You can't make people be who they don't want to be yet. You just be gentle and let them get there themselves. Your mother taught me that. You taught me that. Maybe someday you will be a teacher.

Every time I see any kind of bird now I think of Mama a little, said Pipa, and there was a long silence as the frigate bird drifted away and Taromauri looked away and the minister poked at the fire.

★

Okay, time! said Pipa to her classroom many years later. Now, I *know* you all took this seriously and started something fun, because I trust you, and your homework for the weekend is just keep taking your projects out for a walk. See where they go. Don't plan and plot them much if at all. Just let them go where they want to go. Let them have adventures. You would be surprised where projects go if you let them have their heads and sail off free as a bee. Ideas take on lives of their own and become quite real. One of the most fascinating things about human beings is your imagination and how it can create something that was never in the world before in billions of years and will never be in the world again in that form in billions of years to come. Isn't that amazing? And you yourselves are of course imaginative adventures that never were in the world before and will never be again in this form. Your parents imagined you into being and here you are but you are different every day and every hour and every minute. You are essentially stories yourselves of course, unwinding and unreeling all the time, never knowing your ending; you tell yourselves every moment. Perhaps some aspect of maturity is when you begin to tell the story of yourself rather than other people telling your story.

Mrs. Kuapapa?

Yes, Thomas?

Will you tell us more about that day you were on the boat with your father and the tall lady? When you were little?

Well . . . do we have time? How many minutes do we have left in the hour?

Pause.

Tenteen!

No . . .

Seven! says Thomas, who has secretly been using his fingers beneath his desk.

Seven it is, very good, Thomas. All right, I will tell you one more story, and we will save the last minutes today for singing, and then you will all go home and tell your mothers that they are the greatest coolest sweetest mothers *ever,* okay? And don't forget your homework, to finish your project.

Okay, Mrs. K!

Well, we stayed on that little island all day, and some of us thought maybe we would sleep overnight there maybe, because the weather was fine, but our captain said that islands were dangerous and boats were safe, so we got back on the boat in the late afternoon, and prepared to continue toward these islands.

This island?

This very one, says Pipa. Now here's my story: there was a storm on the horizon, and the captain was worried about that, so my friend Danilo and I sat in the bow and decided to sing the storm away. He said if we closed our eyes and sang from the bottom of the bottom of our bones we could make a song bigger than any storm, and the storm would dissolve and vanish, and the captain would be delighted, so we did it. Believe it or not, when we opened our eyes after singing, that storm was gone!

All gone?

As gone as gone could be, says Pipa. Not a hint or sign or suggestion of a storm. If you had never seen the seed of a storm you would have stared at that sky that day and never consider that there could ever be something anything *like* a storm.

Three minutes, Mrs. K! sings out Thomas.

Thank you, Thomas. All right, now, let us sing ourselves out of class today, out of the week, into the weekend, ready, all together . . .

This fecking hole, says Declan to the hull patch, refuses to surrender. This is a hell of a hole. You wouldn't think water could punch a hole so thoroughly in wood but you would be stone cold wrong about that, my wooden friend. Because this is not fecking *water.* This is the *ocean.* The ocean is a killer, my friend. Everyone's always talking about how beautiful it is and how it's the mother of all life and how it's the food factory of the world and the hope of the future and how a million new medicines are hidden in it and eventually we will be living in it comfortably somehow in undersea cities and everything will be sweetness and light and we will be chatting amiably with the fish and all but that is crap deeper than the ocean in its deepest parts. The ocean is a professional assassin, my friend. The ocean kills more beings per second than you could count in a million years. The ocean is a vast collection of good ways to die. You and me are just fighting a holding action here. In the long term the ocean will eventually rise and wash over everything and we will all start over again from scratch as monocellular beings in the swashing tide. In the short term you know and I know that I will have to eventually retire you and thoroughly rebuild the hull here and stitch all sorts of materials into this hole in a vain effort to make the repair of the hole stronger than the wood which used to be there before the hole. But the ocean *knows* it cut a hole there once, see, the ocean is smart and never forgets, and it will poke and probe and question and examine my work and we will always be niggling and negotiating about this particular piece of the boat forever after. Fecking fecking feck. You, however, my friend, are doing a fine and excellent job of holding off the mother of all life. *You* are a terrific crew member, working harder and saying less than a lot of the people who have supposedly worked on this boat over the years. I name no names. But you, my friend, *you* are going to have a permanent place of honor on the boat. I think I will mount you in the cabin when you are done down here, so that every time I look up and see you I will think you were a damned fine hull patch, yes you were. You were the best hull patch we ever had. In the long history of hull patches you are an all-star patch and no mistake. If ever I sell the boat, God forbid such blasphemy, I will take you off the wall of the cabin and bring you with me, to the ends of the earth, from sheer respect. You did good. Your mama would be proud, whoever she was, deep in the woods. You did good.

★

Taromauri can smell the islands now, full in the face—a rich redolent soiled muddy seething flowering sort of *orange* smell, she says. Smells have colors? asks Danilo. O yes, she says. Don't they for you? They do for me. My daughter had a gray-green smell. My husband for some reason has a brilliant yellow smell, almost golden but not quite. Pipa smells white with hints of green and blue. The minister agrees wholly with this line of talk. O yes, he says, I concur with the lady. I knew a man who had the deepest black smell. You would think this intimated evilry or criminosity on his part but this was not at all true and he was the most calm gentle generous man you ever met. Lovely man. By skin color himself a very light brown, rather like cinnamon, but a deep robustuous black smell as regards personally. And there was a woman in my office who smelled purplish—something like a cross between magenta and maroon. Wonderful woman, remarkably honest. I suspect she is unemployed at present as a result of her unfortunate honesty. A brief woman, but filled with a serene energy that was a real pleasure to work with. A serenergy, as it were. I believe she was the shortest mature person I ever met, but perhaps as a counterbalance to her height her gifts were quite tall. A rich field for speculatory activity, that. Because how very often I have met large muscled powerful men who are quite gentle, and short thin men who are quite violent. Indeed the latter seem to employ the generally reluctant former, as a rule, in matters of criminacious pursuit. If other fields of employment could be found for the large muscled latter, possibly they would retire en masse from service to the short thin former, leaving the former without their usual and traditional troops, and if the violent do not have assistance, would not their efficiency rating, violence-wise, decline and plummet? What good are generals without privates to do their work for them? And imagine the new areas to which the strength and energies of the large muscled persons could be gainfully applied. Ship repair, for example, which would certainly please, for example, our captain. I should say here that even in a career in politics and government, in which a good deal of cursing and foul and vulgar language is common, even quotidian, I have not heard quite the parade and procession of phrases we have heard in the last hour from belowdecks. Imagine that man's verbal acuity and creativity turned, for example, to poetry, or to song.

★

Declan calls a business meeting at dusk, when they are all back on board and Danilo and Taromauri have established Enrique back in the tent, and he says by my calculation this is our last night before we hit the main islands tomorrow, probably in the afternoon. The plan is to unload Piko and Pipa and Taromauri, who have offered to take the burned guy with them and leave him at a hospital; Danilo and the minister have asked to be let off also, closer to a town. I have to stand in at some point for fuel and fruit and maybe bless me a cigar, but after that I am back on the road. Questions?

But for once there were no questions, no answers, no jokes, no teasing, no requests for songs, no moaning about o my God fish for dinner again, no remarks about the terns flickering around Pipa in her chair, no stories unfolding and unreeling of Taromauri's life on her island or Danilo's wanderings through the forest, no halting examination of Enrique as to who he might be and why he had lived his life as he had, no questions for Declan about the boat or his past on land or his plans for the future, no stories of Elly from Piko or Pipa, no discussion of Pipa and the gull, no mention of the albatross who still floated behind them nine feet over the stern in the place where the gull had floated for so long, no teasing the minister for his bright pink feet, no further questions of the minister as to the shape of the immense new blue nation he saw before him like a horizon, no piercing questions from Pipa to Declan about why he doesn't want to come with her and her dad and Taromauri instead of sailing off alone are you afraid of people afraid of us what are you afraid of anyway, no remarks from Piko about the changing color of the sea as they approached a line of ancient seamounts or the subtle change in species of fish, no dark mutterings from Declan about the hull patch or the ridiculous embarrassing fecking sailcloth that looked more like fecking old laundry hung out to dry than it did anything fecking else, no quiet speculation about Pipa's hands working infinitesimally better than they did weeks ago although her feet remain pure useless dangle that's for sure, no declaiming of the wit and wisdom of Edmund Burke as the last light fails and the bow and stern lights were lit, no laughter from below as someone discovered yet another blessed bag of desiccated almonds o my God how many bags of these things did you start out with o my God, no quiet laughter as Piko says to Declan sweet Jesus Dec were you really going to attack that guy with a bow and arrows, no songs from Danilo and Pipa their voices so braided and embracing that Taromauri sat rapt with her hands folded as if in prayer, no halting beginnings of stories from Enrique about his brothers and their dusty childhood and the smell of mesquite and juniper and pine in the mountains above their village, no stories from the minister about how as a boy he and his friends swam down into sea caves and fought with eels and octopus, no halting stories from Pipa as for the first time she tried to explain how she would leave the warm coffin of her body and send her spirit even unto the depths of the sea.

Not a word, not a sound, not a smile; and again they went to bed early, without dinner around the hatch cover, for no one was hungry at all.

★

They sailed all morning without the engine, Declan conserving what fuel he had left, and the wind being perfect for scudding along toward what looked like a cloud bank on the horizon but that slowly turned green and revealed itself as a mountain with a crown of mist, and by early afternoon they could see the soaring green cliffs of a large island and the low brown profile of a lean low smaller island to the west.

As everyone else puttered around the boat doing whatever they were doing, Declan pretended to pore over his charts. West and then west, that was the plan, and here I am going east blessed east. Jesus. There were to be no emotions and no feelings and no discussions or misunderstandings or misapprehensions or expectations or illusions or complications on this trip and now there's nothing *but* complications and emotions. Jesus blessed Christmas. Emotions all over the boat like fish guts. And not even the gull is here anymore. Some fecking crew. I had one who died and now I have six, not counting the albatross. At this rate if I keep going I'll have twelve, soon enough. The Jesus blessed apostles. Weren't there thirteen of those? One got cut from the team. Poor bastard. Like the gull. Should I land with them? Should I? I need food and fuel and I have to fix the fecking hull. You *know* you have to hove to sometime and do that, man. Face the facts. This is the time. Stay with them for a while. Hang out with the pip. I could do with a month of the pip. Maybe work her hands and get her back up to speed. Cigars with Piko. Fresh fruit. Start over. The best captain keeps his crew. Fish a little, farm a little. Sit in the sun, smell the orchids. Watch the pip grow up. Could do worse. Way worse.

But he caught himself musing, and corrected course. Someday. Sure. One of these days. Better keep moving. *Misneach.* Stay with the boat. The old bucket has served me well. We'll be back. Sure we will. We'll check in here and there. Absolutely. No worries. More to see. More sea. There's always time to land and stand. Absolutely. They'll all be fine. They don't need me. I'd be a burden. They have their plans, two by two. Not me. Solo voyage. Safer that way. West and then west. Stay with the plan. Stay with the boat.

But when he turned away from his charts and stepped out of the cabin to reef the sail and start the engine, he felt Pipa staring at him; and for all his sinewy strength, and testy courage, and prickly defiant personality, and absolute assurance that on *this* boat, on *these* worn cedar planks, on *this* pitching little sunburned stage he was unquestioned and unquestionable master and island resolute, his decisions irrevocable and his independence untrammeled, he quailed, and felt a tiny shiver of shame. He stepped back into the cabin. Through the bullet hole in the window he called to Danilo to furl the sail, as the island grew closer and its sharp cliffs ever more clear and distinct.

★

Their last hours on the *Plover* were hurried and harried and there was no time for conversation or lingering farewells. They packed up Enrique, who could now stand and walk with help, and Taromauri furled and stored the tent below; they also dismantled Pipa's chair. Declan insisted that they take it with them but Piko said politely nope, there's chairs there, you'll need the parts for something or other, you know you will. Danilo and the minister packed up and picked up below, and scrubbed all extant surfaces to a shine; Taromauri and Pipa scrubbed the cabin roof, removing all traces of the gull's naturally excretatious behavior, as the minister said. When they were done on the roof Taromauri knelt by the water tank and said something quietly and the warbler came out shyly and flew up on her shoulder. Declan said let's have one last meal on the hatch cover what say but still no one was hungry. Piko apologized for not getting around to fixing the bullet hole in the window, I really should have got to that, Dec, and Declan said no worries, you had a lot to do, I'll get to it, I have putty somewhere or chewing gum or I can always use albatross poop or something. Danilo and the minister shook Declan's hand and said formally that they were most grateful for their passage and while they were not at the moment in a position to fully reimburse the captain for his remarkable generosity they were in a position to make a down payment, which Declan refused, grinning, at which point Danilo said this debt will not be forgotten and will not go unpaid, and Declan said damn right, you guys owe me serious, pay up whenever I am back this way next, plus interest, just kidding. Enrique, supported by Piko, stood and shook Declan's hand and said quietly thank you and Declan said yeh and Enrique said I am deeply grateful and Declan said yeh, good luck. Piko put his hand on Declan's shoulder and said Dec, I can't thank you enough for the lift, we really needed it and you were so generous, you pretend to be a grump but you're not, and Declan said no worries, brother, anytime, we'll do it again sometime, you take care of the pipster, I'll miss you guys, I really will, who ever thought I would say such a sappy thing but it's true. Taromauri sat on the stern railing with Pipa in her lap and Declan knelt and said listen, Pippish, sailing with you has been the most fun I ever had on the boat and I have been on the boat a *long* time, you can come with me on the boat anytime you want in this lifetime or any next lifetimes we get, I think you are a cool and amazing person, and being with you has been a pleasure and an honor, if I ever have a kid I hope she will be half as great as you, and it was cool to see you get your voice back, and I will keep your mom in my heart okay? and Pipa stared at him silently until Piko cleared his throat and she said thank you, Dec, I love you, Dec, I do, I love you, I love you, and she started to cry and Declan went to the cabin to be absolutely sure of his charts because what if he was off course, what if he thought he was headed in the right direction but had got turned around somehow, wouldn't that be bad?

★

Not one but two canoes came out to meet them, somehow; how had they known? In the first canoe, a blue one with a hawk-head prow, was the calm young man with long black hair who had brought him Piko's letter, long ago now; this must be Piko's friend Kono, remembered Declan. In the second canoe, painted a brilliant green, was, to Declan's surprise, a woman, also with long black hair. She was startlingly lovely, he thought—the kind of woman who is so beautiful that you hesitate to look too long, knowing she must endure such stares and gapes constantly. He did stare for a long instant, though, thinking that he had not seen a woman so striking in what felt like years; but then he looked away, feeling uncomfortable, and thinking that his turning away was probably in an odd way a small gift to a woman like her, who would be pleased to not be stared at, for a change. As he turned back to Kono, though, she angled her canoe against the current with a deft infinitesimal shift of her shoulders; and it was this effortless grace, in service to vessel management, that he remembered ever after as the beginning of something else than had been before. A tiny thing, that little confident practiced shimmer of shoulder; but not to Declan.

Piko was standing at the railing with Pipa draped over his back, her head peeking out from over his left shoulder, and Kono smiled up at them, thinking not for the first time that his friend wore his daughter like a bright jacket.

Ahoy the *Plover,* said Kono.

Ahoy the *'Ili'ili,* said Piko, grinning.

Good to see you safe, brother, said Kono. Welcome back.

And good to see you, brother, said Piko. Thanks for coming out.

We were summoned by the Queen of Makana, and came to pay tribute to her, said Kono, smiling at Pipa. Also to thank your friend for taking you on his boat.

Pleasure, said Declan, trying to not look at Kono's companion. Kono saw the effort and said gentlemen, my friend Akia. She has come to help.

Akia, the little bird! said Pipa happily from Piko's shoulder, and Kono's jaw fell open, just like in the movies, and he began to laugh, and said o dear if the Queen can speak now the world has changed forever, o dear o dear, and Piko explained that he would explain it all later. Then there was a flurry of introductions and greetings as the two canoes hovered alongside, and Taromauri and the minister bowed, and Danilo bent down to shake hands, and Declan busied himself in the cabin, trying not to stare at Akia, who now was trying not to look at Declan, either because she saw that he was trying not to look at her, or because she was trying not to look at him for her *own* reasons, he thought, an idea that made his head ring.

No one thought to introduce Enrique, who sat quietly in the stern.

Kono suggested that he and Akia carry the pipster in to the aunties on shore, who would bathe and feed her and make much and merry of their beloved *manuoko,* their little tern, and that way Piko would be free to help unload whatever and whomever; this seemed like an excellent idea, and after Kono hoisted up fruit and fuel for the *Plover*—how had he known to bring that?—Piko hoisted a happily burbling Pip down to the canoes. Kono, with arms like tree limbs, reached for her as you would casually reach up for an apple, but Declan noticed Akia's long hands steadying the child with something like reverence; as she guided the pip into Kono's canoe her hair fell across her cheek and Declan looked away again, rattled.

★

The *Plover* then ran northeast around two massive headlands and into a broad shallow bay, at the east end of which was a long wooden jetty; here Declan unloaded his passengers and what little gear they had. Taromauri hoisted Enrique up to Danilo and Piko like he was a bird she barely needed two hands to lift. They all shook hands again and Declan clambered back down and cast off. The men and woman on the jetty waved until the *Plover* cleared the bay but Declan, mumbling to himself, waved once and then kept his eyes on the surf line.

You never know with these fecking bays when and

where the tide line turns into a wall, and this is no blessed Jesus surfing boat, he said, or thought; was he speaking to the albatross he assumed was still behind him? You just never blessed know.

Well, bird, he said, this time aloud for sure, what do you say, south and then south? I never been south of south. Let's do south. We did west and west and east and east and north is for fecking polar bears. He turned to add something cheerfully rude to the albatross and indeed there it was, huge and calm, hanging nine feet over the stern, just like the gull used to hang in the exact same spot, without even a flicker or shiver of wings, how do they *do* that? But even as he watched, the albatross effortlessly banked away from the boat and headed back to the bay.

Jesus blessed Christmas, said Declan. Even you, Brutus? Fine. Fecking fine. It's you and me, boat. Same as ever. We started out as you and me and here we are again, old bucket. Free as air. Into the blue. The continent of the sea. No—the vast blue nation of Pacifica, as the minister said. What a nut. South and then south! Nature the sturdy adversary, as old Ed Burke says! Difficulty the severe instructor! Amen to that, boat. Amen to *that*. Listen, if you were a *good* boat you would be able to read sight reduction tables yourself and not lean on *me* to do it, but no. Fine. Fecking fine. No more passengers, nobody shooting at us, nobody expecting anything or leaning on us for anything, free free free!

The *Plover* was by now a mile back out to sea, and Declan shut off the engine while he checked his course; he had plenty of room between this island and the next bigger one to slide south between them and then southeast into open ocean, where the next island would probably be Easter or Christmas, sweet weeks away, and I bet the wind will be with us too so we don't have to use any fuel, and we have plenty of fruit, and me, I *like* fish, and *you* are not eating much if I don't have to use up the fuel, so we are set, boat, as far as I can see. No scurvy, no doldrums, plenty of food in the ocean, no expectations, no complaints, no duties, no passengers to deliver, nobody asking for favors, freshwater falling from the sky occasionally, what could be better than this, I ask you that? What could be better than this?

The wind freshened, and he noticed the bullet hole; might as well fecking fix that now as later, he thought. He went below to look for putty, and then remembered that Taromauri had used the putty to help secure Pipa's chair in the stern. Hope she left some on the railing, he thought. He climbed back up the ladder, noticing that Pipa's bed slats were open.

Indeed there were two gobs of putty left under the railing, more than he needed. He rolled them in his palms for a while, to soften them up enough to plug the hole, and then he rolled them together into a single large ball, and then he gently put the ball of putty in the exact center of the railing where Pipa's chair used to be, and walked back into the cabin, and started the engine, and turned the boat half-around, and headed back around the two headlands to the hidden bay from which the canoes had emerged;

and as he came around the second headland, happy and confused, thinking of Pipa's face, the wind shoving him along, he saw a canoe coming out to meet him; and his heart rose as he saw that it was a brilliant green.

THANKS & NOTES

My particular thanks to Admiral Michael McCabe (Ret.) of the United States Navy, who flew combat missions off the USS *Kitty Hawk* in the Pacific and eventually commanded the U.S. Navy's Third Fleet there (the fleet once commanded by Admiral Bull Halsey in the Second World War) for general counsel as regards ships and the sea, and also for great wit and humor, no conversation with the admiral ("Don't call me Admiral!" "Yes, Admiral.") is anything but a delight; to his friend and former shipmate Gary Bean Barrett, once master of the *Pau Hana,* who was a great help to me on cold hard facts of life aboard a small boat in the Pacific; to Dr. Edward Tarlov, of Massachusetts, master of the *Presto,* and his shipmate Dr. Suzanne Roffler Tarlov; to the anonymous authors of *The United States Coast Pilot, Pacific Coast,* a book I came to love with a deep and abiding love; to the memory of my personal and literary hero Robert Louis Stevenson, of Scotland, by all accounts a gentle and generous and open-hearted soul, a great husband and stepfather and friend who also wrote like an angel, especially of the sea, upon which he lived for almost a year, in the Pacific, on the schooner *Casco;* to the Living Treasure of Hawaii called Puanani Burgess, of Oahu, for her great spirit, and for the gift of the *Illustrated Hawaiian Dictionary,* by Kahikāhealani Wight, published by Bess Press in Honolulu, a book in which I have swum happily for years like *honu,* the gentle sea turtle; to the eminent photographer and journalist Hob Osterlund, of Kauai, for introducing me to that most interesting seamount and many of its residents, like *manuoku,* the Fairy Tern, and *moli,* the albatross, not to mention the migrating plover; to Kim Steutermann Rogers, of Kauai, for help with fire-throwing arcana; to Mahealani Wendt, of Maui, for her help with the Hawaiian language and history; to Gaylord and Carol Wilcox, of Oahu, for lending me their house for two weeks, during which I fell in love with plovers and Hawaii; to my friend Suzanne Case, of Oahu, and her friend Leokāne Pryor, of Maui, for their haunting music, which was a lodestar for me during the dreaming of this book (it is their song "Ke Ho'olono Nei," from Leokāne's album *Home Malanai,* that appears in bars throughout this book, for which I especially thank them for permission and meticulous musical notation); to the late Robert Gibbings, of Ireland, whose books of water journeys surely soaked into my unandsubconscious; to Stanley Ayling, of England, for his invaluable *Edmund Burke: His*

Life and Opinions; to the late Thomas Copeland, of Massachusetts, for his heroic editing of *The Correspondence of Edmund Burke* (old Ed wrote thousands of letters, in which, as is the case with many superb writers, the most characteristic and revealing writing is found; this is true, to choose two geniuses at random, of both Stevenson and Flannery O'Connor); to Sir Arthur Francis Grimble, of England, for his lively and beautifully written books *A Pattern of Islands* and *Return to the Islands;* to Sir Arthur again (called Kurimbo by the people of Tungaru, who admitted him to the islands' sun clan) and his editors Harry and Honor Maude, for the monograph *Tungaru Traditions,* from the University of Hawaii Press; to Peter Harrison for his lovely *Seabirds of the World;* to the oceanographer Sylvia Earle of the National Geographic Society, for her clear and useful book *The World Is Blue;* to Judith Schalansky, for her absolutely lovely and idiosyncratic *Atlas of Remote Islands,* an astounding book I swam in almost daily for years; to the marine biologist Edith Widder for her remarkable work with oceanic bioluminescence; to my able consultant in making ropes from fibers found in Pacific Northwest plants, George Schramm of Oregon; to Katrina Van Dusen, of Maine, for the lovely woodcuts in this book; and most of all to Mary Miller Doyle and our children, Lily, Joseph, and Liam, of Oregon, on whose love I have sailed for many years; I am the luckiest ship ever.

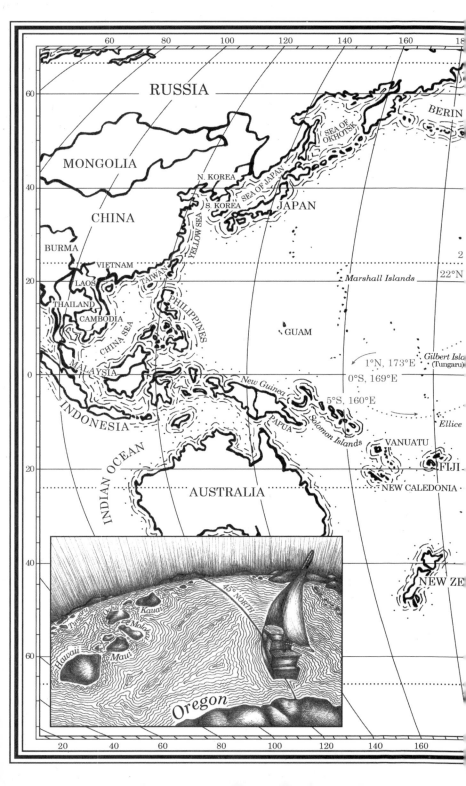